"You have d
must be reb

"It's not a *mullo*," Luke said quietly. "We plan to lift the entire skeleton out of the ground for further study. It's long dead. It won't harm you or your families."

One of the men spat on the ground. "Another sign we have angered the undead."

"It's definitely dead," Annja began to say, then hesitated. "Another sign? What was the other sign?"

"One of our children has gone missing!" someone called from the crowd.

The man with the sword, still sheathed at his back, stepped forward. He was tall and broad, making Annja suspect he could hold his own even without the weapon. "They are frightened and unsure. And now you are uncovering the dead to rise again because their sacrifices have been too few."

"Wait a minute," Annja replied. "Sacrificing what? You mentioned a child—"

"Kill them," the man with the sword said.

ROGUE ANGEL

Alex Archer

BLOOD CURSED

A GOLD EAGLE BOOK FROM

WORLDWIDE®

TORONTO • NEW YORK • LONDON
AMSTERDAM • PARIS • SYDNEY • HAMBURG
STOCKHOLM • ATHENS • TOKYO • MILAN
MADRID • WARSAW • BUDAPEST • AUCKLAND

Recycling programs
for this product may
not exist in your area.

First edition September 2013

ISBN-13: 978-0-373-62164-4

BLOOD CURSED

Special thanks and acknowledgment to
Michele Hauf for her contribution to this work.

The
LEGEND

...THE ENGLISH COMMANDER TOOK
JOAN'S SWORD AND RAISED IT HIGH.

The broadsword, plain and unadorned,
gleamed in the firelight. He put the tip against
the ground and his foot at the center of the blade.
The broadsword shattered, fragments falling
into the mud. The crowd surged forward,
peasant and soldier, and snatched the shards
from the trampled mud. The commander tossed
the hilt deep into the crowd.
Smoke almost obscured Joan, but she continued
praying till the end, until finally the flames climbed
her body and she sagged against the restraints.

Joan of Arc died that fateful day in France,
but her legend and sword are reborn....

1

"Got some interesting local news for you, boss."

Weston Bracks swiveled around on his leather office chair to face the computer screen where he had Skype open and his employee's mug peered at him. This field scout, Wayne Pearce, was reliable, though a bit of a joker, so he waited for the man's "news" hesitantly.

Bracks toyed with the Cellini Rolex on his left wrist, drew a breath through his nose as he looked over Pearce's annoying image and exhaled a disinterested "And?"

"I'm tracking through the Czech Republic at the moment."

"You should have been in London by now. It's been four days since you left the Ukraine."

"I wanted to do some sightseeing."

Bracks closed his eyes and rapped his knuckles against the underside of the desk.

"Just a joke, boss. I missed my flight, so instead I hopped in a car to take me across Europe to London.

I've pulled into Chrastava to have a bite. Did you know this town used to manufacture hand grenades for the Germans during the Second World War?"

"You are a fount of information, Pearce."

"I do pick up things here and there. Though the dialect in these parts changes from mile to mile. There are so many forms of Slavic, it's hard to keep it straight."

Pearce had a dozen or so languages under his belt, which was one of the reasons Bracks tolerated him. Still teasing his college frat boy years, this man. As smart as he was himself, he hadn't the ability, or time, to pick up new languages—a frustrating deficit—so had to rely on Pearce as interpreter.

"Is there a point to this story?" Bracks prompted, rubbing the bridge of his nose with a thumb to make sure his annoyance was broadcasted on screen.

"There is always a point, boss. The whispers in the local watering hole claim that a vampire has been unearthed on a nearby archaeological dig."

"A vamp—" Bracks contemplated hanging up, but then this was probably another of Pearce's jokes. "Very well, I'll bite, so to speak. What in such a rumor could possibly entertain my interest?"

"I don't think it's a rumor. The Gypsies are freaking out. I know the Romani are superstitious and all that jazz. But they seem to really believe that an actual vampire has been discovered."

Superstition. Bracks knew superstition could be a useful weapon. Both for and against him. By using the ingrained beliefs of others, a smart man could ensure the tables were turned in his favor. And he always appreciated favorable odds.

"Tell me more."

THE BOY'S FEET left the ground. He lost one of his tattered, canvas shoes as his body soared through the air. His father would make him do his brother's chores for a week if he lost that shoe. He was held around the chest from behind, while a man slapped him across his mouth so hard he thought he might lose his front teeth.

The foul-smelling guy behind him muttered, "Quiet, kid. We'll take care of you now."

Take care of him? They were hurting him!

Shoved into the back of a shiny black vehicle, before he could reach to steady himself, he was grabbed by another big man with dark hair and dark clothing. Then his eyes were covered with a dusty cloth and another vile-tasting cloth was shoved in his mouth. They tugged his wrists together with what felt like scratchy rope, and then manhandled him into the seat.

He clawed at the unreachable rope, his fingers too short. But he kept trying. His father had taught him he had to fight for his place in this world, and he'd learned that well enough in school where he was ignored simply because he was Romani. Gypsy garbage.

But no one had ever forcibly taken him like this before. How could he, all of eight years old, stop it? They were big men and he was blindfolded.

The vehicle smelled like gasoline and stale, greasy food. He wanted to be home safe with his nana and his dog, Mutt.

"Not a long ride," the man with the awful breath said, slapping him hard on his leg so he cried out against the cloth in his mouth. "You are *wuzho*. You'll be helping people in need. Fine boy."

Helping people? He liked to help people because that showed them he was not the garbage others claimed he was. But *wuzho?* He knew that meant something about pureness or being clean.

Who would help him?

He stopped struggling and tried to breathe through his nose, though the dust and dirt from working in the potato field at the edge of his nana's farm clogged his head and made it difficult to draw in air. His tears soaked the cloth over his eyes, and he choked up a sob. He chewed nervously on the gag.

These men were not nice. They were not going to help people. He'd give up his dog, Mutt, right now to be back in school, taunted and teased by the others.

Would his nana realize he was gone before the sun set? His brother had ditched out, as usual, to go smoke with his friends in the forest. They'd once started a fire on purpose with cigarette cinders and a half a bottle of vodka stolen from one of their parents' cupboards. It hadn't blazed for more than ten minutes before rain had snuffed it out. His brother never got caught. Never got in trouble.

Bet his brother would never get kidnapped by bad people, either. Nobody would touch him. If his brother returned to the field by the end of the day and didn't see him, he might ask his nana about him, he might not. His brother didn't pay much attention to him, other than to shove him out of the way.

The vehicle hit a pothole and his body lurched sideways and smashed against the door. His forehead hit the metal clip on the seat belt and the icy burn of metal digging into his skin made him cry out. But he couldn't hear his voice, only the pounding of his heartbeats.

You'll be helping people in need.

Over and over he repeated the words in his head. Until he believed them.

GARIN BRADEN STROLLED into the containment room, walled with riveted steel panels, in the basement of a building he rarely visited, but owned for business. He kept a numbers of "offices" across the world. The steel floor clanked dully with each stride he took. The room was humid and smelled of rust and rancid water.

His freelance assistant, Slater, stood waiting for him, hands akimbo. The man was in his thirties, divorced twice, adamant about mixed martial arts and a vegan lifestyle and spent winters in a Tibetan ashram. He possessed no body fat whatsoever. Solid muscle.

Garin peered over Slater's shoulder. In the center of the sixteen-by-sixteen-foot room, a bald and barefooted man tied into a steel chair, sweat and blood on his face, defied him with a hardened gaze. Could either have been from exhaustion or desperate fear. Smelled like fear, but Garin knew to never judge a man by his expression.

"What's his break time?" he asked Slater.

Slater rolled a lazy grin across his narrow face. The stub of a cigar was always stuck at the edge of his mouth like a plug to stop the drool. The cigar seemed like an affront to the man's otherwise austerely healthy lifestyle, but then who was he to judge? "I give him forty-five minutes. An hour, tops."

An hour? Slater was slipping. He may be lean and lanky, but he had fists of iron and a vicious determination to get to the truth. And of all the times for expediency, this was it.

"That ship is out there somewhere," Garin said. "Carrying my merchandise."

They'd lost GPS contact because of a storm off the Mediterranean coast. And Garin had immediately suspected foul play. His equipment was top-of-the-line. Someone had broken communications, and he wanted to know who.

Sometimes his hires were not as top-of-the-line as his equipment. It was a risk a businessman had to take.

"I need to get to that vessel before the Syrian authorities do," he said, stating the obvious.

Or someone less law-abiding within the government would take off with his booty. Well, not his exactly. He was just the middleman. The ship was due to intercept with a buyer, a new client Garin did not want to piss off.

"Will do."

Smacking a tape-wrapped fist into his palm, Slater performed a few fighter-style bounces on the balls of his feet and returned to the sweat-soaked detainee. On the floor near the wall lay a length of thick, rusted chain, and on top of that was a battery-powered drill fitted with a diamond-tipped router bit. Slater didn't often use props; they were for show.

Garin didn't linger. If Slater couldn't get the man to talk—and quickly—the night was going to be a long one. The detainee was a contract agent, he guessed. Someone the government had hired for a one-off surveillance job. And he wasn't sure which government that was, exactly. Usually, such agents' allegiances changed from job to job, and tracking their home base was impossible. They were ghosts for hire.

Three hours later, the man finally broke. It was too late to intercept the ship unless they used heavy artillery. Garin did not want to engage with the Syrian government. He preferred the argument with the client instead.

"Sorry, man." Slater wiped the sweat from his face. Now the chain hung about his thick neck, another man's blood brushing streaks across his pumped biceps. "He was a machine."

"You win some…" Garin let the sentence hang there. Clutching his fingers into a fist he fought the urge to grab Slater and smash his head against the steel wall. He'd wanted to win this one, but he wasn't going to get misty over the lost supply. A bigger, better batch was out there somewhere. New clients were also an easy catch. "Did he cough up a name?"

"Yes, it's one you've heard before."

Garin blew out a heavy breath, not having the patience for Slater's dramatic pause.

Finally, with a wincing tilt of his head, the man said, "Weston Bracks."

Garin let out a hiss.

Should have expected as much. Why hadn't he? Bracks had been a tick on his hide for years, nearing nemesis status, though Garin would never admit to it, nor would he allow any man to best him without retaliation.

Bracks kept coming back for more and more. And Garin's pride would not allow him to give the man a win. This game of cat and mouse had gone beyond annoying.

"It's three in the morning," Garin said. "Thanks for your work. I'll be in touch."

Slater wandered out, leaving cleanup to Garin's morning crew.

"Bracks." He blew out a breath and fisted his opposite palm.

Again. And Garin with a full schedule over the next twenty-four hours. He needed to nab a few hours of sleep before tomorrow's meeting in the Czech Republic, a three-hour drive from his home in Berlin. He never did business close to home, but this was a routine stop to ensure smooth operations. As well, he'd arranged a quick pickup in the area. Hell, since he was driving there he was going to do all the business he could.

Yet Garin doubted he'd catch a single wink now that the bastard had made an appearance in his life again.

Roux, Garin's one-time mentor and sometime adversary, got a good chuckle over his and Bracks's tête-à-têtes. Although they were hardly as civilized as that term implied, and commonly involved one or both of them racking up yet another international felony.

Roux said he was reminded of their—Roux and Garin's—own special "friendship." A dubious connection neither one would ever have guessed would last more than five hundred years. That *they* would last more than five hundred years. How that was even possible remained a mystery tied into the sword of Joan of Arc and the pair's failure to keep her alive. It was a mystery that confounded Garin Braden to this day.

He sighed.

Maybe he was finally acting like the old man he should be after all his centuries on this earth, but Bracks's latest hit annoyed Garin more than usual. The shipment had been a result of months of groundwork and careful negotiations. And now it was in the hands of the authorities.

"Too much work wiped out in an instant."

Bracks had gone beyond being a thorn in his side, and Garin intended to end this game once and for all.

EARLY THE NEXT day, Garin's entourage made a pit stop before they crossed the German border into the Czech Republic. Stopping in a small town to gas up, they had been offered free doughnuts with a full tank. His men had taken the offer, while Garin couldn't stomach the artificial sweetness. If he was going to destroy his health, he preferred recreational drugs.

Now they drove south of the border and, following the GPS instructions, arrived at an unmarked warehouse by the edge of a wooded area. In the distance, he could see silver flashes of water. Possibly a creek.

Garin strode into the warehouse, noting it was three stories high. The tin roof had holes in spots where birds perched, yet the walls were secure concrete slabs built in prefab sections. Three-quarters of the warehouse was empty. Two bodyguards—his own—flanked him. They were for show and safety. He wasn't so stupid he thought he could waltz in and out again with some new party favors. One of the musclemen was also his driver, the other just plain muscle.

"Monsieur Braden." A thin Bulgarian man wearing a multicolored knit hat with flannel flaps over his ears bowed and pressed his palms together before his chest in the universal sign for *namaste*. Knee-high riding boots showed a lot of wear and a long red-and-white, zigzag scarf looked like something someone's grandmother might have made if she'd been high on medicinal cannabis. The Bulgarian swept a hand back toward the goods. "Please, look over the product."

The "product" was crammed into the back of a rusted black delivery truck that was scoured with more dents and holes than an Army tanker in Iraq riddled by steel penetrators. The bodyguards assumed stances behind Garin at ten paces, and kept their eyes on the three men who accompanied their host. None were a match to the body shape and strength of his men, but that meant little. A concealed weapon always trumped a swinging fist. Which is why his men carried more than enough artillery to put down a stampede, if necessary.

From the haphazard arsenal pile spilling out of the truck, Garin fished a dusty AK-47. The folding stock swung out freely. Sand spilled from the barrel. Something rattled inside the receiver. And it smelled like…gasoline. This was not good.

He shook his head. He hadn't expected pristine secondhand weapons, but this was pushing his idea of acceptable. And while the assault rifle was a favorite among the military for its durability and ease of use, these weapons were more than a decade old, which shouldn't matter, but Garin guessed they had never seen cleaning oil.

"This is crap," he said, turning to his host.

Knit Cap waved his hands in a salesman's protest. "Oh, no, no, the weapons work perfectly well. Just give it a shake."

"A shake?"

He grabbed a magazine from inside an opened

cardboard box stuffed among the weapons and jammed it into the receiver. An easy fit. Expected. These weapons were designed to be durable, if not long-lasting.

Swinging about, Garin aimed at Knit Cap. The man didn't flinch.

Exactly.

Garin ground his back molars together. He was in no mood for this today.

"Your unflinching stance tells me you're confident this one won't fire," he challenged. "I don't like that."

Knit Cap shrugged.

Garin tossed the gun aside. It landed on the pile of weapons in a clatter, sending not only AK-47s sliding to the ground, but also a spill of fine sand he assumed had originated in the deserts of Kabul, which is where this shipment had supposedly come from. "Is this all you've got?"

"It is what you requested! Quality goods. They are in working order, I swear—"

Angered that the man should continue to insist what he was selling was anywhere in the same galaxy as a quality used weapon, Garin lunged and grabbed the machine gun he'd loaded with the magazine. Swinging wide and high, he fired. The bullets scattered, piercing the tin roof and sending the pigeons squawking—then abruptly stopped. The magazine dislodged with a pop, clattering onto the pounded-dirt floor. Despite the wood grip, the weapon burned above his fist where flesh met steel.

Slamming it to the ground, Garin swung around and grabbed Knit Cap by the scrawny throat.

The seller's guards made a move, hands sliding inside their jackets. Garin's bodyguards snapped up their pistols and stopped them, prompting the opposition's guards to raise their empty hands to their shoulders.

"Your definition of quality is skewed," he hissed at the audaciously fearless Bulgarian. "Where did you get these playthings? Your little boy's sandbox?"

"You expect mint condition for these prices?"

"I expect something that works." Shoving him hard to stumble against the door of the truck, Garin marched away to the sounds of fists meeting jawbones as his bodyguards cleaned up the mess.

"Having a bad few days," he muttered.

The hijacked shipment last night and now this?

He had a phone call to make to a New York auction while they traveled on to Liberce. That call had better lift his spirits.

"I'M SORRY, MR. BRADEN, but there seems to be a problem with your credentials," the woman on the other end of the line said calmly and professionally.

Normally by now, he would have complimented her in a charming tone, but the Germany to New York connection was static, so Garin had to strain to hear her, and couldn't judge if she was young enough to make charm worth it, or old enough to appreciate his efforts.

"We can't allow your bid through until matters have been cleared up."

Item number seventeen sat on the auction block as they spoke. Clearing up credentials would take longer than it required for the auctioneer's hammer to hit the block and close the sale.

Sitting in the passenger seat of the Mercedes SUV, watching the landscape soar by in streaks of green, Garin caught his forehead in his palm. A tumbler of Irish whiskey sat within reach in the cup holder. He wasn't sure whether to tilt it back or throw it out the window. The past twenty-four hours had not included his finer moments.

"Mr. Braden?"

"I'll look into it," he said, and hung up. He tucked the cell phone into a breast pocket.

The priceless black pearl, rumored to have belonged to the Sultan of Brunei—who had made his mistress wear it in a delicate place at the apex of her thighs—during the Ottoman reign would go to someone else. And he had a good idea who that someone else would be.

"Roux," he muttered.

About the only other person on this planet who had an interest in pretty little bits tied up with fantastical histories was Roux.

Garin didn't need the pearl. His goal had been to keep it out of the Frenchman's hands. Hell, he had to keep the old man on his toes. But now that he'd been denied the opportunity to bid on it, he felt as surly as if he'd been denied the whiskey a hand's reach away.

His credentials? His papers did have a tendency to color into various shades of gray.

Sucking down the whiskey, he then poured another two fingers and tilted that back in a couple of swallows. Raking his hands through his dark hair, he stomped the floor of the vehicle with his boot. He was being childish, he knew that. He didn't care.

He had one last appointment this evening. Routine check on an operation that ran smoothly without him, but required his presence on occasion to keep everyone in line.

"Canov, don't screw with me tonight."

He'd gone beyond patience. The next bad thing to happen would push him over the edge.

THE NEEDLE THE nurse wearing the pink dress stuck into his arm hurt. What she wore didn't look like a nurse's uniform, but rather like something one of his father's girlfriends might wear to their house. When he got sent to bed early. She smiled and patted his head, cooing reassurances and reminding him of his nana. Except she was about his father's age. Her hair was blond and her eyes were tired and edged with creases in her darkly tanned skin. He would sleep, she said, and he felt his eyelids flutter as she taped cotton to the inside of his elbow.

When they'd removed the blindfold from his eyes, he'd craned his head to take in the room where he'd ended up. Looked like a doctor's office, but old and dirty. A dingy yellow insect strip, thick with black flies, hung from the exposed lightbulb. The room didn't have a bright light or shiny steel fixtures like the one in Liberec he'd been in last year when his stomach had hurt and his father had rushed him to emergency care in the city. It only had one of those hanging lamps like his father used to see inside the hood of the car when he was working on the engine. And it didn't smell like the hospital, but like the sewers.

He didn't like it here. But he could no longer keep his eyes open. He wanted to scream. Maybe Pa would hear him and come wrap his arms about him?

Opening his mouth, the boy only sighed, and then blacked out.

THE CINDER-BLOCK warehouse was used to store weapons en route to other countries. Munitions passed through the warehouse in a matter of days and were usually trucked out in larger shipments. Nothing remained for long.

Canov ran a tight operation, and had never given Garin reason to question his allegiance. Though Canov took his own pay from the profits before they were siphoned to a bank in Switzerland, if the man was greedy, he kept his greed in check.

Yet this evening, Garin felt a strange niggle at the back of his neck. Something wasn't right in this big almost-empty warehouse. They were forty miles from the nearest town and surrounded by a forest of gnarled oak trees. And there were too few munitions for all the muscle he saw standing around.

If Canov was managing a job on the side, he didn't

want to know about it. But neither did he want it to interfere with this operation.

"You've never questioned me before," Canov said, casting a glance to one of the men, likely security, who stood behind Garin near a sheet of white plastic that hung from ceiling to floor.

Garin wasn't sure why the plastic was there. The warehouse was big enough that they didn't need to partition off areas in such a manner. Its very presence made him want to look behind it.

"You know I am faithful to you, Monsieur Braden."

The man wasn't French, but he'd lived in Toulouse most of his life, and while he'd lost the accent, he hadn't dropped all of the words.

"Smells wrong in here." Garin glanced again at the plastic sheet, which he could not see through. "What's going on back there?"

"It is not your concern. I do as you request and never miss a shipment. You should allow me some freedom to attend other business matters."

"Not on my property." Garin turned and started toward the sheet.

A security guard put himself between Garin and his destination.

"Out of my way," Garin demanded.

The man, who matched him in height and girth, set back his shoulders and had the audacity to lift his chin and look him directly in the eye. One of his own? Or one of Canov's hires?

He was the boss here. And the way his day had been going, no one wanted to piss him off.

The bodyguard placed a palm under his cotton jacket. Unbelievable. The man was prepared to defend whatever was behind the plastic curtain with firepower.

Wrong move.

Garin's anger spilled over like a volcano spewing lava. He swung his left fist, meeting the man's block with the sound of cracking bone. The man did not waver, instead bringing up an uppercut that missed Garin's chin by a few hairs.

A blow from the left staggered him. Another guard must have joined in. Garin swayed. He slashed through the plastic sheeting with his arms and got tangled in plastic tubing attached to a tall steel rod. An IV stand. A bag of blood wobbled near Garin's face before falling and bursting open. Blood spattered his face and he spat out a mouthful, catching a glimpse of someone lying on a wood pallet, prone, unconscious.

Grabbed by the back of his shirt, he was whipped around and tossed toward the guard with the newly broken wrist. Garin fisted him in the jaw, dropping him to the ground. The guard scrambled away. He didn't want this fight? Smart man.

Incensed, Garin turned on his heel and growled at his aggressor. The blood on his face managed to ramp up his anger even more. The guard put up his palms in placation.

Wrenching a look toward his employee, Garin barked, "What the hell are you doing here, Canov?"

"It is a side job. Not your concern," he pleaded.

"I'll show you what *is* my concern."

Garin charged the bodyguard, using his weight to bring the man down. He punched his jaw, over and over. Knocking the man beneath him out cold with a final punch to his kidney, Garin stood. He didn't see Canov.

He headed for the side door. Whatever was going on behind the plastic curtain, he'd investigate later. He wanted to put his hands on Canov first.

Canov's white Jeep pealed away from the warehouse stirring a brume of dust in its wake.

Garin's man called out from the waiting Mercedes, "What is it, boss?"

"We need to pursue!"

He blinked and something blurred his left eye. Garin swiped a finger across his eyelid. Covered with blood. From the IV bag. That's when he remembered he'd seen a person attached to the IV.

He turned in the doorway, eyeing the plastic sheeting, rippled now along the edge where his body had mangled it. Whatever was behind there, Canov was right, it wasn't his business. And it wasn't something he wanted to make his business.

Whether or not he'd approved the operation, he was allied and associated with the dirty dealings.

"Blood?" He wiped his face.

The Mercedes engine revved. Canov wouldn't get away with this. Garin dashed outside for the vehicle.

2

Annja Creed had never been to Garin Braden's estate in Berlin. Last time she'd met up with him in Germany, it had been at his apartment. The man was a world traveler, so she'd never expected him to settle into something this...permanent. She judged the three-story mansion to be from the Tudor era because of the row of redbrick chimneys jutting from above the prominent cross gables. Not to mention the main door was centered beneath what was known as the Tudor arch. The setup was ritzy and the grounds were groomed, from what she could determine in the midnight gloom—she'd expected this of Roux, Garin's former mentor, but not of Garin Braden. She shook her head in disbelief that he was finally putting down roots. It had taken him quite a number of years to reach this adult life stage. She smiled at the thought of just exactly how many years.

A yard light flashed across the trimmed emerald grass as Annja parked the rental car before the mansion's steps and got out.

Drawing in a breath of fresh, jasmine-scented air, she stretched her neck. She needed a shower and sleep, but was running on the fumes of two candy bars and a Diet Coke she'd consumed at the airport. Not the healthiest meal, but it had been convenient and fast. As soon as the flight from New York had landed, she'd hopped in the rental and headed straight here. She had an appointment tomorrow morning, six sharp, so this might have been her only chance to pop in and visit her friend. A friend who wasn't always a friend.

Frenemies? Yeah, she could get behind that better. Every girl needed a man they liked to hate and hated to like, right?

A year or so ago, when they'd met up while either adventuring or dodging bullets—or both—Garin had mentioned he had an artifact he wanted her to look at if she was ever in his neck of the woods. A mysterious artifact owned by a five-hundred-plus-year-old man? Annja hadn't let that enticing invitation slip her mind. Now that she was here in his jasmine-scented woods, best to grab opportunity by the throat.

Annja jogged up the curving limestone steps in front of the house two at a time, finding the more she moved the less the jet lag pulled at her exhausted muscles. She knocked on the front door, foregoing the brass lion's head knocker because…did anyone really use those things?

After several long moments, a butler greeted her with a yawn. As his mouth closed, his eyes opened wider in recognition and he invited her in. Interesting. She guessed Garin must have mentioned her....

"We were not aware you had arranged a visit," he said in a clipped tone.

She almost laughed out loud and had to bite her tongue to hold it in. A British butler? Garin Braden had a British butler and a mansion. Just like his former mentor's setup in France. Except Garin couldn't stand Roux's lifestyle—the two were at each other's throats more often than not. So when had Garin patterned himself after his sometime enemy?

"In the neighborhood and thought I'd stop by," she offered, barely suppressing her enjoyment of this insight into the man she thought she'd known pretty well.

The butler glanced up at the full moon as he closed the door behind her. "Wait here," he instructed. "I'll see if Mr. Braden is available."

Why was it all the butlers Annja had happened to meet were stuffy and British? Did no one but the English aspire to butlerdom?

Annja strained to see along the foyer's dark paneled walls, hung with ancient paintings, each one worth more than a decade's rent on her apartment in Brooklyn, she felt sure.

"Tell him it's Annja Creed," she thought to call out, just in case.

"I know," the butler called back.

She'd never been here before, or met the butler, but she assumed Garin had availed the help with the necessary details regarding all the people that may "stop by." Though, apparently, stopping by simply wasn't done this late at night.

Annja leaned forward to inspect the signature on what looked like a Renoir, and found it was indeed by the nineteenth-century impressionist. She wasn't familiar with this painting of a woman with a red bow in her blond hair, and that gave her a thrill. Could Garin possess art the modern world wasn't aware existed? If indeed he'd been alive since before Joan of Arc's death in 1431, he may very well have received it directly from the artist.

A man who had lived five centuries offered enough hands-on history to interest Annja endlessly.

"Some day," she muttered, "I will pick the man's brain."

She strolled to the next painting and tried to guess its artist before checking the signature. Small dots made up the entire canvas, pointillism, and she had to step back to take in the full picture. Georges Seurat was the only name she associated with the style. Art history wasn't her strong point. She preferred medieval studies, and old bones and pottery to canvas and paint.

Checking the signature, she read a German surname she wasn't familiar with. Well, wasn't like only one artist had cornered the market on the style.

Long minutes had passed when suddenly she heard an angry growl and a door slam somewhere in the vicinity of the second floor and around a corner. Garin's voice carried down to the foyer. "Tell her I am in no mood! I'll see her in the morning."

"Is that so?" She could have taken the train straight to the Czech Republic, her destination. She was sacrificing valuable sleep time to make this visit. And it wasn't as if she owed the man anything.

When the butler reappeared, she put up a hand. "I heard. I know when I'm not welcome."

"He's had a trying day," the butler offered.

"Right. Poor guy. Trying must test his every nerve. Give him my regards. Tell him next time I'm in town, I'll call first. Apparently I'm not on his list."

"If you could return in the morning?"

"I'm headed to Chrastava. Archaeology always trumps a date with Mr. Charming. I'd tell you to give him my regards, but…save that."

She strode out, and instead of driving for more exhausting hours, decided to hop the train south to Liberec, so she could catch some valuable sleep before jumping into a new and exciting adventure. Or at the very least, an intriguing archaeological dig.

ANNJA MANAGED THREE hours of sleep on the train and did half an hour of yoga stretches and sun salutations from her seat before arriving in Liberec, once the unofficial capital of Germany within Czechoslovakia. The yoga woke her up and stretched her travel-weary muscles, and gave her an appetite. She managed to find scrambled eggs and sausage at a mom-and-pop restaurant near the train station—which was more a bar than an actual sit-down diner—then procured a rental Jeep and headed for the dig outside Chrastava. It should only be another dozen miles northwest.

She was footing the bill for this trip herself, though this dig may have potential for an episode on *Chasing History's Monsters,* the cable TV show she cohosted. She'd decide when she saw the site. And she certainly wasn't going to call Doug Morrell, her producer, and fill him in until she knew more. Much as she didn't mind her archaeological adventures being documented for possible show fodder, this one might push the limits of her patience. Her producer had eclectic interests. If Doug heard about Luke Spencer's discovery, he'd put on a black cape and fangs and wield the TV camera himself.

Annja, who'd been in Venice wrapping up an assignment, had gotten a call from Luke Spencer, the dig foreman yesterday morning. He'd said there'd been an exciting discovery that could date back to medieval times. She'd eagerly agreed to meet him today to join his crew.

The dig interested her. But what held even greater fascination for her? Luke Spencer.

She'd met the man a few years ago at a Natural History symposium at the Petrie Museum of Egyptian Archaeology in London's University College. He was a man of few words, smart. Not terrible to look at, either. They'd shared drinks after at the Volupte bar on Tavistock Street, and she couldn't forget his soft Welsh accent.

Driving into the small, industrial town, Annja took in the half-timber housing that likely hailed from early last century. In a quick online check about the city she'd learned Chrastava boasted many baroque-style buildings that hailed from the sixteenth century. There was also a firefighting museum she would love to check out if time allowed.

Word of Luke's find had traveled fast to judge from the hawker's cart at the edge of the city square she drove slowly past, her window open. The young, bearded blond man sporting a colorful Hawaiian shirt looked American, and had a decidedly New Jersey accent, yet his wares were purely superstitious hokum. Garlic wreathes for the doorway and around the neck. Wooden stakes were lined militantly along the red felt tablecloth, and tiny beribboned vials of holy water labeled with a black cross.

Annja couldn't determine if the handful of people looking over the hawker's table were serious buyers or after a silly tourist tchotchke. In this area of the Czech Republic, the modern blended with the classic, and there were many who still followed old traditions and beliefs.

"Tchotchke," she muttered, and smiled. Slavic in origin, a word for toys, actually. "Love that word."

But she certainly didn't want to imagine children chasing one another with wooden stakes. Surely Edward and Bella had blown up all the old vampire myths in an explosion of ridiculous Hollywood *Twilight* sparkle.

The Jeep was equipped with a detachable GPS device that spoke Czech, for which Annja only knew a few words, so she had to split her focus between the navigational screen and the gravel road. Oaks that looked centuries old lined one side of the road.

In the distance red-dirt mountains once mined for copper, zinc and iron stood out against the pale blue sky. Hills and mountains surrounded the city, the northern border of which butted up against Poland.

Riding with the top down in the fresh summer air, Annja was glad she'd applied sunscreen before setting out this morning. The sun wasn't bright but it was going to get hot and she knew she'd burn even if it clouded over.

According to her research, this area that curved the edge of Chrastava used to be a mining center in the fifteenth and sixteenth centuries. After the mines were abandoned toward the eighteenth century, they began manufacturing textiles. Principally Germanic from then on, after the world wars, the area was then inhabited by the Czech and other Slavic nationalities.

Luke was familiar with the local dialects, fortunately, because Annja only knew a few words in Romanian.

The sky was quickly growing overcast. Odd. Annja had checked the forecast from the car rental site and there had been no rain expected for the entire week.

She imagined the inhabitants of this area weren't too pleased with heavy rains. Flooding earlier in the spring had unearthed the area where Luke was digging. He'd been contacted by the local authorities after hikers had found bones sticking out of the thick, compacted mud and had thought they'd stumbled on a murder site. The authorities had figured out that it was instead an unmarked burial site, and attributed it to the Gypsies that had been traveling and setting up camp in the area for centuries. After giving the site a good three months to dry out and acquiring a small stipend and permission from the London University, Luke's team had started to dig.

Annja hadn't noticed much of the scenery last night during the train ride from Berlin, so she drove slowly now, taking it all in. She'd been too tired and annoyed that her surprise visit to Garin Braden hadn't been greeted with the pleased and practiced charm she had expected. Ah, well. She and Garin tended to rub each other the wrong way more often than not, although they worked alongside each other well enough when bullets were flying and quick, defensive reaction was required.

Admittedly, her favorite situation.

Life was meant to be experienced, and if that served up an extra helping of peril, then sign Annja Creed up for the full package. Nothing felt better than surfing the crest of life, fists up and teeth bared.

So she was an adrenaline junkie. There were worse addictions. And since taking possession of Joan of Arc's sword, she'd met more challenges than most would in a single lifetime.

She still didn't understand why she had somehow been chosen as the one to make the long-dead saint's sword whole. All Annja knew was that as soon as she touched the shattered pieces Roux had painstakingly collected over the centuries, the sword was in her hand, as sharp a weapon as it had ever been for Joan.

And when she let go of the hilt, the sword—now

very clearly *her* sword—seemingly disappeared into thin air. But she knew it returned to where it waited until she drew it again. The otherwhere, she called the holding place, for lack of a better name.

Ever since she'd first held the sword aloft, Annja hadn't needed to search out adventure…it had come to her. And as keeper of Joan of Arc's sword, she had no choice but to wield the weapon in defense of the innocent and the wronged.

Pulling onto a winding rutted gravel road, she navigated through a grove of giant beech trees frosted with graying bark before emerging into a clearing that looked out across a vast field of blue lavender. The dig site hugged the edge of a forest, and the land dropped abruptly to the lavender field where flooding had appeared to sheer off the hillside.

Pulling up, she scoped out the setup. Two vehicles. A Land Rover used to haul supplies— probably Luke's ride—and a rental sedan, likely driven by assistants or students. A small dig. Luke was a private man who tended to immerse himself in a project. He preferred to do his own thing, rather than delegate.

Luke had told her he hadn't notified the press, yet she suspected somebody with the dig had been regaling the locals. That hawker had set up shop fast.

Monsters were her TV producer's thing. But the skeptic in her knew exactly where an excursion into the buried undead was going to end, which is why she hadn't called Doug and told him about this particular adventure.

Seemed like some of the locals had followed

Luke's team out from Chrastava to watch from front-row seats. Annja noticed what looked like a family of six, dressed in bright clothing. The women wore lace. They all had dark hair and olive skin tones. The Romani, most commonly referred to as Gypsies, lived all across the Czech Republic and the Slavic nations. A much persecuted and maligned bunch, she was aware that Luke had recently written a paper on the roots of the modern Gypsy and their ostracization through the years right up until their current treatment in the principally German and Slavic schools in the area.

Perhaps they had been hired to assist on the dig. What for, she couldn't know, because she spied no sifters or find tables. And that would work entirely against Luke's M.O. to lead a small team.

She got out of the Jeep, grabbed her backpack and dumped her jacket because, despite the early hour, the day was already hot. She wore a blue T-shirt, khaki cargo pants and her standard hiking boots. At her hip she'd belted on a leather pack with her cell phone, digital camera, notepad and pencils, a few plastic Ziploc bags, a trowel and some local currency. Standard gear for a day spent squatting in a pile of dirt.

She swatted at a bug that landed on her neck. She'd forgotten bug spray, of course, but she'd tough out a few bites. She didn't need to worry about burrowing insects laying eggs under her skin in this part of the world. She hoped. The last time she'd visited Africa, she'd picked up a screwworm hitchhiker in her heel, and had had to trick the thing to the surface by wearing banana peels taped to her skin overnight. Effective, if squishy, but it had attracted fruit flies.

Nodding to the family, she summoned a good-morning greeting in German, but knew that wasn't the local language here. It was likely Slavic.

The beech tree canopy would probably protect the dig site from the harshest sun. It still felt like a sauna here in the clearing marked off by bright yellow pitons and dirt-rubbed white nylon ropes. The flood-sheered wall of dirt offered a place to stand and dig, which two students where doing. Another sat in the pit below it, squatting and intently focused.

Annja wandered to the edge of the pit and, thumbs hooked at her front pockets, looked over the hunched back of a man wearing a khaki shirt and a boonie hat.

"Creed," he said, not looking up to acknowledge her, his focus on the skull eye sockets he was brushing off with a fine sable brush. "No film crew with you?"

"Uh, no." Had he expected as much? "I don't generally travel with an entourage."

The man shrugged, but was that disappointment that pulled down his mouth? "Just so. Come down and check it out."

So much for official introductions.

Annja noticed the Romani family had moved closer as she climbed down into the eight-by-eight-foot pit. She knelt beside Luke, not five feet from the dirt wall where one of the students at least nodded to acknowledge her arrival.

Luke offered her a dirt-crusted hand and she
shook it.

"They your cheering crew?" she asked with a nod
toward the curious family.

"I'm afraid not. They seem to be the proverbial
angry villagers," he said, pushing up his hat with the
wood handle of the brush to reveal a sun-browned
face with white creases in the skin flaring out from
the corners of his gray eyes.

Right. It had been his eyes, she recalled now, that
had made it impossible to say no when he'd asked her
for a drink. And it had been his eyes she'd wanted to
see once again. Yep, definitely worth the trip here.

"They've been muttering about *mullos* all morning," he said, "and the evil eye has been flung about
quite freely. Addison is freaked. Oh, meet Mueller
and Addison. Annja, the guys." Luke gestured to the
two men digging at the wall.

Mueller nodded and tipped his John Deere cap to
her, and the other must have been Addison because
he only muttered, "I am not freaked. Okay, maybe a
little. That old lady gave me the evil eye."

"Don't worry," Annja said. "The evil eye's bark
is always worse than its bite." She turned to Luke.
"Mullos?"

"I prefer to call it a *blutsauger* myself."

"Not you, too." Annja chuckled. "The German
translation of vampire? You've confirmed my worry
that I'd be driving into a bad horror flick. What's
next? Masked knife-wielding stalkers?"

"Who can know?" The man managed a smile at

that one. "Actually, properly translated, *blutsauger* means the chewing dead."

"Right." Annja eyed the skull Luke had been working on, half revealed in the bed of dirt. There was an intriguing object stuck between the mandibles. "The chewing dead. The dead who are feared to rise after death and chew through their funeral shrouds, who will then go after their families and neighbors to satisfy their undying craving for flesh and blood."

"You have to love superstition," he said.

"I don't have to, but I admit the vampire myths never seem to fade."

"You can't keep a good vampire down. He just crawls back into his coffin for a few centuries, then comes back stronger and even more hungry."

Not sure what to say to that one, Annja reached down and stroked the cold, dirty surface of the skull's forehead. It had once been a living, breathing person. She loved the adventure in learning the answers to who, what and why.

Luke's shirt was dusted with dirt and she eyed the plastic pocket protector in his front pocket, filled with a pencil, dental picks and a tiny trowel.

"Didn't think anyone wore those things anymore," she commented lightly.

"What? You don't like my nerd badge?"

She chuckled. "We call them geeks in America."

He patted the pocket. "And bloody proud of it. You hear about the skull they found in Venice a few years back?"

"Yes. Wasn't it dug up at a sixteenth-century burial site of plague victims?"

"It was."

"The skull had a brick in its mouth—*her* mouth. It's one of the first vampire burials known in archaeology."

"Yet another one hit the news recently. A Bulgarian find. Seems like Bulgaria has a lot of vampires. They've recorded over one hundred corpses found with stakes or iron rods through the chest."

Annja settled into a squat next to him.

"I imagine many a 'vampire' was found after the natural stages of decomposition pulled back the skin and hair from the corpse," he said, "making it appear as though the teeth had elongated and the corpse had begun to chew its way through the shroud."

"So the uneducated person sticks an iron stake or nail, or even a brick, in its mouth to prevent the corpse from chewing."

"Right. Or a brick may have accidentally fallen into the burial site and gotten lodged in the mouth. But we can't sensationalize such an accident, now can we?"

Annja smiled. "I haven't had a chance to get to the University of Florence to take a look at the Venetian find."

"You don't need to." Luke tapped the hard, rough object in the mouth of the skull, which, at first glance, most laymen would take for a rectangular stone. "A brick. I'm guessing around sixteenth century if it's at all within the same time period as the Venetian vampire."

"So we're going to go with the label of vampire, then? Nice."

Luke nodded. His eyes glittered. Annja felt the same enthusiasm. Not so much for the vampire aspects of the find, but the whole history and learning about why societies did what they did when they hadn't known about things like decomposition and the fact that, once you were dead, you pretty much stayed that way.

Some of the rumors surrounding the Venetian find had touched on zombies. Even today the sensational story of a zombie waking up from his funeral sets off terror and hysteria. The dead awaking could be explained scientifically today through an unobserved extremely low heart rate and breathing. Back in the sixteenth century, not so much. Ridiculous, considering the word *zombie* hadn't been in use back in the time when the body would have been buried.

"Glad to have you on board, Creed."

"Extremely pleased you invited me here. What made you think of me?"

He bent over the skull again and brushed the dirt around the brick that was exposed to the teeth in the skull. "Truth? Just the other night I caught a repeat of your television program."

Sometimes Annja wasn't sure whether hosting *Chasing History's Monsters* was a boon or bane in the eyes of her archaeology colleagues. It had definitely upped her worldwide recognition, which again was not always a good thing, especially when dealing with the unsavory sorts she now tended to stumble on to because of the sword. It was never cool to have a criminal suddenly nod knowingly and mention an episode of the show. Some even thought they could use her prestige for financial gain.

"I love that you keep the skepticism alive on the show," Luke continued. "Someone has to have their head on their shoulders when the locals are wielding stakes."

Indeed, it was her job to state the facts and steer her producer, Doug Morrell, as close to the truth as she possibly could. Albeit, it was difficult at times when Doug was a master with Photoshop and tended to enhance the monsters they found if the monsters had perfectly natural appearances. He'd even added wings to a bulldog once to create a living gargoyle.

On the other hand, Doug's Photoshop magic proved a ratings booster and if Annja didn't like it she could leave the show. But, admittedly, she loved *Chasing History's Monsters,* fake fangs and all. And it did provide opportunities to travel she'd otherwise not have, as well as a travel budget.

Annja glanced toward the family who, upon seeing her speculation, lifted their fists to their faces and waggled them, pinky finger out and toward the sky.

"Was that the evil eye?"

"You've been blasted," Luke said, and snickered as Addison cursed under his breath. "Scared?"

"No. I thought the evil eye was a sign of protection."

"It is, but it's protecting the giver of the evil eye. Which makes you the receiver, and that's never good."

"I suspect a person has to believe in the power of the evil eye to have it affect them. So I'm good. Do they even know what you've found?"

"I put a guard on the site last night, so they haven't been able to get close enough. Hired a Romani in town, not from the encampment where I suspect the peanut gallery hails. But Daisy, who was working with me yesterday, does have a condition of the running mouth."

"I saw they're already selling garlic and stakes in town."

"Bloody hell." Luke sighed. "There's a Romani encampment about a mile west of here, on the other side of the forest. I suspect the entire camp will be on us by nightfall, torches and pitchforks in hand. If not guns."

"They can't actually believe you've uncovered one of the chewing dead."

"Vampire."

"Right, a pissed-off dead thing that seeks to rise and suck the blood from its family and friends. And even if such things did exist, it's long dead. Can't hurt anyone now."

"Annja, I expect you would understand that superstition and ritual still breeds deep in the DNA of these people. Don't get me started on their elaborate burial rights. But suffice it to say, death is not a natural thing to the Romani, and with it brings great fear and anger."

"Superstition is a powerful force. All right, so prepare for pitchforks?"

The man's smile was genuinely warm and inviting. And those irresistible eyes.

Annja pulled a trowel out from her waist pack. "Mind if I do some digging?"

"Please." Luke leaned back against the dirt wall. "You can take over here for me. There is an entire skeleton attached to this skull. I've uncovered the femur down there, and a few phalanges there." He pointed to the finger bones sticking up from the dirt as if clutching at air. "I'm in mind to take some pictures and have some breakfast while I make a few notes. You hungry? I've got hard-boiled eggs and herring."

Not the most appetizing offer. "I ate before I got here, but thanks."

"Fine, then I'll do the most ungentlemanly thing and eat in front of a woman. While the head and brick are the most interesting, we'll need to dig out the entire skeleton. If you want to work your way down, you're more than welcome."

"I will. You go eat. And keep an eye on the angry locals. I don't want to take a stake to the back."

With a chuckle, Luke hopped out of the pit, and offered Addison and Mueller the same repast. Both men accepted, but Annja suspected only as a means to take a break and not for the culinary treat.

As Luke passed their curious bystanders, he

bowed and then gave a high five to the child who eagerly played along. The kid had dark hair and eyes, and a cute round face. Annja decided that if he hadn't been taught otherwise, he would grow up believing the same lies his parents had learned from their parents.

Sometimes history could be a nuisance.

3

"She said she was headed where?" Garin asked his butler.

"Chrastava. Isn't that where you've just come from, Master Braden?"

Garin muttered an affirmative, and scrolled through the contacts on his cell phone. Why was Creed getting into his business? Chrastava was close to where Canov had set up shop.

"Why is Annja in the one place I least want her to be? Did Miss Creed say what she was doing in Chrastava?"

"No, sir. Well, perhaps she mentioned something about an archaeological dig. Or did I assume that?" The butler left with the breakfast dishes on a silver tray.

Garin scrolled to Annja's phone number, but didn't call her. It was purely coincidence that she was here. He had invited her to stop in if she was ever in the area. She must be doing some research for that television show she hosted.

Would going to Chrastava to investigate look like he was trying to make amends? He didn't do amends. Amends were not required in this situation. But he was curious, and she was only an hour away by private plane.

Besides, he had left unfinished business in the warehouse. Likely Canov had cleared out by now, but he'd give it one last look.

THE PALE AND distant sun began to set. Luke had suggested they cover the site with a tarp for the night. He had arranged for the security guard to come every night at sunset, but the man hadn't arrived yet.

The insects had doubled in number and Annja vowed to find some DEET in town when she returned. Addison had brought over a tarp to help her cover the pit and they were discussing how to cover the wall where he and Mueller had unearthed two other brickless skulls. Those discoveries indicated this may have been a burial site, or even a family grave.

Rising voices from the growing peanut gallery prompted Annja to climb out of the pit and investigate.

Over the course of the day, she'd been cast the evil eye several times, had almost been spat on except she'd managed to step to the side while passing the crowd and had had to take a bat away from a small boy who was swinging wildly at the insects out of his mother's sight.

For what it was worth, they didn't appear angry

with Annja and Luke for digging up the remains of what she'd deduced they believed to be evil. But they certainly weren't pleased the thing existed.

And now the crowd gathered around something, or someone, and the shouting was only stopped by a pistol shot.

"What the bloody hell?" Luke joined Annja, and they approached the crowd, which was backing away from a tall man holding a gun. "Who are you?" Luke demanded. "This is an archaeological dig. There are no weapons allowed here."

Above the crowd's heads, Annja could see the man tuck a Glock inside his dark, tailored suit jacket. To her left an old man muttered, *"Mullo."*

Annja couldn't help grinning. If this man was the image these people formed of a monster risen from the grave, she had to hand it to their imagination.

"I'll handle this," she said to Luke. "He's an... acquaintance."

Shoving through the crowd, she reached Garin Braden, who had arrived in the black Mercedes SUV parked up the road behind the other vehicles. Hands on her hips, Annja looked him in the eye. It was only to her advantage to show the locals she wasn't afraid of the man.

"Why are they calling me *mullo?*" he asked.

"Good evening," Annja said, eyeing an elderly Gypsy who was getting too close with the bat she had earlier confiscated. "I have no idea. You suck on anyone's neck lately? And that doesn't include your dates."

"You're not that funny, Annja."

The crowd moved in closer, muttering among themselves, and Annja ordered them back. She nodded for Garin to follow her to the pit.

"Luke Spencer," she said in passing, "this is Garin Braden. Garin, Luke. Give me a minute, Luke. And watch the crowd. If there's going to be a brouhaha, this guy's the obvious one to start it."

Luke assessed the tall German with a keen eye, then nodded to Addison and Mueller, and as a trio, they went to see what they could do about convincing the audience to leave.

"To what do I owe the pleasure of this visit?" Annja ignored the constant insects buzzing around her head. "Does this have anything to do with your bad mood last night?"

"It wasn't a bad mood."

"Thanks for the hospitality, by the way. After a six-hour flight, such graciousness was mightily appreciated."

"I haven't come to offer apologies. If I had known you'd planned to stop by—hell. You have your moments of hostility, too, Annja, so get over it."

Obviously he was still in that hostile mood. Whatever artifact he'd wanted her to look at was now off her list of must-sees. And the history he'd witnessed? He could keep those secrets. Indefinitely.

She swatted at the cloud of flies. "So what brings you here? And with bullets flying?"

"That couldn't be helped. They were swarming me like crazy people."

"Yeah, but no pitchforks. Yet."

Garin glanced back at them, then eased his big, broad shoulder forward and brushed a palm over the holster strap.

"What is it with you and people assuming you're a creature risen from the dead?" she asked.

"A man lives over five centuries, people start to wonder," he said with no humor at all. "I had a meeting with a few colleagues just outside of Liberec last night—"

"Last night?" she interrupted, confused.

"—before you and I crossed paths in Berlin. Blood was—never mind. Let's just say my colleagues and I experienced a difference of opinion."

He'd been here just before she'd arrived. What were the odds, she thought suspiciously. "Not hard to do with you," she said aloud. "I can say that from experience."

"Yeah, well, tensions were high. Word could have gotten around."

She stared at him. What exactly might the townspeople have heard about his "difference of opinion" the night before that caused them to swarm him now? Had he been caught drinking somebody's blood? Yeah, right. Except that's the only correlation she could see that might have made him a target here.

She pulled the small mag flashlight out of her back pocket and aimed the light beam into the growing shadows of the pit. She lit the skull she and Addison had yet to cover. "I've got my own vampire troubles."

Garin leaned over to look. "I don't understand."

She knelt beside him. "See that chunk of clay in its mouth? Just call that fellow one of the chewing dead. In medieval times—" She stopped and studied Garin. "Well, surely I don't have to tell you that people used to place stones or bricks in the mouths of those they believed would rise to kill their families and drink their blood. You having been alive in the end of the Middle Ages and all."

"Hell." Garin palmed the pistol at his hip. "I do not like vampire references."

"Yeah? Keep it holstered, buddy. These people have cherished their beliefs and traditions for centuries."

"I have a scar on my chest from centuries-old superstitions."

"Right. Wasn't that in Los Angeles where you were almost staked?"

Garin exhaled heavily and stood. His dark eyes took in the horizon where the sun scoured a thin red line across the black treetops demarcating sky and land. "I knocked over an IV filled with blood last night. It was attached to…I don't know. Shouldn't have told you that."

"What? You were fighting in a hospital?"

"Far from it. It's not something I want you to get involved in, Annja. I have the situation under control. My butler had mentioned this was your destination. Just wanted to stop by the site and make amends for my abrupt behavior last night."

"You said you weren't going to apologize."

"Have you heard me apologize?"

Could he make a bigger issue out of muttering a few simple words of regret? Probably.

"I wanted to invite you back to my place for a meal," he said.

Only if he told her more about the person he'd seen hooked up to the IV. He'd been fighting around a sick person and it hadn't been in a hospital?

Annja curbed her voracious curiosity. She had work here that fascinated her, and she had no intention of getting involved in whatever nefarious dealings Garin Braden had his hands in—very likely illegal.

"Sorry, already have a date for tonight. Luke and I are grabbing something in town," she said. "It's been a long, backbreaking day hunched over bones. I need some beer and carbs in a place no one will look twice at my dirty face and clothes."

"I'll have my butler ensure there are clean clothes waiting for your arrival," Garin suggested. "Would you pass over pheasant and centuries-old burgundy for potatoes and kraut?"

"You have my cell number. Call me if you suddenly find yourself on the run from people wielding stakes."

"Why? You want to grab a stake and join them?"

She forced away a smile. "'Course not. You know I do my best work with a sword."

"That I do."

Releasing the smile, Annja strode past Garin to her Jeep and pulled out the steel water canteen. Garin passed her, taking a moment to growl at the locals who followed him to his vehicle. She was worried his driver would back too close to the children at one point, but some sharp-eyed mothers grabbed them up before the angry, growling German and his entourage could do any damage.

"A good friend of yours?" Luke asked, leaning against the hood of her rental.

"More like occasional colleague and sometimes nemesis. For the most part, he's harmless."

It was the other part—the part that did not blink an eye to take down those who threatened him—that Annja wouldn't mention to Luke.

"I'll meet you in town," she said, and hopped in the Jeep. She hoped the security guard arrived soon. "I'm starving, and I want to hear how you landed this dig."

THE TIN-SIDED WAREHOUSE had been emptied of any supplies, weapons and the gruesome bags of blood Garin had seen the previous night. He strolled through the building, bodyguards posted at the doors with assault rifles against any stray, unwanted visitors. The superstitious locals couldn't have followed him from Annja's dig site, but he wasn't going to take chances. How was it possible that the crowd at the dig had associated him with the blood he'd stumbled across in the warehouse? And how could IV bags of blood lead any sane individual to draw the conclusion of vampirism? Events had transpired from annoying to plain weird.

He'd expected this mutiny after his argument with Canov, and he should mark it off as a business loss. Except the man owed him for the last two shipments, and the fact he'd been operating a side scheme under Garin's nose didn't sit well with him. He wasn't sure what Canov was up to, but sensed it wasn't something he wanted traced back to him. If it hadn't *already* been traced back to him. Loose ends needed to be singed to a crisp.

He had put out feelers in Liberec. If Canov had set up elsewhere, Garin would know by nightfall. The man wouldn't be so foolish to press his luck, but he was known to circulate in the area, close to family and friends, a support network of vicious thieves who wouldn't blink at slashing a man's throat.

Or a child's?

Garin eyed the dried brown blood on the floor, littered with rubble from the hasty move. He thought he'd seen a child in this room, but it could have been a small man. Emaciated from blood loss?

Good thing he hadn't mentioned as much to Annja. The woman would be all over it right now if she suspected a child had been hurt. He had no proof. Hell, he could have imagined seeing anyone on the pallet. He'd had blood in his eyes from the fight, and hadn't been thinking beyond his anger.

The stink of foul bodily secretions hung in the air. Someone had been in this room, and whatever had been done to them had not been a cakewalk.

He turned abruptly and marched to the door where one of his men stood guard.

"Dresden, you stay here, and keep your cell on. Give it forty-eight hours. Let me know if anyone returns."

"If so, do you want me to detain them?"

"Yes."

"Dead or alive?"

Garin pondered the ease of the second option, then shrugged. "He'll have more to say alive."

BY THE TIME she'd returned to town the few cafés were closed and Annja had opted for a prepackaged turkey and mayonnaise sandwich from a gas station and a carton of chocolate milk. Luke was staying in a hotel across town from her, and promised her a homemade breakfast tomorrow.

Over milk and questionable turkey, alone in her hotel room, she detailed the day's events on her laptop, but left out Garin's appearance. The vampire superstition was more salacious than intriguing, though she was curious about people who could believe the creature existed. That a buried body could actually rise from six feet under and come after them? But those bones hadn't been six feet under. Maybe that's why they had needed the brick.

Online, she navigated to her favorite archaeology site and searched for info on the Venetian and Bulgarian vampire finds. She had to remind herself, "It's not a vampire, Annja, not even close."

Vampires did not exist. Only superstition and tradition kept them alive in the beliefs of some. And

Luke calling it a vampire would only feed their superstitions.

From the few articles posted, there wasn't much more on the skull than she already knew.

The Venetian skull had been buried with the brick.

The corpse in Bulgaria had been found with an iron stake in its chest. As had a hundred other skeletons unearthed over the years, most traceable to the sixteenth and seventeenth centuries.

One skeleton was on display at the National History Museum in Sozopol, which—Annja found humorous—also displayed six bones believed to have been John the Baptist's.

You've got to love history and its juxtaposition of ideology in museums.

Calling it a night, she went to bed by eleven, congratulating herself on getting some much-needed sleep. Tomorrow promised breakfast and a day spent at the dig.

4

Luke held good to his word, and met her at a cozy little restaurant next to a beauty salon that advertised "Hollywood-style manicures" with a few photos of Angelina Jolie pasted in the window. She chose scrambled eggs and sausage stuffed with savory fennel and garlic.

"No pink slime in this stuff," Annja said gratefully as she bit into a spicy sausage.

"Pink slime?"

"It's a U.S. thing," she said. "Consumer panic. Put a few companies out of business a few years ago. Do we ever really know what we are eating? So many chemicals in our foods nowadays. Although Britain is way ahead of us on GMO labeling. Anyway, you were going to tell me how you managed to land this dig?"

"Right." He sipped his coffee, murdered with cream to a deathly beige, then prodded his overeasy eggs with a fork while he spoke in that quiet Welsh accent that would have put a smile on Annja's face even without the fulfilling repast. "You know I've got Romani blood in me?"

"No. Welsh Romani?"

"Yes. My great-grandfather's side. My mother made sure we grew up with little knowledge of that, though. Only learned about it a few years ago, and that sparked my interest in the Gypsy culture. Last year I spent time in Chrastava studying the Romanis and their beliefs. There's a housing development east of the city that welcomed me and my questions, for the most part."

"That's right. You did the paper on bullying in the schools."

"It's such a shame. And the bullying is widespread across the world, even in my homeland of Wales. Many Roma children drop out or are homeschooled. Yet they are homeschooled by parents who dropped out of school themselves. I wasn't able to complete my research, which included the rich vein of beliefs that runs through the Romani, because my father took ill only a month after I'd been here."

"I'm sorry about that." Annja paused from sipping her Diet Coke. "Is he better?"

"He's got pancreatic cancer." Luke stopped prodding his eggs and looked out the window, clearly not seeing the house special in bright pink letters.

"That's awful. If…you need anything, Luke…" Annja always felt awkward about offering sympathy. It didn't come easily to her. She hadn't known a lot of compassion when she was growing up in the orphanage, although the nuns tried their best to compensate for the children's lack of parental figures. "Sorry. I don't know what to say."

"You don't need to say anything. It's a vicious cancer. The survival rate is abysmal. I spent a lot of time with him after returning from Chrastava last year. He knows I love him, and I also came to understand that he doesn't wish to suffer. When he's ready to go, I won't hang on to him and ask him to stay. And with that, let's change the subject, okay?"

"Right. Sorry." She inwardly chastised herself for saying sorry so much. Sometimes listening was the best kindness a person could offer. "So you were familiar with the area…?"

"Oh, yes, that's why I was called here. I got to know the authorities last year. Made a friend of one of the deputies. And after the flood, and the initial discovery of bones in the mud, the first person they thought to contact was me."

He tilted a grin at her.

"I managed to finagle a grant from the university for the trip here because of the article I'd written. Further research, don't you know." Now the twinkle returned to his eye, and Annja felt some relief that he'd put thoughts of his father aside. "Gypsies and vampires. So much history and storytelling in those two words."

"And yet we're not even close to Dracula's castle."

"No, Transylvania is a good trek east from here. But that doesn't mean the dead don't travel fast."

"Ah, a *Dracula* quote. Luke, I sense a fascination for horror movies and fanged ones in that glitter in your eyes."

"I do love Bela Lugosi's silver-screen rendition

of the prince of darkness. And I confess, I once dressed up as Dracula for a Halloween party. Had the red satin lined cape and ruby pendant. Wore some pointed fingernails and even pointier fangs. You wouldn't believe the women hanging on me that night."

"I can imagine it wasn't entirely because of the fangs."

"You think?" He stabbed the eggs with his fork.

There was nothing whatsoever wrong with making nice with a handsome, smart man who shared her interests. Though vampires weren't one of them.

"So talk to me about the beliefs the Romani have about the dead rising," she said. "Though I know it's possible, I still have a hard time believing people in this day and age can be so secluded as to still buy into outrageous mythology."

"The Romanis have unique burial rites and beliefs. You need to understand those first."

Luke offered her the coffeepot the waitress had left at their table, and Annja pushed her empty mug across the table to receive more of the slap-you-awake brew. She refused the cream, and cringed when his coffee again turned beige.

"Belief in the supernatural is fundamental to the various Roma tribes," he explained, "and varies from tribe to tribe."

"What tribe lives in this area?"

"West Slavics that originally hailed from Germany. The town name was once called Kratzau in German before the Slavs migrated here after World

War II and it was changed to Chrastava. Though the Romas are traditionally Germanic, the Slavs have interbred, and nowadays it's quite a mix. Anyway, to the Romani, death is unnatural, and it may anger those who die."

"I knew that, but why the bad attitude?"

"The living fear the vengeful return of their dead."

"A complete one-eighty from most beliefs," Annja commented. "Most believe death a natural end or new beginning."

"It is fascinating, isn't it? But the Romas do believe death is a continuation of life instead of a final death," Luke agreed. "That's why the newly buried dead person can even be—supposedly—angry that he is now gone from this mortal plane. And before death, when a family member senses death is near, he contacts everyone. Family arrives to sit vigil by the dying, and seek forgiveness for any misdeeds they believe the person might hold against them after death. They want the dying to go to the afterworld without a score to settle against them."

"Sneaky. Gives a person good reason to be kind while alive. What if the death was unexpected?"

Luke shrugged. "Then I guess if I were Roma, and had committed a crime or sin against the deceased, I'd pack my bags."

"And stay away from skulls with bricks in them."

"Exactly. I'd expected the Roma would be more concerned about the recent dead. Apparently, though, the deceased can hold a grudge for centuries— judging by the locals' fear of our discovery at the dig site. I haven't come across any research that concludes one way or another."

"I'll take a look online when I get a chance."

"Please do. You'll find the whole thing fascinating. Another ritual observed following death is to burn or destroy all the deceased's worldly goods. The Roma must never sell an item and be seen to make a profit, and other Roma are particular not to buy or accept articles that may have belonged to the dead. Usually they will try to sell the goods to those who are unrelated or *gorja*."

"Non-Gypsy?"

"You know a little Romani?"

"Less than a dozen words. So the Gypsies must not believe in a hell or an afterlife?"

"Oh, yes, with death they move on to a supernatural existence, sometimes reincarnating as an animal or person. That's where the belief in the *mullo* comes in. The living or chewing dead. Though chewing dead is more a Germanic term than Roma, since the tribes in the city are German in descent I'm using the terms interchangeably. The *mullo* will walk the earth in search of vengeance against those who wronged them, which is why all their belongings are destroyed and, well, why those who can will make reparations with the person while still alive. Once they sense oncoming death, they turn real nice toward the one headed toward death. Can you imagine?"

"Good time to take advantage of those who pissed you off, but if you're on your deathbed, not so good for enjoying it all. So the person dies and, if he's mad at someone, legend says he comes back as a *mullo*. I think that's slightly different from the legend of the chewing dead."

"Yes, well, they start as chewing dead, gnawing through their funeral shrouds, and once risen, I then assume the *mullo* part becomes effective. They say the *mullo* can appear as an animal such as an owl, goat or even a chicken, but most often a wolf. And seeing a wolf immediately after a death brings sure bad luck."

"Didn't Dracula have the capability to shift into wolf form?"

"He did. I suspect Stoker used a lot of the Romani belief system in constructing his protagonist."

"Protagonist or antagonist?" Annja challenged over a sip of her coffee. "Wasn't Jonathon Harker the hero of that story?"

"Was he? I'm not so sure, Annja. Dracula may have been one of the first romantic paranormal heroes to come along, if you don't include Polidori's Byronic Lord Ruthven. Or at least, that's the way modern society labels them—heroes—what with all the vampires running rampant in media of late. I wonder if Dracula sparkled?"

"Oh, don't tell me…?"

Luke laughed and downed the last of his coffee. "No, never. I'll stick with the black-and-white films. I'm not much for the teen *Twilight* movie craze that pairs mythological dead heroes with wide-eyed innocent heroines. If those heroines gave it some thought, they wouldn't in their right minds go on a date with a man so old, or with such hematophagic eating habits."

"There are worse diets," Annja said. "Such as anthropophagy. The leopard men in South Africa used to cannibalize their victims, and the African Maasai include blood as a dietary mainstay. And the Cajuns do make a fine *boudin rouge*. The pork sausage is rather tasty if you don't think about it too much. Still, some eating habits are stranger yet."

"Exactly. You eat processed sugar and shortening under the guise of pink smear."

Annja looked over the breakfast roll smeared with raspberry frosting she'd dug into while Luke had explained the Roma's death rituals. "Yeah, it'll kill me faster than a string of blood sausage might, but I'll enjoy the slow death." She tipped her can of diet soda to him. "I'll follow my death meal with that orange on your plate, if you don't mind."

He tossed her the unpeeled orange, and pulled out his wallet to leave a *koruna* banknote on the table as they rose and headed out. Stopping by the tin waste can outside the restaurant to peel the orange, Annja inspected the gray sky. The air didn't smell electric with the warning of rain, nor did she see any clouds.

"No rain," Luke offered, reading her thoughts. "But the sun likes to play hide-and-seek a lot in this area nestled between the mountains. It'll be another overcast day for sure. Let's head out."

"We can take my car," Annja suggested.

Across the street from where she had parked, the hawker of garlic and stakes had set up his red-and-green cart. Today he wore a white T-shirt that featured the design of a cape and a red cross down the front, as if he were an elegant vampire. He waved to Annja, and Luke cast her a wondering look.

"He may sell me a stake before my visit here is through," she commented, sliding into the driver's side of the Jeep. "You have to give him credit for industry and knowing what the market wants."

"If Daisy didn't have such a big mouth, no one in town would be the wiser to what we are working on. I don't want another repeat of what happened yesterday with the Gypsies staring at us all day. And then that man—your friend—I can't believe they thought he was *mullo*. But where did he come from and why?"

"Sorry about that. Garin was looking for me. He won't return."

"I hope not. But if he does, let's hope it's unarmed and in a much calmer disposition."

"Yes, well, the villagers are packing bats now so don't be too hasty to embrace nonviolence."

"You would defend yourself against women and children?"

"If I had to."

She caught his nodding agreement out of the corner of her eye, and studied his growing grin. She'd said something that tickled him. More and more, Luke Spencer appealed to her.

They passed through a valley paralleled by the mountains that Luke explained had been working coal mines a few centuries earlier. She chose not to let him know she'd already studied up on this. She enjoyed hearing him explain how the area had been rife with precious metals, and mining had briefly reemerged during the twentieth century. Yet with the recent flooding and shifting of the soil and some small hills, Liberec officials had put a ban on mining as a safety measure.

"Lots of Roma deaths in those mines, I suspect," he said as she turned onto the gravel road that wove its way to the dig site. "There have got to be vengeful *mullos* loping all around this area for sure."

"The Romani people don't get a very fair shake."

"Not a lot of places they're welcome," he agreed. "They're a consistently persecuted people, the Gypsies. Unfortunate. They're not all uneducated and not all thieves. It's a terrible stigma. Their skills in the healing arts alone are reason enough to stop ostracizing them and start paying attention and try to learn from them."

"What about the fortune tellers?"

"Really, Annja? That's a little judgmental."

"Sorry, but—"

"All right, I'll give you that. They can spot naivety a mile off, that's for sure. I had my fortune told to me when I visited previously."

"And? You going to fall in love, get married and have kids?"

"Actually, the fortune teller was upset that she couldn't see a future for me."

"That sounds ominous."

"Sure, but if I would have forked over another hundred *korunas* she would have cleared the block."

"Clever. Here we are," Annja said as she navigated beside the parked rental Addison and Mueller shared. "I see our welcoming committee has made themselves at home."

What appeared to be a family of Gypsies—a baby, three children, parents and grandparents—lifted their heads to look them over as Annja and Luke unpacked a few supplies from the back of the Jeep and headed to work. But there were many more Romani than just this one family already gathered.

"Is it like this every day?" she asked. "The audience?"

"Yes. But today is different. Annja, those men aren't the usual locals. And they have guns."

Now she noticed the four men—dark-haired and olive-complexioned—who walked around from behind the family and toward them, their boots crunching over the loose gravel. One had a rifle slung over his shoulder on a leather strap. The other two brandished pistols that looked as if the weapons had seen better days or needed a good cleaning. And yet another, the one standing in front of them, had what looked like a katana slung across his back.

A sword? Ninja Gypsies?

Anything was possible, and she was usually front and center to learn that hard fact firsthand.

"You stay here," Luke said, crossing around in front of the Jeep.

"Yeah, I don't think so," she muttered.

Leaving the supplies beside the vehicle's front tire, Annja followed Luke toward the men. Instinct made her want to summon the sword, but she didn't. Not yet.

Her colleague cast a glance over his shoulder, and winced when he saw she hadn't followed his order to stay put.

"I'm a big girl," she offered, shrugging.

It was always romantic when a man offered to protect a woman. And this man was physically fit and muscled, but rather lean and rangy. Luke could go a few rounds, she felt sure, but he wasn't armed.

On the other hand, the men wielding the weapons didn't appear as though they lifted weights, so perhaps Luke would fare well enough in a knockout. Digging in the dirt did exert a lot of muscle power and endurance levels were challenged after days and weeks under a hot sun. Whoever thought archaeologists were pansies was dead wrong.

Acknowledging the apparent lack of real firepower among the Gypsies, Annja took in the rest of the scene. About a dozen men and women were gathered around the tarp-covered dig pit; they seemed to be the usuals from yesterday. She hoped no one had contaminated the dig, but she didn't see the overnight guard Luke had hired. No baseball bats to be seen, but she could feel the angry vibe rising from the people like a tsunami hitting the mainland.

"You're trespassing on property the University of London has been granted permission to dig on," Luke stated calmly, raising his hands to indicate he meant no harm. The Welshman's normally soft, melodious voice was now surprisingly strong and steady. "We're here to do a job. We're not hurting the land and will return it to its original state when we leave. Now if you'll give us some room?"

One of the men holding a pistol said, "You have disturbed the *mullo!* It must be reburied!"

"It's not a *mullo,*" Luke said quietly. "We plan to lift the skeleton from the ground for further study. It's long dead. It won't bring harm to you or your families."

One of the men spat on the ground. "Another sign we have angered the undead."

"It's definitely dead, not undead," Annja said, then asked, "Another sign? What was the first sign?"

"One of our children has gone missing!" someone called.

"What has that got to do with this skeleton?" Annja replied "It couldn't have hurt anyone. Surely the authorities are exploring the kidnapping of your child…."

The man with the sword, still sheathed at his back, stepped forward. He was tallest and broader, making Annja suspicious he could hold his own even without the weapon. "They are frightened and unsure. And now you are uncovering the dead to rise again because their sacrifices have been too few."

"Wait a minute." Annja stared the man down. "What sacrifice? Sacrificing what? You don't mean your chil—"

"Kill them!"

The man with the sword fisted an angry gesture toward the woman who had shouted. His wife? She looked to be in her mid-thirties, around the same age as the man with the sword, but a hard life tended to age people much quicker, so she could be still in her twenties.

"We do not sacrifice our children," the man with the katana said in disgust at Annja's implication. "They disappear. Sometimes they return, sometimes they do not. It is the work of the *mullo!*" he said, raising his voice, apparently wanting everyone to hear him. He spat, then looked at Annja with a glint in his dark eyes. "You are responsible for bringing this nightmare to my people."

Luke's raised eyebrow indicated his skepticism matched Annja's own. If someone or something was taking children from the Roma camp, it wasn't a vampire. Especially not a "vampire" that had been reduced to bones in the pit yonder.

"The *mullo* is legend," Luke tried to explain. "There is no such monster. Monsters do not exist."

"Luke," Annja cautioned, but the man with the rifle lunged forward and peeled aside his jacket to reveal an emaciated shoulder criss-crossed with thick, silvery scars. Annja would need a closer look, but she'd guess a brown bear, which she knew lived in the area.

"A bear," Luke also guessed. "I'm sorry for your pain, but—"

"It was a monster!" the man protested, beating his shoulder for emphasis.

"I thought the *mullo* appeared as a wolf?" Annja posited.

The man shook a fist in the air. "Wolf-monster! It lives in the forest!"

"What could you possibly have done to anger a skeleton that could be centuries old?" Annja defied the man. "And even if the legend were true, the *mullo* only goes after those who have provoked its vengeance."

"The *mullo* is after our children," the woman who had spoken earlier broke in. "The bones must be burned. It is the only way to ensure the safety of our children and families."

"No." Luke started toward the dig pit, ignoring the click of the pistol triggers behind him. "This is an important find." He shoved aside the Gypsies standing in his way. "We've got to unearth the skeleton completely and bring it in to study. It is not animate or alive in any manner. It simply cannot return from bone to torment you. It cannot!"

Her colleague was unaware of the growing danger. Annja kept an eye on the man with the sword, which he'd quietly drawn out of the sheath at his back and held, blade down, near his thigh. The guy, she noticed, watched carefully as the one with the pistol rushed up behind Luke. The lackey raised his pistol hand, preparing to smash it across the back of Luke's head, when Annja shouted, and drew all eyes to her—and her battle sword.

As Luke went down to his knees, having received an abbreviated blow to the back of his neck, she swung toward the two gunmen still facing her. They dodged the swing of her blade, and one fired haphazardly. The bullet shattered the Jeep's left headlight. Annja swung wide. She didn't want to cause damage, just scare the men more than the skeleton apparently already did. She succeeded in backing them toward the crowd, which now moved as one toward the nearby forest.

A wolf-monster? This was fast becoming a *Chasing History's Monsters* episode.

With a throaty shout, she sent them all running toward the brushy edge of the forest. Only the man with the katana stood firm, blade held high and over his head, ready for her.

Someone called out encouragement to him to "send the *gorjas* running."

"This isn't necessary," Annja said, holding the battle sword out to her right in a sign that she would not engage if he did not press her.

She hated revealing the sword to Luke, but hadn't seen any other way to stop what had already turned violent. Besides, at the moment, Luke was discombobulated at best.

"You are making it necessary," the swordsman said. "You know nothing about the ways of my people. The dead travel fast."

Again, that line from *Dracula*. And that he used it to defend a ridiculous belief in the impossible didn't impress her. Something about the man was off. He wore a pristine black shirt, the collar pointed with silver tips, as were the toes of his boots. At his ears, thick diamonds glinted. A bit flashy, if truth were told.

"If you are concerned about what we will do with the remains removed from the earth you can assign a man to watch over us," she said. "We'll keep you in the loop regarding where the bones are brought when the dig is finished. We've found three skeletons so far, so we'll be here a few more days—"

The man swung his sword, cutting the air. Behind him, his people had gathered in a pack, eyes wide.

Out the corner of her eye, Annja took in Luke sitting at the edge of the pit, rubbing the back of his neck. Staying out of trouble. Good boy.

The man swung the tip of his sword out near her hip, and she heard it cut across the steel loop hanging from her belt loop where she often hooked a canteen. He stepped back, and by the look in his dark eyes, she realized he'd orchestrated that strike. Intimidation tactics, then. When bloodshed was what the angry Romani wanted.

The fact he'd found opportunity for such a move put Annja on guard. He was no man to take for granted.

"You're seriously going to take on a girl?" she taunted. It worked sometimes.

"I will do what I must to protect my own," he replied. "But if you put down your weapon first, I will follow. Perhaps we can talk about this?"

She liked the idea of an exchange between blades much better, but Annja consented with a nod. She wasn't about to lay down her sword, though. Not until he put his away, which he did, sheathing it behind his back.

She walked over to the vehicle and made a show of putting the sword in the backseat. By the time she'd returned to stand before her aggressor she knew the sword had returned to the otherwhere, until Annja once again needed it and could call it forth with a thought.

"Let's talk, then," she said. "But not with your angry crew flanking you. Can Luke and I take a look over the site to make sure no one has caused it any damage, then we can meet in town? Over lunch?"

With a nod toward the others, he said, "They will leave, but I will stay to watch over you."

"Fair enough." For now.

That spoiled her plans to make a hasty lift of the skull from the ground. But she hadn't mentioned how long it would take her and Luke to "look over" the site. If they played their cards right, they could finagle a few hours' work and perhaps lift the skull without the Gypsy swordsman being the wiser.

Annja strode over to Luke while the man spoke to the others in the Romani dialect Annja couldn't decipher.

"You okay?" she asked Luke, who slowly nodded. She inspected the back of his head and found an inch-long gash at the base of his scalp. "A little blood, but it looks like an abrasion. You're tough."

"Hurts like hell, but...where did you get that sword?"

Always difficult explaining the sudden appearance of a medieval battle sword in her hands. So she never tried.

"Just something I like to keep handy. Oh, hell."

She noticed the tarp had been lifted and the dig pit had been covered over with loose dirt. The skull, which had once been visible, was now completely buried. The dirt wasn't packed down, though, so they should be able to recover it. Enough to make her and Luke's day a long one. And that was if they weren't interrupted by more Romani. And if the man with the katana let them.

"I think there's a first-aid kit in the car," she said.

Luke nodded and she went back to the vehicle, the Welshman in her wake. She cast the Romani a glare, but he ignored her and made a show of slashing his sword once or twice in front of him. The Gypsies, and the three gunmen, began to drift into the forest. There must be a path through the forest to their encampment, Annja guessed.

Luke muttered something and she turned to see that he'd stumbled over to the Jeep after her and Katana Man. Luke was now gripping the Jeep door, leaning against it and not hiding the pain. She sensed the workday for him had already ended. "Sit down before you fall down. You could be concussed."

"It's not that bad. Just wasn't expecting a headache so early in the day."

She rummaged through the glove compartment and found a white plastic box filled with Band-Aids and alcohol. She had no idea where the Roma camp was, but it must be either in or on the opposite side of the forest. They could live in town, but she guessed most didn't.

Five minutes later, she'd treated Luke's wound, but hadn't put a Band-Aid on it because of all his hair. It was thick and soft and she tried not to run her fingers through it after she'd taken care of the wound. Smelled nice, too, like spicy aftershave.

"I'll survive," he said. "Now let's get to it. If we want to lift the skeleton out of the ground it'll have to be sooner rather than later. I don't suspect they'll stay away for long."

"You're thinking the same thing I was thinking," she said. "Their leader isn't going to take his eyes, or his sword, off us. You know some thugs we could hire to stand guard while we work?"

"Not particularly. The night guardsman has a day job. You?"

The image of Garin Braden's growling mug popped into Annja's brain. "Nope. Guess we'll have to hope the evil eye suffices."

5

It was high noon. Annja sat at the edge of the pit and tilted back the remainder of the warm water from a canteen. Luke spread out a small canvas tarp in preparation for laying their work on it. They had decided to lift only the skull because that was the most valuable part. The rest of the skeleton would have to wait until they could put in another two or three days of digging. Foremost, they wanted to protect the skull and brick from being stolen.

The Gypsy leader had situated himself at the base of an oak tree not thirty feet from the pit. He hadn't said much, but his keen dark eyes had crept along Annja's skin all day. He wasn't going to let them walk away with the skull, she suspected. But then, what did she know? That he was sitting aside, allowing them to do their work, did impress her. And confused her.

What was his story? He'd stood on the side of the angry villagers, and yet now he had settled in and was content to allow them to do what he'd vowed could never happen—remove bones from the site. Of course, she hadn't wandered over to see if his lowered head included closed eyelids. Was he napping? If so, they had to hurry.

"You ready?" Luke asked, and she turned her attention back to the task at hand.

They'd dug under the skull, leaving a good two inches of soil to support the fragile bone and make lifting it out easier.

"Do you find our silent sentinel disturbing?" Annja asked as they worked.

"More interesting, actually. He's been sleeping most of the day."

"No, he hasn't, he's—" At a look to the tree she could see that the man's head was bowed and his eyes closed. "Then we'd best work quickly before he starts taking inventory."

The skull, filled with dirt, and the brick weighed about four pounds, Annja decided as she placed it on the tarp. Luke then carefully wrapped it and tied it firmly with twine before gesturing she hold the plastic bag open to keep it all together.

"Did you encounter that man when you were here a year ago?" she asked, remembering now Luke was not new to the area.

"Not that I recall. And I certainly would remember a character like him, diamonds in his ears, sword and all. But I do know the encampment on the other side of the forest. I was only able to interview one person from there who was willing to give me any information on the troubles her son had had in the school. And that was only because she was moving in a week, and wasn't afraid of retaliation. Gypsies are secretive and don't trust easily. They are misunderstood. That's the reason for the mistrust."

"You seem like a man who can gain another person's trust easily. Your voice has just the right amount of authority."

"And yours has an interesting cadence," he offered with an eye-crinkling grin. "Brooklyn."

"You know my history from watching the show."

"You have me there, but I do like it. Your voice, that is. You, uh…" He wiped a hand over his chin and looked aside, then shook his head as if dismissing something he didn't know how to say.

"What?" she prompted, suspecting from his inability to meet her gaze head-on what he might have wanted to ask. No sense in making it easy for him. She did have her standards. "Do I dance with the Gypsies at night around the campfire while you're not looking?"

That made him chuckle. "No, Annja, I was wondering if you were, well—are you seeing anyone right now?"

"Not at the moment."

"I suppose relationships are difficult with your travel schedule."

"A challenge. But I do enjoy challenges."

He tilted his head. "You must get propositioned a lot."

"Not nearly as much as I'd like."

Annja stood, leaving that one hanging out there.

She'd had her share of dates and always managed to fit them into her schedule when the man was worth it. If Luke asked, she would definitely clear space for him.

Grabbing another tarp that they'd used to cover the pit, she unfurled it carefully, not wanting to wake their sleeping guard.

"How did you chase them away?" Luke suddenly asked, not looking at her as he carefully laid the tarp over the remaining skeleton.

"I would never chase away a proposition if I liked the man," she said.

He laughed. "Not the men who proposition you, but the men with guns who were here earlier."

He wanted an answer to something she couldn't explain. "I wield a mean evil eye."

"Doubt it." Luke straightened and wiped away the sweat from his neck, wincing as he fingered the abrasion, which had colored to a deep red since being pistol-whipped this morning. "I've watched your television show. You can handle a weapon well, though I assume that is production and editing. Never saw you with a sword, though."

So he'd seen her with the sword. Probably everyone else in the dig area had seen it, too. But she'd needed to call it to hand and it had served its purpose of showing the swordsman she was not to be trifled with.

The swordsman. She was curious how he'd come to own the katana and how he'd trained with it. From the few moves she had seen, he could be a skilled swordsman.

With a sigh, Luke leaped up out of the pit and took the bagged skull from her. "Fine. None of my business. Let's hope the Gypsies have gone. The sleeping guard we can deal with."

She could imagine Luke might hold his own on an adventure. That glint in his eye broadcast lust for something more. A something more she experienced often.

"I don't think so," the Gypsy said as he joined their walk to the car. Before Luke could set the skull inside the Jeep the man touched his sword tip to the string-tied blue tarp in Luke's hands. "That must be burned."

"We've discussed this," Annja said, putting herself between the two men. "The skull has to be dated and studied, but we can't do that here. Mr. Spencer is going to send it on to the archaeology department at London University where he works. I promised we'd keep you in the loop. You'll know where the skull is at all times."

"There was no such discussion." The man gave her a narrow look that bored through to her gut. What was it she had heard about Gypsies being able to read a person's soul? She filed that one along with Luke's fortune teller. "You said what you *wanted* to happen. I did not agree to that."

"I thought you didn't want the thing around? That it was a curse unearthed from the ground? What better than to take it out of the country, far from here, and remove all possibility of that skeleton returning from death to haunt your people? It surely can't rise without a head."

"Legend aside," the Gypsy said, "that is the head of one of our deceased. Some believe it is dangerous, but it will not be once it has been reburied. It stays."

"How do you know it's one of your own?" Luke asked. "This skull is likely centuries old. There is no apparent graveyard in the area."

"What of the other skeletons in the wall over there?" the Gypsy countered. "This site was obviously used for burial, marked or not."

"Sure, it could be a burial ground," Annja agreed, trying to keep him calm. "Yet how can you know the bones are Romani?"

"We bury our dead close to our homes to appease the deceased."

"Wouldn't you mark the graves?" Annja asked, but Luke didn't wait for an answer.

"You weren't even alive when this body was interred," he said. "And besides, your people have no real home in Europe. They bury their dead along the trails they travel from town to town. You claiming this skull as one of your own is like me staking claim to the entire cache of graveyards across Wales."

Annja, sensing the Gypsy's growing irritation, grasped his wrist as he flicked up his sword hand. The blade stopped under Luke's chin. Both men held each other in a deadly stare. Luke did not back down, showing her the mettle she'd suspected he possessed, while Annja was surprised at the tension in the wrist she held. The swordsman was strong, and wasn't about to back down from two unarmed *gorjas*.

"My home is where I lay my head each night," the leader hissed at the Welshman. "And if you cannot understand a man's right to honor the dead, then we will never come to accord on this matter. Release me," he said to Annja. "I will not harm him."

"Then sheathe that sword now."

The Gypsy stepped back angrily, but did as he'd said. He sheathed his sword with an elegant move that gave credence to her suspicion he'd done so many times before, and that the weapon wasn't just for intimidation.

"Have you trained?" Annja asked, hoping to deflect some of the testosterone toward male pride. "With the blade? I've not come en garde with you, but I guess that you're skilled."

"My father taught me. He was a master swordsman." He hit a fist against his chest. "This is my home. And I will not be chased out by you, or the Czech, or even the *mullo*'s angry spirit."

"We've no intention of chasing you anywhere."

"You don't understand, you—" The man pointed a finger toward Luke, then Annja. "You are an American, yes?"

"From New York," she said. "Brooklyn."

"The home of the great Statue of Liberty and freedom to all who walk your shores, yes? Well, I am Romani. We are not accepted anywhere we go. For generations we have been persecuted for simply existing. Can you understand that?"

"I may not be able to relate to it," Annja said calmly, "but I can understand. We're not here to offend anyone, only to research."

"Always science is the answer to intrusion upon another man's rights."

She was about to argue the whole rights issue, but the Gypsy continued his tirade and she wanted to keep an eye on his sword and make sure it stayed sheathed.

"We are not welcome in the city. They sniff at our money. Our women are called whores. And if something strange occurs, like a child who has gone missing, it is always the Roma. The authorities blame us because they think we are lazy and uncaring for our families."

"A missing child...." Annja caught his eye as he paced. "One of the Roma here earlier mentioned it. When did that happen? We're not talking about *mullos* now, are we? What's going on?"

The man spat on the ground and sneered, jerking his head up and away from her. When his eyes widened, Annja noticed the arrival of a black pickup truck. It stopped a hundred yards from where she had parked the Jeep but the driver didn't get out. The Gypsy waved to the driver, signaling him to either stay put or wait for him.

Then he turned and eyed the skull Luke still held tucked under his arm as if it was a football he was ready to throw for the long pass. Another glance to the truck. His driver waited.

Annja narrowed her eyes on the waiting truck—

dented, probably twenty years old—but couldn't make out the driver's features to know if he was Romani, as well. Not that it mattered.

Finally the Gypsy said, "You will not leave Chrastava with that skull." And then he turned and walked to the truck, leaving them with the skull and the means to pack up and drive off.

Annja tossed Luke a look. "What kind of threat was that?"

"If you've got that sword available," Luke said, "perhaps now would be a good time to get it out?"

The two stood there, watching the Gypsy get into the truck. Annja waited for the vehicle to drive toward them. Would this be an attempt to take them out? But instead, it backed down the gravel road and turned to drive away.

Again she and Luke shared glances that could only be interpreted as gobsmacked. That victory had been too easy.

AFTER A MEAL of pork and dumplings swimming in thick, savory gravy, Annja and Luke made their way back to Luke's hotel room. There he had a nifty setup of microscope, digital voice recorder and an iPad loaded with apps suitable to an archaeologist's needs that made Annja jealous.

"I've stopped using pencil and paper," he said when she asked about the technology. "Ever see a crew chief lugging around ten pounds of ring binder, paper and notes?" He lifted the iPad. "Mine weighs less than a pound and I can fit more material on it, and access my research back in London."

"Yes, but you have to recharge, whereas paper is always charged."

He dug out a small black box from his backpack. "Solar charger."

"Touché. And you have the geek badge. I can't compete."

He tapped the plastic pocket protector. "You want some coffee before we get down to business?" he asked.

"I'm good for now. But don't let me stop you."

Luke filled up the coffeemaker, then unpacked the skull, while Annja opened her laptop and checked on her email. An instant video message popped up in Skype and, seeing it was from her producer, she settled at the head of the bed, legs stretched before her, and answered the call.

"Hey, Doug, what's up? Must be early in the morning there in New York."

"I'm in Spain actually, finishing up a segment for the show."

The man's mop of brown hair hung in his eyes. His smile was always eager and a little goofy. In his twenties, he liked to wear geek-shirts—as Annja referred to the T-shirts emblazoned with pop culture logos—and today was nothing new. His brown shirt featured a bat-shaped design formed by white silhouettes of what appeared to be horror movie vampires including Bela Lugosi, Elvira and Count Chocula.

"Spain? You don't normally travel for the show,

Doug. At least, you're always complaining that the budget won't allow it. What's up?"

"Call it a working vacation." He skimmed his fingers through his hair and flipped it out of his eyes. "And I wanted to take in a few bullfights after hearing about your adventures in Cádiz. It's warm here!"

"That it is."

"And the women are gorgeous. Dark hair and eyes and the skirts that swirl when they dance."

"I never would have pegged you for a fan of flamenco, Doug."

"Is that what you call it?"

Annja smirked. Of course, the man only had eyes for the women in their swirling skirts. He always saved the technical details for the small research staff the show employed.

His face moved awkwardly close to the screen as if he were trying to peer through the monitor glass. Not a flattering view of his nostrils, at all. "Where in the world are you, Annja?"

"Why? I don't have an assignment for *Chasing History's Monsters* I've forgotten, do I?"

"No. Can't a guy call and check in on his favorite TV host now and then?"

"Sure, Doug. I hear your other favorite TV host is in the Bahamas filming about Lusca, the half shark, half octopus."

"A tiny bikini opportunity, if there ever was one. Why can I never talk you into a bikini for a segment?"

"That's Kristie's job. I'm sure it's even in her contract. I, on the other hand, prefer to leave something to be desired."

She caught Luke's quirked eyebrow from over the unwrapped skull, and shrugged.

"But seriously." Doug's face filled the screen again, and she never realized how bushy his eyebrows were until now. "What are you up to? On a dig?"

"Yep. Just toted a skull with a brick in its mouth back to the hotel and I'm going to have a look over it."

"A skull. With a brick?" Doug's eyes widened and his jaw worked furiously at what Annja guessed was a piece of gum. "You mean you dug up one of the chewing dead?" His triumphant fist pump filled the screen. "Yes!"

"What the—how do you—? Oh, right, you are a big fan of vampires," she said innocently. "I almost forgot about the little club you are in that dresses up like vampires and plays." She rolled her eyes.

"Play? We don't play, Annja, we reenact. And you bet I'm a vamp fan. I'm heading to Club Dread next month for the annual Halloween ball. I've got my Dracula cape and had the dentist make a new set of custom fangs for me. Annja, you've dug up one of the chewing dead? Why aren't we filming this for the show?"

"It's not a vampire, Doug."

Why wasn't she filming it for the show? It was exactly the kind of sensational fiction they produced. Annja knew the answer. Because right now she wasn't too sure how the angry townsfolk would react to a film crew.

"It's just a skull with a brick in its mouth. In medieval times the people were superstitious and—"

"And that's what *Chasing History's Monsters* is all about, Annja! Chasing. History's. Monsters! Seriously? Are you trying to keep this one from me?"

Yes, well, she had hoped to. Why had she opened her big mouth now?

"I need to fly out there and get a good look at the thing. Film it. You have a video camera with you, don't you?"

"Just the one on my digital. Nothing good enough for television filming— Doug, don't come out here. It's a dangerous situation right now."

"Dangerous? Oh, Annja, you are only stirring the fires. How can a dirty old skull be dangerous? Unless—have people been bitten?"

"No, no one has been bitten. Please, calm yourself. It's not the skull, it's the locals, or rather Gypsies, who are upset that the skull might belong to a real vampire that might rise from the grave to torment them."

"Really? Rampaging villagers? Oh, dude! And you're not filming? Annja, you're killing me. Right here." He pounded his chest. "Like a stake through the heart. Footage of torch-toting villagers is exactly what the show needs."

"No torches." Yet. "And *Chasing History's Monsters* has done vampires to death, Doug."

"And yet, the suckers keep rising for another bite.

Ha! I have to book a flight right now. You're in the Czech Republic, right?" He bowed his head, and Annja heard the clatter of keyboard keys. "Yes, I have you on my Find a Friend app. Ah, Chrastava. Where the heck is that?"

She could've kicked herself. A television crew was the last thing she needed on-site when they had no idea what to expect day to day from the Romani. On the other hand, when had she balked at taking a film crew through treacherous situations?

When said crew consisted of one vampire-crazy producer. She felt sure if Doug didn't find what he was looking for some supersonic Photoshop skills would kick in.

A glance to Luke found him leaning against the table where he'd set up the microscope, arms crossed over his chest, shaking his head.

"Eavesdropper."

Luke shrugged. "I don't see what's wrong with having a film crew to record our information. It might prove beneficial. I haven't yet mastered the camera with the iPad, or rather, I haven't taken the time to learn. I'd love to have another means of documenting my work."

"That's why you wondered where my film crew was when I first arrived." She figured out his misplaced enthusiasm just now.

Luke had the decency to look guilty.

"Yes, but you don't know Doug Morrell—"

"Got it!" Doug made the thumbs-up gesture on the computer screen. "My flight leaves in four hours.

I should be there by midnight. Where are you staying?"

Reluctantly, Annja gave Doug the address for her hotel, and warned him not to wake her when he arrived after midnight. By morning, she'd be prepared for his macabre enthusiasm for the undead. She hoped.

"See you later, Doug." She closed the laptop and apologized to Luke, though she suspected it wasn't necessary. "He's my producer. Always looking for an interesting idea. I suppose you're right. Any chance to document the research on film shouldn't be overlooked. I just worry about the crew's safety."

"This skull will prove sensational. Much like the Venetian and Bulgarian finds did. I could get a paper, or an article, out of this, maybe *National Geographic*'s interest. Though the link to vampires is slightly off. The word *vampire* didn't exist in the time period I suspect this was laid in the ground. Of course, no matter what you label it, it all meant about the same in terms of revenants and horror."

"Right. But *blutsauger* has been in use a while. And *mullo*. I should look that up." She reopened her laptop, and made sure Skype was off. She didn't need a play-by-play of Doug's flight to the Czech Republic. "*Revenant* would be the best word for a dead being that rises from the grave."

"I vant to suck your blood."

She glowered over the edge of her laptop at Luke's horrible impression of Dracula, and quirked a brow.

"Just what I need, two grown men wearing capes and fangs."

Annja focused back on the Google search. Not all links led to vampires. She'd forgotten *mullo* was also the name of a Celtic god associated with the planet Mars.

"If we're going to film," Luke said, "do you want to hold off on cleaning the skull?"

Annja thought about it. "I suppose. Action shots of me dusting bones are no money shot, but they do serve to show archaeological process. Necessary to balance the sensationalism on the show. Doug will bring a video camera with him. But let's figure out the time period, if we can."

"Without radio carbon dating, we can merely guess. I'm no anthropologist, but I'd place it mid–nineteenth century, only because I have a suspicion about the brick."

"Much more recent than originally suspected." Annja considered the skull. "Were they still placing bricks in mouths in the 1800s?"

"By then I believe they'd graduated to running pipes down through the ground and into the coffin. By affixing a cord or twine to a bell, if the dead were suddenly to come to life, the ringing bell would alert everyone."

"I thought that was to get help in the event of being buried alive—" she rolled her eyes "—not a vampire alarm."

"True. And by then, embalming had grown popular for the very purpose of keeping the dead, well, dead."

"And look where it's taken us. To hundreds of thousands of graveyards filled with chemicals contaminating our planet."

"How can an archaeologist like yourself possibly prefer cremation?"

"Let's just say that when I die, I hope it's fighting for my last breath as the lava flows over me. Or gasping for air five hundred meters underwater."

"You want to go out in a blaze of glory."

"Nothing wrong with that."

"Indeed." Luke stared at her a moment. Suddenly, he suggested, "Well, then, how about wild roses and thorns to keep the blokes down?"

"Why *do* you know your vampire mythology, Luke? I hadn't taken you for a vampirologist."

"A man glances over all sorts of esoteric information in the process of research. And I have read up on the Romanis. So many delicious beliefs and social customs with the Gypsies. It's difficult not to run into the undead while reading up on the people."

She clicked on *mullo* and read details they already knew about the legend of rising from the dead to seek vengeance.

"Do you know how to get rid of a *mullo?*" she asked Luke, who now tapped the brick with a dental pick he'd pulled from his geek badge. "You hire a *dhampir*—"

"The son of a vampire and his mortal bride,"

Luke filled in. "I believe the Marvel comic book hero Blade was a *dhampir*."

She looked up quickly. "Please don't mention comic books to Doug." He seemed confused by that, but she ignored him and went back to her research. "Hmm…there's no mention of bricks in mouths in the *mullo* legend. The Gypsies would drive steel or iron into a corpse's heart at the time of burial to keep it down."

"You've read about the Bulgarian vampire finds?"

"Yes. But refresh my memory."

"Excavating a monastery near the Black Sea town of Sozopol, archaeologists uncovered close to one hundred corpses with stakes driven through their chests."

"I didn't hear there were a hundred of them. Really?"

"You do seem to resist the whole vampire legend. The discovery has boosted tourism in the area. One of the skeletons is currently displayed at the National History Museum. It's dated to be over seven hundred years old. I believe the man was Krivich."

Annja searched her memory of medieval who's who. "The Crooked?"

"Yes, a notorious pirate and aristocrat, possibly a master of witchcraft, as well. Which was a good reason for the iron stake."

"I just read about this—isn't the National History Museum also the place where some of John the Baptist's bones are on display?"

Luke smirked. "Quite the variety of history they have on view there."

"So, an iron stake through the chest… That's similar to Dracula's wooden stake through the heart," Annja said.

"Iron used to keep back mythical creatures. Faeries most often. And, of course, iron swords were the weapon of choice for decapitating suspected *mullo* corpses."

"Well." Annja looked at the skull sitting on the table. "The decapitation part has already been taken care of, so if the Romas protest again we can use that in our defense. Decapitation means the dead can't rise."

"Good. So we've got our story straight."

They both chuckled.

Luke tapped the brick with the dental pick again. "Did bricks have holes in them by the mid–nineteenth century?"

"The holes first appeared when the extrusion process was developed to make clay bricks. Why?"

"I think this one has a hole in it. It could either be original or created by time and erosion. We'll have to remove some more soil to be sure, but I'll save it for filming," he suggested eagerly.

Annja glanced up into the man's gleaming eyes. "You're excited about the arrival of my producer, aren't you?"

He shrugged. "Isn't every day a man has the opportunity to work with a film crew."

"It's a crew of one."

"And you. That makes three of us. I'd call that a crew."

She smiled. "All right. We'll reconvene in the morning at the dig site. I have to head back to the hotel and wash…and prepare to meet Doug in the morning."

"I'll pick you both up at seven?"

"Sounds like a plan."

6

Santos eyed the lanky young American man who got out of the taxicab in front of a grocery store. He knew it was an American from the flashy gestures. The man had apparently wanted the cab to wait, but as the taxi drove off, leaving him waving frantically, he settled down and kicked the street pole beside him. He had a load of gear strapped to his back and carried a long black duffel.

Tourists always made their way through the town, but this one was unusual in that he wasn't with a friend and didn't wield a map or GPS on his phone to find his way about without bothering to lift his head to take in the sights.

Taking note of the hawker who was setting up his stand, Santos could only shake his head when the American man started picking up stakes and a garlic necklace. He handed over American cash to the hawker, who gladly took the currency.

With a spring to his step now that he'd claimed the ridiculous items, the American walked into the small grocery store.

And Santos waited to observe his exit five minutes later, beef jerky stick in one hand and a bottle of soda in the other. His hand itched for his katana. No wonder the media claimed Americans were all obese. Did they never eat real food that came directly from the ground or tree? This man, though, was skinny. It was a wonder he could heft what appeared to be some weighty baggage.

Santos decided to help him with that. He dialed up his buddies and made sure they found out exactly what this American was doing in the city. After his experience with the two archaeologists out at the dig site, he couldn't risk more eyes on this operation. And the last thing he wanted to report to his supervisor was a fouled plan. A media frenzy was not going to go down well.

"NO PRODUCER?" LUKE asked as they headed out of Annja's room the next morning. "I thought he was arriving at midnight?"

"I got an email that his flight was delayed a few hours. He's not answering his phone."

"You worried?"

"Yes and no. Doug's a big boy. He may have decided to do some sightseeing, maybe even film scenery for a segment."

Grabbing one of the complimentary sweet rolls from the dinette area as she followed Luke out of the hotel, Annja choked down the dried-out pastry.

"I've got coffee brewed and packed in the Range Rover," Luke said as he pushed open the swinging doors and they strode into the parking lot that was vacant except for a few vehicles. Not a lot of tourists in this area, and it wasn't peak season. "What the hell?"

A black van had parked beside the Range Rover, the side doors open to reveal a man sitting cross-legged, his arms wrenched around behind his back, and a burlap sack over his head. Annja recognized the Vans sneakers immediately.

Two men carrying pistols, scarves concealing most of their faces, approached Annja and Luke. Khaki pants and jackets made them indistinguishable from each other, except for the different colored scarves. Could these be the same men who'd held guns on them yesterday afternoon?

Quelling the urge to call the sword to hand, Annja erred on the side of caution and waited to see what would happen. They heard a sudden shout from inside the van.

"Doug?"

The man in the burlap hood struggled with another khaki-clad gunman.

"This is your friend, Annja Creed?" one of the men asked. She didn't recognize the speaker. And she didn't see Katana Man, either.

"Depends. I can't see his face."

"He says he's arrived to see you and talk about vampires." The guy with the gun tilted his head. "A strange man, if you ask me."

"Yes, he has his moments."

From behind the hood, she heard Doug whine. "Annja, please!"

"What's with the hood and the guns?"

"We've come to invite you and Mr. Spencer to meet our boss."

"An invitation?" She exchanged looks with Luke, who betrayed none of the nervous energy in his face that she could feel wavering off him. It was never good when the bad guys knew your name. "What's your boss's name? He is the guy with the katana sword?"

The men exchanged looks. "You'll know his name when you are introduced."

"What if we've already got plans?"

"Then the strange man in the van will be shot." The blue scarved man grinned widely and swung the barrel of his gun toward Doug's head.

Annja's instincts charged to the fore and she struggled not to move. Sometimes it was best to follow the trail and hope it led to answers.

"When you put it that way, perhaps we've got a few hours to spare, eh, Luke?"

"I imagine so."

"Where exactly is your boss?" she asked.

"Step inside the back of the van, Mr. Spencer. We'll have to put a hood on you, as well, for precaution. And you, Miss Creed, you'll run back inside the hotel and fetch the skull you removed from the site. My boss is particularly interested in getting a look at it."

"It's too delicate to transfer," she tried. The machine gun nudged her bicep. "It would be better if your boss came here to view it."

"We'll drive carefully. As you can see, we've already got precious cargo. Now move!"

GARIN BRADEN TOOK an MI-17 helicopter to Liberec, a private chopper he'd had retrofitted from a gunship to a personal carrier. A car rental waited at the small airstrip near the train station, and Garin now sat outside the Chrastava hotel where Annja was staying.

Hadn't been his first guess. He'd checked another hotel first, asking after Annja at the reception desk, explaining he'd wanted to surprise an old friend. The fact that the receptionist had been young and blushed when he'd given her a charming smile had helped his cause. Good thing the town was small and only boasted a few hotels. He would have never pegged Annja as someone who'd choose the only family-oriented hotel in the city. It offered miniature golf and free in-room family movies.

He did like that woman's surprises.

Now, he sat in the parking lot, observing the commotion. He'd been considering going in to knock on Annja's door until the black van had driven up. Strange sights like men carrying pistols and tugging along hooded hostages usually indicted Annja Creed was in the vicinity. And sure enough, she walked out of the hotel, toting something wrapped in blue tarp. One of the men gestured with a gun for her to move quickly.

"Creed, how do you always manage to get muddled in all the wrong situations?" he muttered. "I thought you were here for a job? Who would have thought archaeology could be so dangerous."

Was Annja's situation related to his difficulties in the area? Such a coincidence tested the odds. Bracks couldn't have learned that he and Annja were friends. It didn't feel as if this was another ploy to show him up. Hadn't the stolen ship been enough, anyway?

By rights, it was Garin's turn to retaliate against Bracks.

Until Garin knew exactly why she was being forced inside the back of the black van, carefully cradling a plastic bag the size of her head against her gut, he'd sit back and see what he could learn. He would follow the van, and move when it felt right.

WHILE ANNJA COULDN'T see where they were going, it only took ten minutes to arrive. She assumed they had driven southeast to the larger town of Liberec, six miles from Chrastava. The hotel room was small as far as hotel rooms went, and Annja, Luke, three armed guards and the still-hooded Doug had to cram themselves in. In the chair by the window a man wearing a fedora sat, cigar smoke curling up around his chin.

Cherry tobacco, she assessed. Loved the smell. Hated that she loved it right now, she thought.

One of the guards pulled the hood off Doug's head, and her producer blinked and looked around. His eyes landed on her and pleaded for an explanation.

"I told you," she muttered, "the situation is dangerous."

"Nice," he managed to say. "They broke the video camera. That's a huge red mark on my expense account."

The guard who'd removed his hood slapped the burlap sack across Doug's face. *"Drz hubu."*

"That means—" Annja started.

"I know. 'Be quiet,'" Doug finished.

Correctly translated it meant "shut up," but she'd allow Doug the gentler admonishment.

Annja's eyes went straight to the small arsenal on the bed. One assault rifle, a few Glocks, half a dozen blades and two military-issue grenades. The grenades worried her—she didn't want the hotel going up in an explosion should someone feel the urge to exert control over them.

Luke, his left shoulder against her right, remained silent. He wouldn't get in the way if she took action. It was Doug she couldn't rely on to not get his head blown off.

"Three?" the cigar-smoking man said, not lifting his head to acknowledge them. "I expected two. Who is responsible for making this a ménage à trois?"

"We found this man on the way to the site in Chrastava. Your contact alerted us to him. He looked suspicious, and when we questioned him, he gave us the woman's name."

Contact? This just got a lot more interesting.

The man in the fedora, his face still shadowed by his hat, turned to them. After a long moment, he stood, tugging at the lapels of his pinstripe suit and shaking out his arms so the sleeves fell properly. In wingtip leather shoes, he seemed to have stepped out of a gangster movie. His complexion was pale, not the olive tones of the Romas. His accent sounded distinctly British.

"Annja Creed. Archaeologist and television personality." He strolled his gaze from her head to her dirt-dusted boots, and back up her legs and torso in a manner that should have made her squirm, but only fired her anger. "And you are Luke Spencer, the supervisor on the dig site. A part-time professor of Sociology at the London University."

"You've done your homework," Annja said.

"Information is power, Miss Creed. But I don't like it when someone tosses a wrench into my events calendar." He stabbed his cigar in Doug's direction. "Who is this sorry-looking man?"

The guard kicked Doug's tennis shoe, and he blurted out, "Doug Morrell. Producer of *Chasing History's Monsters* and media celebrity. If I go missing, there will be people looking for me."

Annja contained the urge to roll her eyes. On the other hand, *Go, Doug.*

"And why would you go missing?" the man asked in an accent Annja thought had a touch of Cockney to it. "Do you expect to tumble into a dig pit and break your neck?"

Doug delivered the man a moaning wince. "We don't know anything!"

"What is there to know?"

"Who you are and why you kidnapped us?"

"Doug," Annja cautioned. "My producer has only just arrived in the city this morning to film a segment for our show," she explained to the Brit. "He has no idea what's going on. I could claim the same. What is your interest in us, Mr....?"

"Weston Bracks. International business opportunist."

Which, in Annja speak, meant a criminal with an inflated assessment of his freedom.

He smoothed a finger along the brim of the fedora, and Annja wondered if he'd watched too many gangster movies.

"It seems you've riled my townspeople, Miss Creed. Which isn't necessarily a bad thing for my line of work. Just...annoying. The balance between too much and just the right amount of media coverage is a difficult tightrope, eh?"

"Your townspeople?"

"Yes, well, I claim a certain concern for their well-being."

And she believed that one as much as the holy water in the hawker's cart was actually blessed. "What are you doing here?"

"I moved operations to the area after I'd learned about that fascinating skull. Where is it, by the by?" He eyed the wrapped package Annja held. "I might take a look at it. Always on the lookout for valuable artifacts."

"As I would expect from a business opportunist."

He winked at her. "I like you, Miss Creed. Feisty. Now hand it over."

"It's delicate."

Annja held out the wrapped skull. All instincts screamed for her to draw the sword and lay them flat, taking names later. "Let me unwrap it, please."

"Of course." He gestured to the bed arrayed with weapons. "Be careful of my pretties."

Annja laid the plastic bag next to the grenades and went through the motions of carefully extracting the skull.

Doug gave a low whistle, his eyes wide.

It had held together nicely, though a sifting of fine soil had been scoured off and scattered onto the bed as the tarp was carefully folded down.

"There was only the head?" Bracks said from over her shoulder.

"No, the full skeleton remains in situ," Annja said. "But we decided to remove the skull for fear someone might desecrate the site. They're superstitious in this neck of the woods."

"Superstitions are often rooted in truths."

She shot a glance at the misplaced gangster. She could feel the heat of his body along her arm, and she didn't care for the proximity. "Do you believe in vampires, Mr. Bracks?"

"Of course not. But belief can be a powerful thing especially for a—"

"Business opportunist," she finished for him.

He preened a hand over his suit sleeve. "The Romas call it *mullo*."

"You know your supernatural myths."

He shrugged. "I am a man of knowledge. Graduated first honors from Cambridge."

"What major?"

"Business and accounting. Step aside, will you? Back beside your companions."

She did so and watched with fists tightened near her thighs as Bracks looked over the skull. Surprisingly, he took care and only touched it lightly with two fingers to move it side to side. The brick was still firmly wedged between the mandibles thanks to the dirt they'd left packed in the skull. A thorough cleaning would loosen it, and confirm whether or not it had a hole in it, which would place it in the nineteenth century. Or perhaps even the twentieth.

The skull could be even more recent than either she or Luke suspected. Which would give more credence for the Romas believing it was one of their own.

"The *mullo*," Bracks said grandly. He glanced to his guards, and one of them made the sign of the cross. "You see?" Bracks looked to Annja and winked. "Superstition is deeply rooted in these parts."

"You said something about it not being bad for your line of work," Annja mused. "You moved operations to Chrastava after hearing about the discovery? That means you're either a vampire or a purveyor of fear."

"Both would be considered in the same line of work, yes?"

"In a manner, yes. Care to enlighten me on this particular business opportunity?"

Bracks chuckled, and with a gesture over the array of weapons spread across the bed, Annja decided she'd framed that question incorrectly.

"Gunrunning and vampires don't logically mix," she said.

The man scoffed. "I'm a businessman, Annja, and I take offense at that suggestion."

"Right. An international entrepreneur who thrives on the illogical beliefs of others?" She couldn't piece together the weapons and the lure of a possibly centuries-old skull, and she suspected he wasn't going to do it for her.

Bracks stubbed out his cigar on the edge of the nightstand, then tossed the butt in the tin waste can across the room by the door, making a basket.

Annja exchanged looks with Luke, who offered her a calm nod. In vast opposition to Luke's cool, Doug was sweating despite the rickety air-conditioning unit in the window that kept the room reasonably cool.

"So you've seen the skull," she said. "We'll wrap it up and take it along with us, and be on our merry way."

With a lift of his chin, Bracks silently commanded one of the men. A gun barrel poked into Annja's spine.

"I need to ensure this precious artifact does not fall into the hands of the ones who wish to burn it,"

Bracks said. "Can't snuff out the superstition before my work here is done."

"Don't worry. It's a valuable archaeological find. If anyone steals it they'll be looking at jail time."

"It's easy enough to destroy something without taking it away from the owner." Bracks reached for a Glock, checked the magazine and aimed it at the skull.

Luke tensed beside her. "Annja," he said on a breath.

Bracks was going to destroy the only evidence of the fascinating legend.

Annja curled her fingers about the intangible hilt of her sword. Was one damaged skull worth revealing Joan of Arc's sword in front of Doug and Luke? Or further endangering the two?

On the other hand...

At a knock on the door, they all froze. Annoyed, Bracks waved the gun toward the door. "Who is it?"

A kick against the wood slammed it inward. And standing in the doorway, Garin Braden flashed a devilish smile. Until he met eyes with Bracks, and then his charm dropped like rain. He growled and raised his fists.

"You!"

7

Only pausing at the surprise of seeing Garin in the doorway for a moment, Annja used the distraction to kick the backs of one man's knees with the hard rubber sole of her boot. He went down, his gun hand flailing out, and she grabbed the pistol by the barrel and easily twisted it out of his fingers.

His cohort was more on the ball, and swung a punch that connected with Annja's bicep. She almost dropped the weapon, but instead used the force of the punch to swerve and roll across the end of the bed, gun still firmly in hand. At the last moment, she remembered the skull on the bed. It was near the pillows, safe for now.

At the door, Garin pushed Doug and Luke aside. One of his meaty fists crunched as it met the jaw of one of the gunmen. A pistol round echoed in the small room.

Annja scanned the scene as she righted herself from the bed. Abruptly an arm went around her throat from behind. Her attacker's other hand crushed her wrist and squeezed relentlessly, compressing the ulnar nerve so she dropped the pistol onto the bed. Still, there was a nice assortment of weapons to choose from, if she could get her wrist free.

Luke had backed his shoulders up to the wall, watching helplessly. That was fine by her; he was out of immediate danger. Doug had crouched on the floor, arms before him in defense.

She couldn't place Bracks, but at the moment had to hope Garin's bulk blocking the doorway would keep everyone inside from leaving before they had permission.

The arm about her neck squeezed and lifted her jaw, compressing her throat. The attempt to kick off the bed and crush her attacker against the wall was only halfhearted, and Annja managed to stumble backward, being dragged as her aggressor lost his balance and they both went to the floor. Choke hold released, Annja rolled off him, gasped for breath and searched the floor for the gun she'd dropped.

One of the gunmen knelt in the doorway, spitting blood. He looked up in time to catch Garin's fist against his skull. Processing the impact, the man wavered, but didn't go down. Garin lifted him by the shirtfront and swung him around to land on the bed. While his attention was focused on the bed, Annja saw Bracks in his sleek pin-striped suit slip out the door, followed by the one who had been choking her.

She spied the pistol under the bed, but determined it was a long reach, so instead lunged up for a bowie knife on the bed. She threw it out the opened doorway, but the fleeing men had already turned a corner.

"Shoot." She grabbed another knife and asked Luke if he was okay.

The Welshman nodded and winced. "Who is that?" he asked with a nod toward Garin, who now loomed over Annja's shoulder. "Wasn't he out at the site the other day?"

"A friend—" Annja started.

"You said he wasn't a friend."

"Nice," Garin commented as he turned to check over the fallen man's body for weapons. He pocketed a switchblade and tucked the pistol inside the back of his jeans. "Not a friend?"

"Not always," Annja insisted as she grabbed Doug's hand and helped him to stand. Her producer was shaking, but he'd rally in a few minutes. "Who were they, Garin?"

"No time for chatter."

"Really? I'll lay bets that you're not here just to see me. You know those guys? What's up?"

"I hadn't expected him to be here. We'll discuss this later. Get your *friends* to a safe location. I'm going after them."

And with that, Garin strode out of the hotel room as quickly and mysteriously as he had appeared.

Annja blew out a frustrated breath at being left behind to babysit the menfolk. Whatever Garin was involved in, she was in it, too. How that had happened, she had no clue. So she would do her best to get that clue.

She dug in her pants pocket for her hotel room key and slapped it into Luke's hand. He now held the skull to his chest.

"Is it okay?" she asked.

"Think so. Now what?"

"You and Doug catch a cab and head to my hotel room. Although it isn't safe anymore. Just gather up my laptop and things, will you? Two minutes. No more. Then go to your hotel. It should be safe because Doug didn't know where you were staying to tell anyone. Got it?"

Luke nodded, then he pointedly looked toward the bed, scattered with weapons. "What about that stuff?"

"Grab a few if you're so inclined, but they're probably black market."

"I think I'll stick with the skull," Luke said.

"But, Annja." Doug sucked in a breath and blew it out, shaking out his shoulders and bushy hair as if preparing for a race. "They knew who you were when I mentioned you on the way to the dig site. Who were those men?"

"I honestly don't know, Doug. But I'm going to find out. And what was that about, anyway? Do you often walk up to armed men and announce you're looking for me?"

"No, they jumped me and tossed me in the van. I was standing in front of the grocery store drinking my soda, minding my own business and waiting for a cab."

"Then someone must have seen you were American and put two and two together. I'll check in with you later. I have to catch Garin."

"The man who is not a friend, yet apparently you'll not let him out of your sight," Luke commented.

Annja twisted a look at the archaeologist and wondered if that had been jealousy on his part. Interesting.

"Sometimes it's a good idea to keep the enemy close," she said. "I'll be back as soon as I can."

"I should come along," Doug said as he followed her swift exit down the hotel hallway. "I can film you in action."

Not if she had anything to say about that. "Where's your camera?" she called over her shoulder.

"Oh, hell. Those assholes busted it when they searched my bags."

Exactly.

"Doug, keep an eye on Luke. He's more skilled in history than espionage." She knew that word would bring a glint to Doug's eye. "The two of you go to Luke's hotel and wait. I'll be back. Promise."

Handing him some responsibility was what he needed to boost his confidence. "I can do that, Annja. I have everything under control!"

Annja dashed out of the hotel and scanned the parking lot for Garin's black Mercedes SUV. She spied it driving north a block away, and set off at a run. Surely, she could catch him. The town had a speed limit for vehicles, but not runners.

Annja heard a few car horns honking in the distance and determined the noise was due to Garin's pursuit of Bracks. The commotion sounded to be about a quarter of a mile to the west. She veered left, and caught sight of the black SUV as it slowed to a rolling stop.

She pushed off the balls of her feet, pumping her arms and legs. Since taking possession of the sword her athletic ability, which had been exemplary to begin with, had increased measurably, and she was still thrilled by her faster speed and greater strength. If she could ever figure out a way around the unfair edge the sword gave her, she'd like to run the Boston marathon. Although she'd need at least a month free to train.

Like that was ever going to happen.

Her momentum slammed her against the passenger door of the Mercedes and she pounded on the window to get Garin to unlock the door. When he did, despite his obvious exasperation, she opened the door and slid onto the passenger's seat.

"Annja!"

"I'm as thick in this as you are."

"You have no clue what you're dealing with." He pulled left, and she swung the door shut and buckled her seat belt.

"But you know what's going on, and that's what counts. Why am I suddenly chasing the same people you seem to be chasing? Or was that just a valiant rescue effort back there at the hotel?"

"Much as the idea of sweeping in to rescue the

damsel in distress appeals to me, I know there's no damsel in distress in this car with me."

"You got that right. I don't think the glass slippers would fit. Besides, I'd break them the first time I tried to walk in them. Who is this guy? He and his men kidnapped us. I need to know who and why, and I think you have the answer to that question."

"Would you believe me if I told you I didn't?"

She eyed his square-jawed profile as he navigated the street, which headed out of town and toward the hilly, forested terrain between Liberec and Chrastava. His jaw pulsed as he stared straight ahead. His dark hair swept his black shirt collar and he was currently wearing a goatee—perhaps to hide the scar she knew dipped from his lower lip to his chin. The man was vain about his looks.

Garin's fingers wrapped tight about the steering wheel. He liked to keep information close to the vest, and rarely doled out all the intel he knew. She accepted that about him. He wasn't an upstanding citizen by any measure, though he had shown her rare heroic moments that made it difficult to label him friend or enemy.

"Man's name is Bracks," he provided.

"I know that. He introduced himself. A business opportunist, of all things. And he's British and apparently educated. What else do you know about him?"

"That's all I can give you, Annja."

"That's all you're *willing* to give me, but I'll take it."

The car swerved onto a gravel road and gripped the surface with ease.

"Now answer this one," Annja said. "Do Bracks and his men have anything to do with vampires?"

She gripped the hand bar above the door as the SUV accelerated. Loose pebbles drilled out from the back wheels, spitting into the close ditches and pinging the interior metalwork.

"Vampires? Are you still on that kick?"

"It's become a common thread in my troubles lately. And you did almost get staked the other night. My mind just put two and two together."

"Vampires aren't real, Annja."

He had once shown her a scar on his chest from when someone had actually attempted to stake him because they'd thought he was a vampire. The former soldier who had once mentored under Roux to protect Joan of Arc had clearly lived a long time.

"I know that. You know that. But some people, most especially the Gypsies in this area," she continued, "steeped in tradition and age-old beliefs, don't know that."

Bracks had wanted to capitalize on the superstitious for reasons that evaded her. What kind of capital could a skull and frightened Czech citizens provide him? Didn't sound like the guy was dealing in illegal artifacts. He wouldn't need to scare the locals for that. Would he?

"The vampire connection doesn't feel right to me, Annja." Garin took another turn, and she saw the vehicle he was following. The road was well traveled by trucks so they went unnoticed as a tail.

"Well, something about the vampire myth has lured these guys to Chrastava. Bracks wanted the skull we'd lifted from the dig site."

"The one with the brick in the jaws?"

She gaped at him.

"Twitter," he explained.

"You're on Twitter? Wonders never cease."

"I change with the times. Unlike a gray-haired old bastard we know."

"Roux is pretty modern. And, hey, you seem to be trying to pattern your life after him—the big mansion, the British butler—so I wouldn't knock him if I were you."

Roux was the one Annja had to thank for Joan's sword. Of the two men, he was older, wiser and calmer than Garin Braden, but he'd never give up gambling or women.

"I don't get Bracks's desire to steal your discovery. It's a damn brick in a skull. And a dirty old brick in a skull, at that."

"It's valuable only historically to researchers. And yet, if the media picks it up in a big way, it could prove a tourism boost. I don't think Bracks is the sort of entrepreneur who's after the media and tourism angle, though."

"Too honest. Not his scene."

"Belief," she muttered, tapping the window as the foliage whisked by outside. Bracks had been keen on exploiting the local belief in vampires.

Men had committed terrible crimes because of strong beliefs. The Jonestown suicides. The Nazi concentration camps. The Trojans' belief in the wooden horse as an omen had supposedly brought them to their knees.

Briefly, Annja wondered what she believed in. She wasn't particularly religious, even having grown up in a Catholic orphanage. Leave it to the sisters to chase the faith out of her with a ruler and a stern demeanor. As a rule, she didn't believe in mythical monsters unless there was compelling archaeological evidence of its existence. And some monsters did exist. Some of them were even human.

She believed in owning her strength and following the way of the sword she controlled. Sometimes it seemed as if the sword controlled her. As if the sword demanded that if she could help someone she must.

Vampires? Not so much. But men who lived for centuries...

She glanced at Garin again.

The road had narrowed and both ditches were hugged by thick forest and roadside scrub. The car they'd been tailing was nowhere in sight, yet Garin still drove with determination.

"You know where you're going, don't you?"

He nodded, and didn't say anything else.

He knew what was going on, but he wasn't ready to tell her. She'd have to stay close to him, and hope they weren't driving into a nest of real bloodsuckers. The human kind who wielded weapons.

LUKE AND DOUG RETURNED TO Chrastava and gathered Annja's things from her hotel room. Luke's hotel was on the opposite side of town, a five-minute drive. Luke directed Doug to carry in Annja's backpack and laptop, while he handled the bagged skull.

The producer, who acted like a kid but was probably in his mid-twenties, had gotten over his scare. He'd complained about his broken equipment all the way from Liberec.

Luke wasn't sure how to take what had occurred back in Liberec. He'd experienced strange happenings related to artifacts found at dig sites before, though. He'd spent half a year in Egypt fighting against pot hunters who would sneak on-site after midnight, dig random holes in search of valuables he and his team hadn't yet discovered, then be gone by morning, possibly absconding with artifacts that would never know legal provenance or see the inside of a museum. These kind of thieves were generally a nuisance, but sometimes they carried weapons, and Luke had learned to keep his distance. Or else hire security, which was usually not accounted for in a dig's budget.

Of course, he wasn't comfortable at all with Annja having seen him cringing by the wall, trying to stay out of the way, while she fought the men with guns.

"Does this sort of thing happen often to Miss Creed?" he asked Doug as they went into his room and took a few moments to unpack. Doug tossed Annja's duffel in the open bathroom doorway; it was unzipped to reveal some clothing and a digital camera.

"Not sure." Doug set Annja's laptop on the desk next to the microscope. "Well, yeah, I guess it does. She does like adventure. Sometimes I swear she purposely seeks out the most dangerous route when we're filming, but that's all good. Then again, she keeps a cool profile about the stuff she does that's not involved with *Chasing History's Monsters,* so who knows?"

"You're her producer. You seem to know very little about Annja."

"I've known her for years, and the weird thing is, she grows more enigmatic every day. A mysterious woman. And she's gorgeous and smart. How can you not like that?"

Luke nodded in accord. How could he not indeed?

Still, he should have at least swung a punch or two.

"If only she would record her adventures today," Doug said. "Whatever it is she's up to has got to be interesting. What about the man she went after? The big bruiser who showed up to the rescue. He looked like real muscle. Someone I can entirely see Annja having on her side."

"He's not her friend, or so she says."

Luke sat on the end of the bed, holding the skull in the plastic bag. He smoothed the blue tarp. "So you think there's a television show behind this?"

"Oh, yeah. Vampires are hot. Even vaguely hinting at that old bone being capable of rising from the grave to stalk the living will hike up our ratings. I already know how I'll market it to teens. We'll use the tagline Beware: The Chewing Dead. Ha! I'm going to run promo on that one right around Halloween."

Doug joined Luke on the bed and nudged the plastic bag.

"So can I have a look?"

"Sure. It's been banged around enough as it is today, more handling isn't going to make it any worse."

Yet still, he took care in unwrapping the artifact. More dirt had fallen away, and he felt the brick move. If it dislodged, it might damage the mandible.

Laying it out on the plastic on the bed, he set it with the lower jaw down as the weight of the brick gave it the best position. Doug whistled as he had when he'd first seen it in the other hotel room, but he didn't touch it. He tucked his hands in the pockets of his sweatshirt jacket.

"To think someone thought this guy was going to survive being buried, chew through his funeral shroud and return to kill them all," Doug said. "But, hey, shove a brick in his mouth and that'll keep him down. Isn't it crazy what people once believed?"

"You mean to imply we still don't have similar crazy beliefs?" Luke challenged.

"I'll give you that. We all have our own weird beliefs." He leaned forward, sniffing the skull. "How old do you think it is?"

"Annja and I originally thought sixteenth century, though that was a guess. The brick seems newer, perhaps nineteenth century. Without radio carbon dating and an anthropologist to take a look at it, that's as close as we'll get until I can bring this home to the university's lab in London. I also want to get back to the remainder of the skeleton at the dig site. Can't leave that sitting out to be destroyed."

"You want to head out there now? I can help you dig. Hell, wish I could get some footage during the day. Do you have a digital camera that takes video?"

"I have an iPad that has a camera," Luke said slowly. "Annja said we should sit tight, though, and I'm compelled to follow her wisdom after the morning we've had."

"Yeah, but guys who sit around in stuffy motel rooms miss all the action. Come on, Luke old buddy." Doug flexed his biceps and assumed a superhero pose. "If the Romani are afraid of vampires, then don't you think it's our duty to remove the suspicious skeleton to keep them from chasing after people?"

"The bones aren't going to harm anyone. But the Gypsies may do harm to the bones. And I had only hired the guard for the site during the night. You're right. We can't let the skeleton remain in situ."

"In situ means in the ground, right?"

"Exactly—where we originally found it. But I want to secure this skull before we go. Hopefully there's a safe in here. Why don't you dig out my iPad and familiarize yourself with the camera while I wrap this back up?"

"Already know how to use it, but I will probably need to download video editing software apps. You mind?"

"Go for it," Luke said.

GARIN PULLED UP along the gravel road about three hundred yards away from a red-brick country house edged by high shrubbery. The shrubs prevented those driving by from seeing into the yard and house. They also prevented those inside from noticing anyone parked down the road.

He'd been surprised to see Bracks in the hotel room, standing over a scatter of weapons on the bed—and Annja. Then again, why did it surprise him that the woman now sitting beside him was in his business?

He didn't need Annja barging into his game with Bracks. It was a two-man board, and any extra pieces must be sacrificed. So now to sit tight and wait out the man inside the building.

And figure out how to get rid of the nosy archaeologist staring out the window to his right.

8

"Stakeout is fun," Annja muttered after they'd sat outside the vine-covered country house for an hour. Of course, that was a lie. She was antsy. The sun beamed onto her side of the vehicle and the sun visors did little but deflect the rays from her face to her arms and legs. She was thirsty, and Garin had no water in the car.

Scrolling through the daily news on her cell phone, she tried to not think about charging inside and swinging her sword to get some answers. "I could use some snacks."

Garin huffed and cast her a sideways glance, but didn't comment. She couldn't tell if he was seriously into this sitting about and waiting or as bored and anxious as she was.

"So," she said, "you show up at a dig site unannounced and quite a surprise to me, I must say. Then later you arrive in time to break up a tense meeting with a man who has ties to the dig—and, I presume, to you—though I can't figure out either one of the connections. Then you drive off, leaving me behind like it's your war and you're not going to share the spoils. You going to tell me what we're dealing with here? Or am I supposed to figure this stuff out on my own?"

"What does the weather report say for today?"

She snorted. She wouldn't award him points for that clever redirect. She had a weather app, but she refused to open it.

"A cargo ship carrying artifacts stolen from an Iranian museum that was destroyed and looted during the war," she read instead, "was detained by the Syrian authorities a few days ago."

"Is that so? Doesn't sound like the weather to me."

Ignoring him, Annja read more. "The captain was shot dead, and the rest of the crew was missing. Sounds like someone was shipping stolen artifacts and got caught. Good for the authorities. Too bad they didn't catch the bastards behind the shipment."

Garin grunted, and Annja eyed him curiously. She would not put such an escapade past him. And just when she started to ask him about the possibility of his involvement, a tinny jangle inside Garin's suit pocket prompted the man to pull out his cell phone.

He looked at the caller ID, made a face, then with a heavy sigh answered it. "What do you want, Roux?"

"Say hi from me," Annja chimed in, faking great enthusiasm because it got her a head shake from Garin in return.

"Annja says hi.…He says *hi* right back at you."

"Such a dear."

"So, to what do I owe the pleasure?...Ah. Of course, you're welcome. But I didn't throw the auction. There was trouble with my credentials. I hope you enjoy the pearl."

Annja could just make out Roux's voice from where she sat and heard him say, "...plan to use it in the same manner the sultan once did."

That made Garin growl. The man was very growly today. "Is that all you wanted, old man?" He paused, listening. "No, we found each other's company entirely by accident. I'm tracking..." Garin looked at her.

She offered him a sweet smile, much sweeter than she could normally manage. She was getting loopier by the second sitting here doing nothing.

Turning toward the driver's side window, Garin didn't lower his voice, but his tone was clipped as he added, "Bracks."

So, apparently Roux knew him by name, as well. Interesting.

"No, I'm not going to get her involved any more than she already is. Goodbye, Roux."

He snapped the phone shut and tucked it away. He cast her a dark glare. "I can hear your thoughts screaming at me, Annja."

"Yes, well, then I won't have to repeat them if you can hear them loud and clear. Answer?"

"The men who took you to the hotel, the men we followed here, are...or were...my men." Tension laced his tight voice. "Except for Bracks."

"Huh."

"I thought they were working for me, but whatever was going on in that hotel room was not my call."

Definitely tension. "If you say so. What happened? Have a falling out with the fedora gang?"

"They are not my gang, nor are they in any way employees."

"But if they were your men...?"

"I have occasion to deal with freelancers."

"And those freelancers did something that wasn't ordered by you."

"Like you, I'm trying to figure this out. What's going on with the men I had dealt with, and how the hell Bracks is involved."

"A man you know well."

Jaw pulsing and fingers squeezing the steering wheel, he finally conceded, "Well enough."

"Does this have something to do with you being so grumpy the other night when I stopped by?"

"Annja, that morning I missed a...shipment... because the double agent who was spying on us wouldn't talk. Later, the munitions I ordered from Kabul were shoddy and filled with sand. I lost an auction for the Sultan of Brunei's black pearl to Roux—of all people. And then the men I thought were taking care of tying up some loose ends for me are also doing something on the side that I don't want to be involved in. And they are apparently also working for—"

"Bracks," she said. "Sounds like Garin had a very bad day."

He sneered at her condescending tone. "Let's call it a bad couple of days, and leave it at that. Okay?"

"Fine by me." She'd had days as bad as they could get—fending off sharks, getting swept out to sea by a tsunami, fighting ninjas on the streets of Tokyo, the associates who had died because they'd got involved with her—so she wouldn't push. "So the shipment you missed... Did the Syrian authorities detain it?"

The look he cast her chilled her blood. And answered that question.

"Okay." She turned in her seat to face him full-on. "And this something on the side you don't want to be involved in, it has to do with vampires and Romani coming after you with stakes?"

"You keep bringing up vampires, which surprises the hell out of me, knowing you to be a skeptic."

"I'm using the term facetiously." She turned off her phone and tucked it in a pocket. "The belief in vampires is strong in this region of the world. And Bracks apparently wants to capitalize on that belief for his gain."

"Did he say that to you?"

She nodded. "He was forthcoming in the hotel room. Wanted to take the skull from me, or at the very least damage it."

"The skull with the brick in it. The one everyone thinks belongs to a vampire?"

"Yep. Yet if the man wanted to perpetuate the belief, I don't understand why he'd want to destroy the skull. He almost shot a hole right through it. And how is he of concern to you? You said he wasn't one of your freelancers."

"Never. He's just gotten mixed into a vicious tangle that I am trying to unweave. The two of us…"

"Yes?"

"Annja, why are you so damned nosy?"

"It's what I do," she replied cheerfully. "Archaeologist. We dig deeper."

He lifted an eyebrow at that one.

"Bracks and I have been dancing around each other for some time. It's not your concern, Annja. Even though we find ourselves sitting together right now, waiting for the same men, I believe it's for vastly different reasons."

"No vampire for you?"

"No. And yet…"

The man scrubbed a hand through his hair and then clenched the steering wheel so tightly Annja prepared to dodge the pieces.

"What is it? Come on, Garin. Spill."

"Every time I think about vampires," he conceded, "my thoughts go back to the night in the warehouse. There was blood. And lots of it."

"Like someone had been murdered?"

"No. Maybe. I don't know. The blood was in bags."

"Ready for transport? For donation? Transfusion?"

"Yes, it looked like the sort of medical-issue plastic bags that I've seen holding blood. The thing that bothers me is I thought I saw…" He blew out a breath and rapped the steering wheel with a thumb. "I think I saw a child in the warehouse."

"You mean slave labor?"

"I'm not sure of anything. It was probably a frail man. I may have imagined it. I was dodging a fist at the time. But whatever's going on doesn't feel right to me. And I certainly didn't order it. I would never involve myself in anything that would bring harm to a child. You know that about me, don't you?"

She nodded. She hadn't seen proof of his honor, but instinctually knew the man could never bring himself so low. "So you want to control the actions of the freelancers you work with?"

He turned to stare directly at her and it wasn't a friendly look. More chastising, and *I'm going to punch you if you don't shut up soon*.

"Ah. I see. You don't want to be held accountable for what your freelancers might be doing with children for other clients."

"Like I said, it could have been a frail old man. I got a quick look while fighting off Canov's thugs."

She hadn't heard that name before, and was pretty sure it had just slipped through Garin's carefully monitored list of Details He Was Willing to Divulge. So she wasn't going to call attention to that slip, but instead tucked it away for future reference.

"Okay," she said, "so we're dealing with assholes."

"Good call."

"Assholes who also work for you. What does that make you?"

Now he tilted his head to her and she couldn't

define the look he gave her, though she could feel it melt her skin.

"I've never claimed to have an upstanding nature," he said.

"That you have not."

"We can't all be Annja Creed, out to protect the innocent and downtrodden."

"All right, enough of that."

"Somehow Bracks has taken charge of them. I don't know if it was purposeful or not. Canov is a free agent. He works for many."

"We're dealing with some kind of belief in vampires combined with lots of blood and maybe children. And weapons? What kind of weapons were these men running?"

"All sorts. But I don't think it's related to your situation in any way."

"There were a handful of weapons in the hotel room."

"Random pistols and grenades, Annja. It was a display of firepower, a threat to frighten you."

"Yes, I suppose. Didn't work."

"I need to get inside that country house and see what Bracks is up to. I counted two going in, but I have no idea how many were inside before they got here."

"The shapeless shadows moving in front of the windows don't help much, either. How about I go out and reconnaissance while you stay here and keep an eye on the front door?"

"Why you?"

"I'm smaller and more stealthy."

"Is that so?"

"Says the muscle-bound man who is a half a foot taller than me. I can slip into small spaces, like through the hedgerows. So I win. I go out."

"I don't even want you here, Annja. This is not your battle."

"Right, you get to keep all the spoils. But when Bracks kidnapped my producer he made it my battle."

"Would it matter if I asked you to stand down?"

"No. I'm in it for the win now. You got a pistol?"

With a reluctant sigh, he took the pistol from the holster under his left arm and checked the magazine. The semiautomatic gun was fully loaded.

"What is that?"

"A .380 ACP. Not for civilian ownership. Fifteen rounds. It packs a kick, so watch it."

"Nice."

He handed the pistol to her. "No sword?"

"Again, small and inconspicuous is the theme here."

"Guns are noisier than swords."

"Yeah, but bullets work better at a distance, which I'm hoping to maintain. Give me ten minutes before you start worrying. Otherwise, I'll break out my 'help me' sneeze to alert you."

"If you go missing during reconnaissance I will be better off."

"Then you should have stayed away from my dig.

You don't think I can keep my mouth shut regarding your nefarious deeds?"

"I know you can, but there are some things I don't need you to know about at all."

"Fair enough. I'll try to forget all the bad stuff you've ever done—wait. That could take a while." She grinned and tucked the pistol into the back of her cargo pants. "Back in a few."

THE VINES MUST have been growing for decades on the single-story house. Red brick only showed through here and there. Must keep the place cool in the summer, Annja mused. Thick shrubbery skirted two sides of the property, and beyond a short stretch of field she could see forest. Just another unassuming cottage on the edge of the city, set off from the neighbors by woods and an empty lot crowded with rusting farm equipment and fence posts tangled with barbed wire.

Somewhere in the distance a rooster crowed.

The fresh air didn't calm her pounding heart. Of course, she didn't want calm, only stealth. She had to remain alert for periphery guards, even though they hadn't seen any on stakeout.

Tracking across the dry lawn that crunched under her hiking boots, she ducked below a window and was thankful there were none of the thorned shrubs on this side of the house.

It was risky to attempt surveillance in daylight, but Garin was parked close by, and though Annja constantly vacillated on whether or not he was friend or foe, when the chips were down, the man did tend to rally to her side.

On the other hand, he was obviously keeping information from her—had even said he'd be better off without her—so she wouldn't grow complacent. It was not out of character for Garin Braden to stab a friend in the back if it suited his needs. Or drive off, leaving her to fend on her own.

From where she knelt, she couldn't hear voices from inside, but she did pick up the gurgle of running water around back of the house. Sounded larger than a stream. She guessed they could be close to the Jeřice brook, which she'd noted from the train as they'd neared Chrastava. Almost a river, the Jeřice provided a convenient escape route if those inside the house were suddenly pressed to leave in a hurry, and in a different direction than they had arrived. And if they were spooked by Garin's SUV.

Annja crept along the side of the brick house. Cool vines brushed her arm and leg. The back shed, where the car they had tracked was parked, sat only ten feet from the house. She scampered from building to building, keeping low. The pistol pressed against her spine had warmed and she liked the safety of feeling it against her skin, though she wasn't keen on guns. Murder was never right. Except sometimes she had no option but to make the kill. She never did it lightly.

A peek inside the shed through a dirt-frosted window showed her it was empty, except for a few garden implements, hoes and a rake leaning against one wall, and beside them some stacked tin buckets. This place may have once been a thriving farm or even a vast garden.

Angling around the back of the shed, she spied a dirt path that led to a narrow copse of oak trees, and beyond that...

"The brook." Running low and quickly, she reached the tree cover and passed through to the other side where a sturdy wooden dock boasted two boats with their motors propped up at the hulls. "Getaway vehicles?"

But to where? And from what? Liberec would be the closest town, though she wasn't sure if the brook wended that direction. The mystery of what exactly she was dealing with was driving her nuts.

Katana Man had said something about a child gone missing. Was there even a connection?

She hoped Doug and Luke had reached Luke's hotel room safely, and with the skull intact. Doug was probably upset he wasn't alongside her filming the action. The guy could be annoying at times with his overzealous dedication to recording the weird and wacky train wrecks that the show's viewers tuned in to watch.

But whatever the men who had shored these boats at the dock were involved in did not include vampires, she felt sure.

Turning, Annja looked into the barrel of a gun. The arm extended beyond the pistol grip met a narrow shoulder and the face cracked a grin glossed with tobacco juice.

"You weren't the one we expected, but you'll do," the man said.

She slowly moved a hand around her hip, but the guy wasn't stupid. He shoved the pistol barrel between her eyes. "Hands up!"

Not wanting to risk reaching for her gun and taking a bullet, Annja complied, raising her hands slowly. He moved the gun across her temple and to the back of her head, and gave her a shove to walk toward the house.

She sneezed, and hoped the sound would carry.

9

Garin saw the shadowed figure stalk toward the back of the property. Leaning across the shift, he palmed the Heckler & Koch he'd stashed in the glove compartment. With the growing darkness as cover, he made way across the gravel road and down to the house, using the high hedgerows to conceal his approach.

Annja's signal sneeze had told him she'd been discovered. Already he heard shouts inside the house. He rushed the front door, shooting at the doorknob as he did. A bullet pierced the doorplate and, when he arrived, one kick pushed the door in.

Half a dozen shocked faces turned toward him—but not a single one belonged to Bracks. Damn it, where was that shifty Brit?

Annja took advantage of the element of surprise to kick away the man who'd been holding her wrists behind her back. She returned with a roundhouse kick to his jaw, the force of her strength and the hard boot toe dropping him flat. He lay on the floor, unconscious.

Garin fired at a man who aimed a pistol at him. Cartilage and blood split out from the man's knee. Another shot to the man's bicep injured his weapon arm. The semiauto went flying.

The rest of the team rallied, grabbing weapons and shouting to kill him.

The one man he had most hoped to see wasn't here. Could Bracks be in another room, or had he already escaped? But how and where? They had sat watching the place for over an hour. And he'd followed the car since Chrastava. Had Bracks slipped out before or after he'd begun to tail them? This made no sense. He didn't want to take the time to go through his former freelancers one by one to get to the core of the problem, but right now, the low men on the rack were forcing him to keep Annja safe.

The sound of a sword cutting through air filled the room. Annja's battle sword sliced a clean line through one of the thug's thighs. He yelped, going down, gripping the wound. Garin did love it when she wielded Joan's sword. It was an extension of her body and mind. A beautiful thing to watch.

If there weren't a pistol aimed at him. Shifting his own aim to the left, Garin fired. When he heard the opposition's weapon report first, he instinctually ducked. Plaster from the wall behind him spattered the back of his head.

"That one is the brains," Annja said, nodding toward the skinny man in a red vest who was reloading a rifle. "Please try to control yourself and keep him alive."

"The rest fall," Garin announced, ignoring her protest. He took no pleasure in killing men, but unlike Annja felt no angst in defending his own hide.

Two men were down and wounded. Annja dropped a third and the fourth, but didn't kill them. That bothered Garin. They would prove messy if he allowed them to live. But he wouldn't put a bullet in their brain with Annja watching him. The woman had morals, and he couldn't argue with them.

Because she'd just argue back.

The skinny guy, whose magazine had jammed and he couldn't get it placed, was down on his knees, pleading for them to spare him. Garin backed him into a corner.

Annja's blade swept before Skinny, the tip of it cutting into a framed needlepoint pronouncing Home Sweet Home hanging on the wall and blockading him with the deadly weapon at his neck.

"Where's Bracks?" Garin growled. "He was here."

"He wasn't! He got out before we got here. Told us to go ahead without him. The pickup is—" His eyes went wide, darting back and forth between Garin and Annja.

"Pickup?" Annja prompted. She kept an eye on the room behind Garin, where the others lay moaning.

Garin followed Skinny's gaze along the wall and to the floor where a white plastic cooler sat. "What's in there?"

Skinny shrugged. "Not supposed to look. It's sealed. To open it will break the seal and damage the contents." He patted his shirt pocket. "I was doing as I was told. I don't know Mr. Bracks other than for this job, I swear. I never meet the bosses."

Wise business practice, as far as Garin was concerned. Since the punk had just double-crossed one of them. Him.

"When and where is the pickup?" he asked.

"Outside, across the sunflower field. Soon. Don't kill me."

"Did I kill any of your colleagues?" Garin asked angrily.

"Uh, I think you took out Schweps. And the woman is scaring me. Where'd she get that sword?"

"You don't like a girl with a sword?" Garin said. "Come on. Who doesn't like a girl with a sword?"

Annja pulled the blade out of the embroidered wall hanging and with a sweep of her hand sent it off into the otherwhere. That continued to baffle Garin. When she needed the sword she could call it to hand. And when she didn't? It just disappeared when she released it. That was more incredible than his longevity. He didn't like not knowing the answers to things. He wanted to know what made the sword tick, and if, when it had been joined together from scattered pieces years ago and Annja had claimed it, it had somehow altered the length of his life. Until that point, ever since Joan of Arc's death by fire, he'd felt…immortal.

He could still take a bullet and survive, but did he have a shelf life now? He and Roux were both tied to that sword, for good or for ill, because they had been there when the soldier had broken it into pieces while Joan burned at the stake. That sense of immortality wasn't a gift Garin was willing to give up. Neither was he willing to let Annja hold some kind of power over him simply because she held the sword, now whole again.

The only way he'd ever understand would be to get his hands on the sword—and break it again. Restoring it to the form it had been in when he'd felt certain he'd live forever.

They heard the sudden juddering pulse of a helicopter above the cottage.

Annja lunged for the plastic cooler.

"Don't open it!" Garin shouted. He had no clue what was in there, but what he'd seen the other night gave him a clue. Sealed? That meant the contents had an expiration date or were volatile.

Searching Skinny, he pulled a small piece of paper out of the man's front pocket. A business card with an address. "Grab the cooler, Annja. Let's get out of here."

He shot Skinny in the ankle, putting him down in a dead faint. Stepping over the fallen, Garin followed Annja outside and toward the sunflower field.

"WHERE ARE WE going?" Annja asked as they ran out the back door. Twilight dropped a gray cloak over everything but she could still see well enough.

Garin took the cooler from her, which was fine. It weighed about twenty pounds—not overly heavy, but she liked to keep her arms free in case anyone followed them.

She twisted a look back toward the house. Everyone inside was out cold. She appreciated when Garin used restraint.

"To see where this all leads," he replied. "I'm hoping it's to Bracks."

They entered the sunflower field, the heavy yellow heads hitting them in the faces. Moving into the lead, Annja took out her sword and used it as a machete. She heard Garin's approving growl from behind. They passed through half an acre before arriving at an open dirt field.

About five hundred yards beyond them, a helicopter landed on the rough-plowed dirt. There were no business logos or identifying marks on the drab olive green exterior, not even a registration number. Private, and from the rust lacing around the rivets at the metal seams it didn't look as if it could carry anyone more than a dozen miles.

Garin waved to the pilot as if he knew him. The pilot returned the wave and made a circling signal with his forefinger. Not much time. Hurry it up.

Ever curious, and not about to let Garin leave with whatever was in the cooler, Annja said, "Let's do this."

"This is not an *us* adventure, Annja."

She saw his fist plow toward her and blocked it with her forearm.

"I'm going," she protested, and twisted at the waist, bringing up her foot to kick his thigh.

The man returned an uppercut and skimmed her jaw. Before she could straighten and prepare for the next blow, the man's iron fist found her gut. She doubled, expelling her breath in a painful clench of abdomen muscles.

"Sorry, Annja, stick to skeletons. This is my battle. The spoils are mine."

Lifting her by the hair, Garin then punched her in the jaw, knocking her out. She didn't feel the ground catch her body as she collapsed.

TREKKING ACROSS THE field, Garin knew Annja would be okay to leave behind. Even if the men in the cottage rallied and went looking for them, they'd have to deal with a warrior armed with a sword who was pissed off at being cut out of the deal by him. He chuckled to think of the fight those idiots had waiting for them.

He hadn't a clue who the pilot was, or what was going on, but sometimes the best way to get anywhere was to blend in and act like you're a professional. That ingenuity had gotten him into and out of more than a few perilous situations.

Garin climbed into the helicopter and buckled in. The pilot, wearing eye goggles and a headset, turned and gave him the thumbs-up. "We'll land in Berlin in forty-five minutes. Buckle in!"

"Roger that." Berlin. Taking him back home?

"Wasn't there another?" the pilot asked. "I only have orders to pick up one, but I thought I saw—"

"Staying behind," Garin summoned quickly. "Let's head out!"

Apparently the pilot didn't know the identity of the passenger he was to pick up. Good for Garin. Between his feet sat the white cooler.

For the first time, dread trickled down Garin's neck, and that was a rare and ugly feeling. If all suspicions were correct, he didn't want to look in the cooler.

They lifted off the ground, and soared into the gray sky, high above the pinpoint lights from the small town of Chrastava below.

Should have left Annja the keys to the SUV, he thought. Oh, well. She was an industrious woman. She'd find a ride back to town somehow.

THE FLIGHT BACK to London was quiet, the plane dark and the few other passengers all reading quietly on their electronic devices or snoring. Weston Bracks closed his eyes but didn't find sleep.

He expected Braden to pursue him, to come back at him with something bigger and better than the shipping heist. He had almost snagged a nice load of artifacts with that one. Braden's security had been lax, easy enough to slip in a spy. Though he'd have to write him off as a loss. Surely, Braden had tortured the man to find out who was behind the theft.

The almost-theft, that is. Damned Syrian authorities had charged in at the last moment and overtaken the ship. Thankfully, Bracks's men had been well trained. They'd shot the captain and, wearing SEAL wet gear, had deployed into the ocean. They'd rendezvoused with a pickup five leagues north.

A loss, but so long as Braden hadn't gotten the goods Bracks was going to tally that one in the win column.

But what an interesting surprise to take care of business with the immensely fascinating Annja Creed and to have Braden walk in on that. And it seemed Braden and Creed knew each other.

How to figure that one? Was she working for him? Yet he'd thought the job in Chrastava had been completely unrelated to anything Braden was doing. One of their employees must be moonlighting with the other. And Bracks pinpointed Canov. He was the only one in the Czech Republic he'd dealt with lately. Could he also be on Braden's payroll? Possible, always possible.

The fun had only just begun in Chrastava. He couldn't pull out now. And to sit back and see how Creed and Braden worked together would prove fascinating. Was she someone Bracks could ultimately use against Braden?

"We shall see."

PICKING A FEW stray sunflower seeds out of her hair, Annja trudged back to the SUV by way of the red-brick cottage. The place was empty, the car they had originally followed gone. She peered in the windows, but didn't see any bodies, which gave her some solace.

She rubbed her jaw where Garin's fist had landed

solidly. That was going to leave a bruise. The bastard. She had no clue where the helicopter had been headed, so she now stood at a dead end. And she'd tried Garin's cell number. Of course, he wasn't answering.

As she neared the SUV, she felt thankful the tires hadn't been slashed, or the car trashed. But though the doors were unlocked, the keys were not inside. They were probably in Garin's pocket eight thousand feet above the ground right now. They had driven a good ten miles out of Liberec. She didn't look forward to the walk back.

Climbing through to the backseat, she folded down one side to get into the trunk. Shuffling around in the trunk, she lifted the floor mat and found an emergency kit. Inside she found a flat-head screwdriver, exactly what she needed.

Sliding onto the driver's seat, and pressing a foot to either side of the steering wheel on the dashboard for torque, she forced the ignition lock out and inserted the screwdriver in the slot beneath. The engine revved.

"Nice. Thanks, Bart."

Her good friend and confidant, NYPD detective Bart McGilly, had once explained how to start a car without a key. Just in case she ever needed the skill. She did love his willingness to corrupt her with all his secret police knowledge. She looked at the damage she'd done to the ignition. Good thing this vehicle was registered under Garin's name and not hers.

The SUV had half a tank of gas. The day wouldn't end entirely on a bad note, after all.

WHEN GARIN TOOK in the landing strip below he realized they would touch down at an actual airport, or something very close. It was small, and there were only a handful of buildings nearby, but it was marked with landing lights, designating it a landing strip.

When the helicopter landed, he unstrapped himself and opened the door. As he stepped out from the cabin and cleared the blades, he sighted a white limo driving down the landing strip. The night had grown long and the moon sat low behind high trees to the west. Had to be close to a town or city, but he couldn't see any smoke or air pollution that would clue him to a direction. He'd been unable to get service on his cell phone in the helicopter to track by GPS, so he pulled out the phone now.

His instincts told him, *Get out now.* Yet he walked forward, his long, sure strides moving him toward the limo with its tinted windows. Behind him, the helicopter hadn't lifted off. Waiting for a return ride home? It would probably need to refuel.

Fingers crossed that whoever was in the limo didn't know who he was expecting to pick up, Garin heaved out a breath.

A man got out of the limo, slim and dark, nondescript. He waved him toward him impatiently. "Hurry, the plane is ready to taxi!"

A plane?

"A dropoff point," Garin muttered.

This had just been the first stop. That little mail plane sitting outside the airport had to be his next ride. The plane didn't look like it could carry a pilot and a passenger, let alone mail.

He slid into the backseat of the limo. The car wheeled around and less than a minute later had delivered them. An elaborate escort, considering he could have walked down the runway to the plane. If anyone were going to overdo the power play, leave it to Bracks.

Garin tucked himself into the back of the plane. Alone with the cooler. He wasn't going to look inside. He should look. What was keeping him from looking? If he was going to be informed, and fight Bracks with as much power as he had, he needed to look. Especially since the cooler might be forcibly taken from him at any point, given that he had no idea who was controlling this journey he was blindly taking.

Sliding a hand over the rough plastic cover, he determined with a lift of the handle that the lid wasn't vacuum sealed. He wouldn't be able to see anything in the darkness of the plane. Relieved, he was able to put off opening the thing. He could at least wait until he had more privacy. If that was meant to be.

THE PILOT HAD told him he'd have to sit in the back because the passenger seat was filled with packages spilling out of a box. Garin assumed this wasn't an official mail plane, and probably everything inside was illegal.

The back wasn't officially the back, either. It was

right behind the pilot's and passenger's seats, and was three-quarters stuffed with mailbags and plastic shipping containers. There was no seat. Garin sat wedged into a space on the floor where a seat might normally have been positioned, and was thankful a seat belt was available. The whine of the engine did not bode well for this trip. Neither did the odor of gas.

He'd been in smaller aircraft and had flown in an open cockpit biplane fighter in World War I. He could handle a puddle jumper like this for a few hours.

His right elbow resting on the cooler because a mailbag was suspended from a bright orange netting overhead, he eyed the pilot from behind. The guy hadn't given him more than a nod of his head and directions to buckle up in the back. He was clearly just the transport pilot. Nothing more, nothing less.

Their destination was Gatwick, it turned out, thirty miles outside London. The flight would take a little less than three hours, so he hunkered down to catch a few winks while he could. He would probably sleep through any turbulence. He could sleep through an invasion, as he'd proved a few centuries earlier.

Funny thing about him and Roux. They'd walked through the ages together, reluctant companions who kept their distance. The other had once been his master, teaching him the ways of the soldier and martial arts skills. He'd at times been a father figure, a stern and demanding father, and at other times had been a brother soldier in arms. But they both knew they were in it—life—for themselves.

Tough love, that. Though Garin would never actually admit to loving the old man. A strong measure of like, for sure. And frequent annoyance, always. He supposed Roux was lounging poolside right now, a bevy of bikini-clad women purring around him. The man had taught him the value of luxury and women, and Garin would never begrudge him that.

Garin's last thoughts before he fell sound asleep were so what if he wasn't a morally upstanding man? He wasn't preaching his nefarious ways to influential children or young athletes, so what the hell? He was fine with the life he led. And it wasn't as though he had a family who looked up to him to show them the way. Any family he'd once had was centuries gone and forgotten.

At the tail end of a rainstorm, Garin awoke to see that they were soaring over the English Channel. Carefully, he tilted back the plastic cooler handle. It wasn't locked, and the cooler was cheap, so by sliding back the handle, that released the grip on the cover.

Sealed? Not in any particular manner that would keep him, anyone, from opening it.

It popped open and a faint meaty odor trickled into his nostrils. Inside the cooler, ice packets lay on top but he saw the dark murky crimson color beneath and immediately knew it was blood bags. Like those he'd seen hanging in the warehouse?

What the hell was going on?

He didn't want to risk digging inside the cooler, but a long tag, written on with black marker, stuck out along the inner wall of the cooler. He leaned in to read the words, which he believed were Slavic. *Játra*. He wasn't sure if he was translating it correctly. His grasp on languages covered many, but not all, and the Romanian dialects were tricky.

Did it translate to *liver*?

Garin closed the lid and rapped his thumb on the cheap plastic, but his thoughts soared far away, back to the Czech Republic. Blood and a liver. They had come from a dirty concrete warehouse in the middle of nowhere.

Were they transporting human organs? For transplant? Impossible. Official medical connections needed to be made. Even black market organs had to be transported in a more secure manner. The organ couldn't stay viable in a simple plastic cooler. Neither could the blood. Not for any amount of time.

Who would accept an unviable organ, and for what purpose?

And since when had Bracks involved himself in the trade of human flesh and blood? He'd always been an arms and art kind of man.

This was disturbing, but the only way to truly know your adversary was to step into their shoes. Bracks did tend to slip into anything and everything. Seemed like the man gave new ventures a go, and if they were successful, he stuck with them. If not, on to the next project.

Garin tapped the cooler. Surely by exposing it to

air he had decreased the viability rate, or whatever you call it, for the objects inside.

No, this wasn't right. If indeed it was a human liver inside, it couldn't be intended for transplant. No black market dealer would send an organ this way and expect repeat business.

So whoever was receiving the contents had a different use in mind.

He searched the archaic knowledge that floated in his memory for something, anything, that would clue him in to what was going on.

Of all the times he could have used Annja Creed's esoteric knowledge, that time was now. Yet she would flip to know exactly what was in the cooler. And then she'd adamantly suggest they contact the authorities.

Not an option.

Wishing he had cell phone service to do some online research, Garin shifted a hip and eased his spine to fight the growing ache from sitting in this cramped position.

Soon enough, he'd have answers. He hoped to get them directly from the horse's mouth. And then he'd silence that horse forever. Bracks was one man he couldn't allow to live.

THE PILOT FOLLOWED him down the runway toward the waiting limo. Garin had considered him innocent beyond being a means for transportation, but Garin could be wrong.

A man in dark clothes waited outside yet another

limo, a thick black envelope in his hand. An exchange? It was beginning to look like it.

What if he refused to play along? He needed to keep a fix on the cooler because he knew that would lead him to the man he sought. But to refuse would reveal him as an imposter and he'd have to take out both the pilot and the man waiting, and possibly the driver. Which would put him back to square one.

There was one other option.

The man held out his hand to receive the cooler, and tucked the envelope under his arm. Garin didn't hesitate in handing it to him. Flipping open the lid, he merely glanced inside, then shut the lid and slapped the envelope into Garin's palm. "Thanks. See ya."

And he got into the limo and the car took off, leaving Garin standing alone on the dark runway, only the flash of the signal lights moving the airplane toward the hangar.

"So much for not breaking the seal."

And so much for him staying close to the cooler.

Garin reached inside his suit jacket and drew out the business card he'd claimed from Skinny.

"All righty, then," the pilot said from behind him. "Shall we return?"

"Thanks for your service," Garin said, strolling away from the pilot toward the small airport's only building. "I'm going to stop in town for a bite to eat. I'll find my own ride home."

"I was instructed to bring you back, but if you've made other plans, then have a good one. *Ciao!*"

The send-off only reminded Garin of the week-end in Venice he was missing because he'd decided that silencing Bracks once and for all was a better idea than lounging between two scantily clad blondes while floating the Venetian canal on a gondola beneath a brightly striped sunshade.

He could taste the two-hundred-and-fifty-year-old Lafitte right now. Some days he really hated playing games.

10

Once back on the main road and headed toward Chrastava, Annja found she had cell phone service. She dialed Luke's number and he answered on the first ring.

"Annja, where are you?"

"Just outside town." She realized now she'd been gone all day. Both men must have been wondering about her at the very least. "How are things there? You and Doug get my stuff out of the hotel?"

"Yes, we're fine, and we've moved you to my room for now. The skull is intact despite all the joggling. We went to the dig site earlier and managed to get the torso of the skeleton unburied before it began to rain. No signs of the guy with the sword or any protesters. Curious, don't you think?"

"Maybe the rain kept them away."

"It wasn't raining for the first few hours we were there."

"I should arrive at the hotel soon. I'm going to stop to pick up something to eat. Can I bring you and Doug anything?"

"Anything sounds great. So you didn't catch your man?"

"I did. And we followed the guys who kidnapped Doug out of town. How is he?"

"Only a little battered and bruised."

"Is that Annja?" she heard Doug call from the background. "Tell her, wherever she is, she should be filming."

"You should be—"

"I heard," she said. "No camera. And this is not related to vampires. At least, I don't think it is."

On the other hand, she had no idea what had been in the cooler, but the idea of what sorts of things could be kept in a cooler made her angry.

"What's up, Annja?" Luke asked. "I don't understand what's become of our innocent foray into skulls and bricks."

"I don't, either. But I don't think the chewing dead or some wolf-shaped *mullo* has much to do with the trail Garin and I picked up. Unfortunately, Garin decided to go it alone. He left me behind to follow the trail of breadcrumbs, which has disappeared."

"And you let him?"

"I didn't have much of a choice." She stretched her aching jaw. She needed ice to keep it from swelling. "I'll see you in a bit. Talk later." She hung up and swerved into the parking lot beside a local restaurant.

ANNJA HANDED LUKE the brown paper bags of food and he immediately dug into them, laying out the paper-wrapped sausages and plastic containers of salad and potatoes. The restaurant had included plastic plates and utensils and napkins. She'd stopped by a gas station to pick up Gatorade and soda, and some protein bars to restock her dwindling supply.

Luke turned, and as she was walking by him, he caught her by the wrist. His eyes went directly to her jaw, narrowing. "Annja, what happened?"

"Has it bruised?"

"It's dark purple."

"The bruise should match the shape of Garin Braden's knuckles." She strode into the bathroom and grabbed a hand towel, wrapping it around ice from the bucket Luke must have filled earlier. She pressed the improvised ice pack to her jaw. "I'm fine," she answered Luke's worried look when she came back out.

"Food looks great, Annja." Doug downed an entire can of orange soda before dishing up a plate. "I'm starving." He swirled what looked like a wooden dowel as if it was a baton, then dove into the food with the plastic fork in his other hand.

"What is that? No, wait, don't tell me what that is." Annja stared at the wooden object Doug tapped against his knee.

"It's a stake, Annja," he replied, his mouth full of food. "I picked it up from a merchant in town. I got holy water, too. You want to see?"

"Help me, please." She flashed a pleading look toward Luke, who smiled from behind a bite of sausage.

She grabbed one of the sausages for herself before the men claimed them all. Mounding salad on her plate, she then settled onto the bed, stretched out her legs and, before eating, tilted back her head and closed her eyes a moment, placing the ice at her jaw.

She was angry at having been cut out by Garin, but was also determined not to let it get to her. She'd come to Chrastava for this dig. Shouldn't she focus on that?

Not if an innocent child was somehow involved, her conscience nudged her. A conscience that was inextricably connected to Joan of Arc through her sword. *Her* sword.

And to top it off Doug was going to make a production out of the whole thing, stakes and all.

"Here."

She opened her eyes, and accepted the bottled water Luke handed her. He sat on the end of the bed, while Doug had claimed the chair by the table where the microscope was set up.

"Did you tell her I'm using your iPad?" Doug said around a mouthful of food. "I love this! I can film and edit all with the same device. The resolution isn't optimal, but it'll serve for scenery segments. And long shots."

"You're filming?" she inquired. "What, exactly?" She looked to Luke. "Please tell me he hasn't gotten you to wield a stake menacingly for a shot. If there's a silk-lined cape around here…"

Luke laughed. "Not yet." He winked at her. "Doug is showing me how to use the apps I've never had time to sit down and muddle out," he said. "I wanted to get your take on the fact that we didn't encounter any protesters at the site."

"I wish you guys would have stayed away from there. I warned you."

"You don't think the mild-mannered archaeologist can handle an angry crowd?" He puffed up his chest.

Annja laughed, shaking her head. "It's the over-zealous cameraman with a penchant for creating drama where there is none that worries me." She caught Doug's openmouthed gape. "I just don't want you to get carried away. When you start suggesting fake fangs and blood—and you will—then I will cut you off, okay? And I'll have Luke to back me up."

"Though the holy water is cool, Annja," Luke said.

"Yeah," Doug cut in. "The label claims it's been blessed by the Roman Catholic Church."

Annja couldn't help it, she rolled her eyes.

"We're going to head out again after midnight," her producer added, and then caught Annja's castigating look. "Best time to stir up the undead is under the full moon." He tilted his can of soda at her defiantly.

"So much for practical," she said.

"Don't argue with the producer. I know what sells, and fangs and blood sell. Though I was disappointed by the site this afternoon."

"Just a bunch of bones?" she guessed.

"Right. I can never understand why you love your job so much. It's always just a bunch of bones. And for what?"

She and Luke exchanged knowing looks. The thrill of discovery trumped any labor spent under the hot sun and backbreaking hours hunched over the dirt with the tiniest of brushes.

"For history," Luke offered, "and the knowledge that comes along with it."

"I'll join you on your return to the site," she said. "You'll need a narrator for the clip."

"Nice," Doug said with enthusiasm.

"Did you get a chance to inspect the skull further?" she asked Luke.

"Cleaned out most of the dirt from the brick and almost have it dislodged—"

"While I filmed!" Doug chimed in. "Although, brushing away dirt in a hotel room won't make it into any highlight reel."

"Another hour and I should be able to remove the brick," Luke said. "I would prefer to take it back to London and work on it there. All the equipment I need to date the artifacts is at the university."

Despite having been ditched by Garin, Annja was glad to be back with this pair. Doug would provide for some intriguing and adventurous fieldwork. And Luke continued to appeal to her sense of play. A girl couldn't always be all about the work.

EVEN THOUGH THE iPad didn't photograph well in the dark, and they needed proper lighting to do any narration shots, Doug played around with the apps to get some interesting effects as he wandered along the edge of the forest.

Luke pulled back the tarp and zoomed the flashlight beam over the pit to show Annja the progress he'd made that afternoon. Another day of both of them going at it, and the skeleton could be out, so long as they didn't have any interruptions from protesters. Once it was out, he had an agreement with the country's government, and the paperwork to prove it, to ship the find back to London, along with the skull. The other two skeletons would be exhumed, as well, but they would have to wait. Mueller and Addison had both gone home since their work visas had expired, and Luke was reluctant to call Daisy back on the job.

Annja was glad it was taking a while to unearth the complete skeleton, because that meant she had more time to inspect the skull. Even though all her instincts screamed that the safest path was to get the skull as far from the superstitious Gypsies as possible, she let herself believe it was secure in the hotel room.

Unless Bracks's men were still in town. She would keep an eye over her shoulder.

If Bracks was related to whatever was in the cooler, were the cooler's contents more valuable to him than the skull? Or did he want both? If so, why had he threatened to shoot the skull?

She'd tried Garin's cell phone once more on the drive out to the site, but of course she hadn't expected him to answer. Briefly, she wondered if a call to Roux might help in her efforts to reach Garin. Roux was not Garin's keeper, nor did he always get along with him or know his whereabouts. But on occasion Annja felt Roux was more on her side than Garin could be, and she had used the one against the other a time or two. Roux was a little like a father figure who didn't want to be bothered too much by the child, but should she happen to be in his company he was always glad to teach her what he knew. He had been the one to help her hone her sword-fighting skills after she'd taken Joan's sword.

Bending at the waist to stretch out her spine, Annja did a sun salutation there before the dig pit, lifting her arms high to the moon.

"I love yoga," Luke commented as he was pulling the tarp back over the pit.

Doug still wandered the edge of the forest, getting what he called mood shots.

"Just stretching out the kinks," she said, spreading her arms wide and exhaling deeply. "It's been a long day. You practice often?"

"Most days. Ever tried Bikram?"

Bikram yoga involved performing vigorous poses in a room heated to one hundred and five degrees. "Once. I don't like sweating with others. It's gross. I'll stick to ashtanga and hatha and save the group sweat for gallivants through the tropical rain forests of South America."

He climbed out of the pit and landed on his butt close to her, his legs hanging over the edge. In the darkness she sensed he was looking over her face, which was illuminated by the moonlight. Doug was not to be seen, though he could be heard, crunching the branches in the forest. And she was glad for that. The moment she couldn't hear him, she'd have to go looking for him.

Abruptly Luke kissed her just as she was in the middle of upward dog, preparing to move backward into the downward dog stretch. Awkwardly, she plunked back on her heels beside him at the edge of the pit.

It had been too quick for a real kiss. She had, after all, been in the middle of sun salutation. But that kiss had left her wanting to pull him back to her mouth for a longer connection.

"Hey now, that's enough, you two," Doug teased them as he walked up to the pit. "Though—wait a minute. A little romance would beef up the ratings nicely. Yeah! Kiss again."

"You're out of line," Luke said, and stood. He punched Doug's arm as he passed. The Welshman strolled over to lean against the hood of the Range Rover.

"Sorry," Doug offered to Annja as he folded the cover over the iPad and nodded toward the vehicle. "We heading back?"

"Yes, the site has been covered for the night. Luke and I intend to unearth the rest of the skeleton tomorrow. You get some good shots?"

"I'll know in the morning when I can do some editing." He yawned. "Let's go, Annja. Today has been a long one."

"You're telling me."

ANNJA DRIED OFF after her shower, and smeared the fog from the mirror with the back of her arm. Out in the other room, the two men munched more sausage and potatoes for breakfast. Doug was bent over the iPad to edit last night's film footage, and Luke perched over the skull.

She didn't mind the roommates, and hadn't even thought to rent another room for herself. She could manage the expense but since no one had grumbled about sharing the room, why bother?

Now, she anticipated settling down with her laptop to research Bracks. Not that she expected to find anything on the business opportunist, but it was worth a shot.

She tugged on a T-shirt and her cargo pants, which were in need of a wash, but they'd do for another day. The hotel offered laundry service, but she'd grown accustomed to wearing her things well beyond their expiration date. Twisting her wet hair back into a ponytail, she secured it with a ribbon-wrapped elastic band, then tossed her towel onto the wet pile started by the guys, who'd had first dibs at showers. Chivalry? Ha!

Annja dove into her egg sandwich and was thankful for the orange juice Luke had mind to pick up from the grocery store when he did the run to the restaurant.

"Your jaw looks much better," Doug commented. "That guy is an asshole. If I see him again—"

"You'll what? Defend my honor?"

"You don't think I'm capable?"

He was no match for Garin Braden, but Annja would never be so cruel as to say so. Very few could stand against that man. "You are, Doug. I guess chivalry isn't dead, after all."

Her producer beamed proudly.

"Well, this is interesting." Luke gestured for Annja to join him at the table, and she crawled across the bed and leaned over his shoulder. With field tweezers, Luke carefully extricated a sliver of paper from inside one of two holes he'd discovered in the brick, which confirmed the find to be from the nineteenth or early twentieth century.

Annja felt Doug breathing over her shoulder. "Narrate, Annja," he instructed, his arms holding the iPad out.

Jumping into her role, she turned to face the camera and gave details of the brick while Doug filmed Luke's dramatic removal of the paper, which he held up so Doug could get a good shot.

"What does it say?" Doug whispered. He moved closer, nudging Luke in the back.

"You're too close, man," Luke protested.

"Oh." Doug gave him the thumbs-up. "But what's so interesting?"

"We can film this later," Annja said. "Even reenact the removal process. Right now, we need to give Luke some space so he can look at the paper. One wrong move and he could damage it beyond repair."

"Thanks for the vote of confidence," Luke tossed out.

Doug set the iPad on the bed and, tucking his

hands under his armpits, leaned over the desk Luke had commandeered for a lab table. The tarp was spread to catch the dirt from the skull.

Using tweezers, Luke carefully set the small coil of paper on a lab slide. "I'll need humidity to properly unroll it."

"Cool. How are we going to do that?" Doug wondered.

"Annja's shower did run well into twenty minutes."

Both men averted their gazes in a weirdly accusatory silence. What was this, the brotherhood of the shower patrol?

"I thought you were going to drown in there," Doug finally commented. "But go, you. Now we've got the humidity the man needs to do his job."

"That's me," she said, "always foreseeing the future."

Luke carefully carried the slide into the bathroom, and Doug settled beside Annja to show her the footage he'd edited so far. He was good, she had to admit. Even using a device not designed for film work, he'd managed to get some great mood shots of the full moon silhouetted by dark, spindly tree branches, and the eerie forest shots were perfect. He camped it up with a running sequence, as if the person holding the camera was being chased, but she liked that, as well.

"When do you put on the fangs and ask me to chase after you with that fancy stake of yours?" she asked slyly.

"Annja, would you do that?" Doug handed her the

iPad and stood, looking around the room. "Where are my fangs?"

"I was just kidding, Doug," she said.

"Yeah, but I'm not. Give me a second to find my fangs!"

Grabbing her cell phone, she excused herself to get out of the room, and once again attempted to call Garin.

11

A black taxi dropped Garin off at the corner down from his destination. Strolling the sidewalk that fronted a neighborhood of brick houses, his eyes shifted side to side and his strides moved his head occasionally to take in the periphery. The Chelsea neighborhood wasn't far from the bustle of London's city center. It had been bohemian in the sixties and punk in the seventies—its heyday—but now it was a quiet, wealthy area that offered the odd private business such as the massage salon he was currently passing, and the Happy Aging Clinic next door to it.

The day was growing long, but it wasn't yet closing time. The next brownstone featured a small brass plaque on the iron gate that announced Middleston Antiques: Private Queries Only. Not what he was looking for, but it could be a clever front, and this was the address listed on the business card.

Garin shoved open the unlocked gate and strode up the brick steps to knock loudly on the door. He didn't wait for an answer, and pushed open the door.

The mood in the small reception area was subdued, furnished as it was in dark wood and Berber carpeting. An Adele song whispered out of the overhead speakers.

The receptionist pressed her black-rimmed glasses up her nose and said, "Oh, Mr. Thurman?"

"Yes," Garin replied, sliding a palm down the immaculate cut of his Armani suit. He'd stopped to catch a few hours of sleep and purchase some new clothing after the flight last night. The Ritz was always top-notch, and catered to him as if he was a king.

The business card had brought him—Mr. Thurman—here. Now, to learn what was up.

"We've been waiting. Though you are a bit early."

"Wasn't sure how long it would take to get here."

"I understand, you being from Germany."

She had that one right. "Exactly."

"The goods have arrived and we're just now authenticating them for the ritual. If you'll come with me?"

"Of course." The ritual?

He strode after the squat secretary whose nylons shushed with each step that brushed thigh against thigh. The goods were presumably the items in the white cooler. But the mention of a ritual clogged the back of Garin's throat. He felt a little sick. Nothing good came of rituals.

There were four doors down the hallway, two on each side, and he noted the distinct odor of disinfectant. Taking a deep breath, he couldn't place any other scents, and didn't know what to expect. He was shown into a small, spartan room with two chairs and a stainless-steel sideboard. Much like a doctor's exam room, without the hazardous waste disposal and rubber gloves.

"Will this take long?" he asked. "I have dinner reservations."

"Not at all, Mr. Thurman. I'll send someone in to process your purchase momentarily." Closing him in the room, the secretary shushed away.

"Not feeling good about this," he muttered. "Wonder where Mr. Thurman is?"

Obviously they hadn't expected anyone but Mr. Thurman to arrive. Otherwise, they wouldn't have so willingly invited him in, and without so much as an ID check.

If Annja were here, she would have never allowed them to be closed in this tiny room. Of course, she would have already called the police by now, which is why he'd had to knock her out. Bet she sported a beauty of a bruise. He could only feel a modicum of guilt for that.

Garin put his finger to his lips, and visually scoured the corners of the room. It could be bugged, even outfitted with a camera. He rotated his head on his neck, tilting it side to side. Antsy, he shook out his arms and began to pace.

There were no clues he could get from the room, or the little he had seen walking from the reception area and down the hallway. The smell bothered him. He wondered if some kind of medical shenanigans took place in any of the other rooms. It was the obvious guess, having seen what was contained in the cooler.

He needed to take a look in the other rooms. And the best way to do that would be...?

Garin opened the door to find himself face-to-face with a tall, thin Indian man holding a titanium box against his gut as if it were a prized relic. In fact, the box was decorated with arabesques and tiny red jewels that reminded Garin of Moorish design from centuries past.

"Mr. Thurman, I've got some instructions for the ritual. You have the cash?" he asked Garin.

Smoothly, Garin slid his hand inside his coat and produced the black envelope he'd received at the exchange. "We had agreed to...?"

"Five large," the Indian man said huffily. "Hand it over."

The exchange was made, and the man gingerly handed Garin the box. It wasn't heavy, the only weight, he guessed, produced by the case itself. He decided against shaking it to see if anything rattled about. Was there a human organ inside? If so, he was breaking too many laws right now, and would not look.

"It must be tonight," the other man said quickly. "Beneath the full moon. We've already emailed the ritual to the address you provided on your application."

"Yes, of course," Garin said.

"I cannot express how important it is to follow the

ritual to the letter. If you wish to receive your greatest desire, then you must be fierce and bold. Do not be repulsed by the ritual."

Now that didn't sound like something he wanted to give a try. "I have a few questions first."

"Ah? But those should have all been answered in the emails. I don't do customer service, Mr. Thurman." The man's brow was rimmed with sweat beads. "I merely act as liaison, as you have been clearly told. You did read the emails?"

"Er, yes."

"If you'll excuse me for a moment, Mr. Thurman. I've just one more thing."

He left the room and closed the door behind him, leaving Garin staring at the silver box. His thumbs worried at the raised decoration. He suddenly felt as if he were standing in the middle of a gun range, all barrels aimed directly at his head. Open, exposed, he didn't feel right holding the mysterious box, yet he hadn't brought anything along to put it in.

The idea of looking inside seemed obvious, but apparently he was supposed to have been informed, in an email, no less, about what was inside and what to do with it. And to follow the repulsive ritual to the letter. Whatever organ or blood he'd carried in the cooler was now inside this box; he knew that with strange certainty.

And it was time to start asking questions of the good doctor and his receptionist. Palming the pistol holster under his left arm, with his other hand clutching the silver box, he tried the doorknob. It was locked. Garin jammed his hip against the door but felt no give.

"Dead bolted from the other side," he said. "Guess they figured out I'm not Mr. Thurman."

Garin scanned the room, his eyes tracing along the ceiling and floorboards. No windows, either. Again, he charged the door, knowing it was going to hurt like hell. He swore. The door didn't budge.

And now he smelled smoke.

Not the kindest way to put a man down.

"The bolts," he said, looking around the room for a tool to use to pry out the hinge bolts, but there wasn't much to search. A file cabinet, which was empty, and two chairs.

Setting the box on the floor, he grabbed one of the aluminum-legged chairs, inverted it and banged it up under the highest hinge. Unsure he wanted to open the door if he could hear the fire—he might open the door to a flaming wall—he continued to pound at the bolt. The first bolt popped free and landed on the carpeted floor with a muted thud. The next quickly followed.

He touched the door carefully, finding it wasn't hot, but smoke purled under the bottom in a creepy wisp.

"Good thing I'm hard to kill."

Yet if he inhaled the smoke, the oxygen deprivation could knock him out. And if the building burned, he'd be burned along with it, and, longevity aside, he didn't want to test his ability to survive a blaze and recover from third-degree burns. He wore scars from injuries over the years, but he'd never tested fire. Not like Joan had. And after witnessing her death so many years ago, he never wanted to test it.

Besides, if the scars had stayed with him, so would the burns.

Using the hinges to pull the door inward released spumes of choking smoke into the room. Flames glanced at his legs as he rushed out of the room. Down the hallway where he'd wanted to investigate is where the fire had originated. But it was creeping along the bend where the floor met the wall, all the way up to reception. They must have laid down gasoline.

He cleared reception and ran out through the front door and immediately veered around the side of the building and to the back in case they were still there, waiting to count the casualties. The windows on this side of the building were already letting out smoke. He could see flames, as well.

Splaying his hands open, Garin realized he'd left the box inside.

"Damn it."

The box was the only evidence that something shady had been going on here, and a feeble tie to Bracks, at best. He could go back for it, but the flames had already entered the room he'd been in.

He pulled out his cell phone, and dialed the London emergency number. He was not going to get any information now, and he worried the houses were so closely spaced it wouldn't be long before the flames jumped to the next building. He reported a fire and gave the address, and decided he had about five minutes, tops, to get the hell away from the scene.

At the back, a tight alleyway marked with black tire treads revealed signs that someone had left in a hurry. Garin swore again.

"What the hell are you up to, Bracks?"

LUKE DROVE THE Jeep toward the dig site. In the back seat, Doug filmed the scenery. They'd muddled over the brick for most of the afternoon. Annja had made no headway in searching for information online about Bracks.

They'd decided to head back to the site before the sun set so Doug could get some local flavor shots. Later he would dub the narration into the edited footage, but he liked to record while filming, as well. There was a lot Luke didn't know about what went into producing a television show, so he soaked it all up.

Of course, Doug wasn't a cameraman or a film editor. But even Annja had to agree some of his footage wasn't bad. He clearly knew enough to get by.

Quite the pair, these two.

Annja sat in the passenger seat, her focus on the laptop. The vehicle hit a rut, jogging Doug so that Luke grasped quickly over the seat, caught the man's shirt and managed to yank him back to safety before he keeled headfirst out of the vehicle.

"Would you buckle up back there?" he said.

"Can't get a good angle if I do that." Doug did

shift back onto the seat and, turning, began to film behind them.

That wasn't where the action was, though. When Annja saw the black smoke billowing into the clear gray sky on the horizon, her heart sank and she swore. "Step on it," she directed.

"What's that?" Doug slid to face forward over the passenger seat. "Is that the dig site? There's a fire! Hurry up, man. This is going to be good!"

Rolling her eyes at the man's macabre enthusiasm, Annja gripped the row bar as Luke stepped on the accelerator. The bumpy road tossed them in their seats and the trowels and buckets in the back clattered. As they rolled onto the grounds before the dig site, Annja spotted the usual crowd.

A man stood out, holding a lit torch and shouting in triumph as he spied the Range Rover. The three hopped out.

"Guess they don't have flashlights in the Czech Republic, eh?" Doug said, clearly delighted to see a burning torch. "Can either of you see anybody waving a pitchfork? That would be the money shot."

"Do you know who that is?" Luke asked, ignoring him.

"Do you?" Annja saw that the guy with the torch wore a black T-shirt with some kind of death metal logo on it, but he didn't look familiar.

"It's the American hawker who was selling stakes and garlic," Doug said. "What the hell?"

Luke stalked up to the man in the T-shirt. "You've destroyed an archaeological dig. I will notify the authorities and this won't go well for you. What the hell do you think you're doing?"

"We slayed the vampire, man!" the American shouted, and fisted the air. "As for the *mullos* over there…" The seller crossed his arms and nodded in pride. "They aren't going to rise again any time soon."

"Rise again? They've never risen!" Luke kicked the dirt. "I'm surprised at you. Is this how you increase your sales? By erasing the reason for selling the stakes in the first place?"

"I know these people. They needed a hero," the man shouted. Another fist thrust rallied his odd crew of followers.

Luke punched the man in the jaw, and he went down without another word.

At that moment, another man appeared from out of the forest. The one who wore a sword on his back. He looked at Luke, who held up his fists ready in defense, then shouted for answers.

Annja shoved past one of the local protesters and a path was cleared for her to approach the dig pit where she smelled the kerosene and couldn't get too close because the blaze was twelve feet high. All her life she'd had nightmares about fire. Because Joan had been burned at the stake? Or was it deeper? Something to do with the loss of her parents, of which she had no recall?

Wrapping her arms across her chest, she shivered even as the heat scorched her cheeks.

Doug joined her side, the tablet computer's tiny

camera eye aimed at the fire. "I'm sorry about this, Annja, but you know if I document it, you might be able to use it as evidence."

"Thanks, Doug. Doesn't look like you're going to get your show, after all."

"Don't be so sure about that. If this is the reaction to the possibility that vampires exist, it's perfect."

Around them shouts that they had "stopped the *mullo*" were greeted with cheers. Annja, however, received more than a few evil eyes. The audacity of ignorance burned her more viciously than this fire. She felt sure the blaze wouldn't completely reduce the bones to ash—it took a higher temperature and longer burn to do that—but the remains would be damaged beyond rescue.

"A total loss," Luke shouted, joining her side. "Hell, the security guard must not have been around. I should have camped here overnight. Kept an eye on the area. I should have hired security for more than the evenings."

"It's out of your hands," she said. "They were going to destroy this site one way or another."

"Yes, but I can't believe the idiot selling stakes was the one who helped them do it."

"Good left hook," Annja commented.

"The guy with the sword seems as surprised as we are at the fire and he's questioning his people right now. He may prove an ally."

Scanning the surroundings and determining that the fire was contained in the pit, that it shouldn't leap the forty or fifty feet to the forest, Annja stepped back, arms crossed, and watched as Doug panned across the crowd with his video camera. The crowd played to him with exaggerated gestures. And—oh, yes—there was the proverbial pitchfork poking the sky in triumph.

"I did not authorize this!" the man with the sword said, at Luke's side. "This is no way to create peace. It was unnecessary. You and I both understand the *mullo* does not walk this earth."

Stunned at that confession, both Annja and Luke gave their attention to the man.

"Then why play to their superstitions?" Luke insisted. "Isn't it the old beliefs and ways that keep them from integrating with modern society? Isn't that what you want for your family?"

"I want peace, not fear. The old beliefs and ways will never die. I can fight it all I want, but until the fears die with the elders, I must do what I can. The elders, my parents and cousins, they believe. They have lost two children in the past year. And myself…" He heaved in a sigh and looked away from them, up over the tree line.

Himself? What wasn't he telling them? Had he lost someone? Annja wanted to ask about the missing children, but right now her attention was divided between making sure the flames didn't spread and keeping Doug from stepping too close to the fire.

Abruptly turning back to them the leader said, "And for you to bring this horror into the lives of my people has pushed them over the edge. This bonfire was started by fear and yet…it will serve to cleanse them, do you understand?"

Annja did understand, but that didn't mean she had to like it, or approve.

"They've lost children?" Luke asked. "Don't tell me your people believe a mythical creature rose from the grave to—what? Suck their blood?"

The leader shook his head, bowed it, then lifted his gaze to land, Annja presumed, on the parents in question who must be in the crowd. This was the first clue she'd been given and she wasn't going to let it go.

"We've not been formally introduced. My name is Luke Spencer," he said. "And this is Annja Creed."

"I know who she is. And I know you are the man who unearthed this nightmare."

"And you are?" Annja interjected angrily, trying to calm the urge to call up the sword and let him have it right now.

"Santos Shaw."

"Tell me, Santos," Luke continued, "tell me what it is that sparks the horror in your family's mind? You said that you understand it is myth. Don't you want to discover what really caused the loss of those children?"

Santos's jaw tensed, his eyes fixed on the amber blaze. Annja understood that his people could deem him to share sacred family secrets with an outsider, and she didn't want to press. Hell, she was here to dig up skeletons, not investigate the mysterious disappearance of children.

I think it was a child. What had Garin seen in that warehouse? And if it had been a child, was it the missing Romani child? If so, the place the kidnappers were keeping the child may have been close to the abduction site.

"He's hiding something," Luke said to her. "I need to learn more about the families. The ones who lost children."

"I don't think he's going to have a friendly chat with you. The blaze has been set. They've defeated the *mullo* without having to hire a *dhampir.*"

"Annja, don't start."

The American salesman had served as the Gypsy's *dhampir.* "Ask him, then."

"Can I speak to your mother or father? An elder?" Luke asked. "Ask someone about the missing children? I promise to be respectful of their loss. But I need to understand. My job is all about understanding the social structure of a people through the ages by studying bones and the everyday articles of living. Anything related to the bones they have burned only enhances the picture and could help archaeologists worldwide to better understand your people."

Santos winced. "We are not a project for you to put under the microscope and study."

"I didn't mean to offend." Luke splayed out his palms in an open, nonthreatening gesture. "Help me to understand why the bodies were buried the way they were. I suspect the burial is more recent than the many centuries I'd originally guessed at. They could be recent relatives."

Santos crossed himself at that statement. Annja wondered if Santos feared revenge.

"Please." If Luke's gentle tone couldn't convince the man to talk, then nothing could. "Just a few minutes to talk with your family? Someone, an elder, who may have information of those who have passed perhaps three or four generations earlier? The truth can calm their fears."

Firelight glinted in Santos's dark eyes as he studied Luke's earnest expression. The Gypsy nodded.

"I will see about that. You get that *gorja* with the camera out of here, and then perhaps my mother will talk to you. But I will not promise you anything."

"Deal." Luke shook the man's hand, and then went after their rogue cameraman.

GARIN PACED THE floor of his hotel room, cell phone to his ear as he spoke to Slater. Wine decanted in a silver ewer beside his waiting caviar. He'd showered and wrapped himself up in the thick hotel robe, and now all he was missing was a sexy blonde—but there was business first.

"You recall Bracks's interpreter?"

"Indeed, I do. A slimy Irishman, he was."

Garin smirked at the age-old clash between the English and the Irish. Came in handy when selling Irish arms to the Brits, though.

"I need to bring him in," he said. "Can you be ready?"

"Always."

"I'll be in contact." He hung up, but didn't set down the phone.

Dipping a finger through the tiny jewels of black roe he licked off the salty treat.

The phone rang, and his second taste of caviar got stuck at the back of his throat when he saw it was Roux.

Before Garin could even say hello, the old man began talking. "You and Bracks. I've been thinking."

Of course he was on top of what was going on in Garin's life. Garin expected as much, though he was always baffled why Roux was ever concerned about him.

"Don't tell me not to do anything foolish," he said. "You're not my father."

"On the contrary. I think it's time you took the man out. And I'm the closest you've ever known to a paternal figure, ungrateful son that you are."

"Taking Bracks out is tops on my list. Glad you agree, old man. Anything else?"

"Speak to Charles at the concierge. He'll hook you up with the quality of woman you're accustomed to."

Shaking his head, Garin couldn't help a smile. "I'll do that. Goodbye."

Roux clicked off.

Annoyance rippled through Garin.

"Annja," Garin decided. "She's your spy, isn't she, Roux?"

Why the two spoke about him behind his back bothered him.

No, it didn't.

Perhaps a little. He was aware Annja Creed didn't consider him an upstanding citizen. He was what he was. He couldn't change. He'd been forged this way over *centuries*. He answered to no one but himself.

So why did it bother him when he heard the disappointment in Annja's voice?

Garin dialed up the concierge and asked for Charles.

12

The leader of the Roma protesters escorted Luke, Annja and Doug through the woods on what he explained was a mile trek to his mother's home. Annja was nervous about leaving the dig site behind with the flames still licking the sky. Annja had wanted to kick the American hawker into the ditch and leave him there, but when he'd come to after Luke had decked him, he slunk away toward the forest, and she'd been inclined to let him scamper off like the coward he was. Nothing she could do now to change the damage he had created.

Santos had reassured her that his people would stay until the fire died. Not only did they have safety on their minds, but he also suspected they wanted to ensure the bones had been reduced to ash. They would also keep watch because a forest fire would ravage their small community. They lived at the edge of the city in houses, not the apartment complexes designated for the Roma. And they did not camp in trailers or tents, he added, implying that he suspected she'd pinned him for the traveling vagabonds most often associated with his nationality.

Annja detected the pride in the man's tone as he explained this, but he was clearly still cautious and distrusted them. The Gypsies were a private people. She should be thankful Luke had managed this introduction, and only hoped when they did meet others, they would be willing to talk and to shed some light on the fears that had led to the destruction of the dig site.

Of course, she looked a mess smeared with dirt, and the sweat had made it into a sticky kind of mud facial she sincerely hoped had some kind of skin-improving agents in it. Otherwise, the look would just be sorry.

Santos had demanded that Doug leave the iPad behind; he didn't want him filming the conversation with his mother. Luke, however, had refused to leave the valuable electronic device back in the Range Rover, so Doug promised to keep it tucked in his backpack. Annja had caught Doug's wink, but she intended to make sure the man held to his word.

The authorities should be contacted regarding the fire at the site, and certainly, if a child had gone missing, shouldn't the police be working on that, as well?

"Just ahead," Santos instructed as the moon slipped behind the jagged black tree line and smoke from the distant blaze furled up. "I told my mother about you already. She is curious."

"Do you get a lot of Dracula references living in

this section of the world?" Doug asked as they hiked over thick tree roots coated with lush moss.

Santos flashed a grim look over his shoulder, chilling Annja in its trajectory toward the cocky producer. No reply. None necessary.

"Dracula could have been deemed a *mullo*," Doug continued, unaware that he'd been cast the evil eye. "He did shape-shift to wolf form—"

"And he was also fictional," Luke reminded him. "Could we abandon all references to the undead for this visit? Please?"

Doug shrugged and shoved his hands in the front pockets of his jeans. "Just doing my job, man."

Some kind of animal howled.

"What was that?" Doug asked.

The foursome slowed their pace, and Santos's footsteps fell more lightly now, so Annja followed stride. Could have been a dog. Very likely a dog. Wolves did live in this country, but she had no idea if they were forest-dwelling and stayed away from populated areas.

Annja caught Santos's wary look, his jaw tight and pulsing. So he was worried about the animal, as well. Interesting.

"My mother has a husky," Santos finally offered.

"You see?" Luke admonished Doug with his own brand of evil eye, but it skimmed right over the producer's head.

They arrived at a clearing with four small houses—more like shacks—surrounded by vehicles, some stripped down to the iron innards. They passed through a wrought-iron gate and walked by a laundry line hung with bedsheets. Annja noted the rain barrel beside the house and guessed they didn't have running water out here, though she did see an electrical pole behind the house. The strong scent of lye made her wonder if they had been making soap or perhaps curing olives. She had seen an olive tree when coming out of the forest.

Santos welcomed them into the home he shared with his mother. He hadn't mentioned a wife or children, and Annja didn't see a ring on his finger, but that didn't mean much.

The slender, dark-haired woman who stood in the kitchen wiping her hands on the apron she wore over her dress was beautiful. She stepped up to take Annja's hand in greeting. She may have been aged, but she could probably still bring a man to his knees, Annja decided as those bright black eyes twinkled with good humor.

With further introductions—Santos called his mother *Dai,* the Romani word for *Mother*—but introduced her as Mamma. "*Dai,* this is Luke Spencer. Mr. Spencer, this is Mamma."

She shook Luke's hand and held it, turning it over to inspect first the back, tracing her finger over the wormlike veins scrubbed with dirt and soot, and then flipping it over to touch his palm.

"A man of labor," she said, "but not too hard. You are one with the earth, the stones, the water and the air, yes?"

An obvious guess, the skeptic in Annja silently

screamed. The archaeologist's hands were covered with dirt.

Luke nodded, wobbling from a yes to a no, and then to something in the middle. "I'm an archaeologist. I do spend a lot of time digging in the dirt in an attempt to learn about the past."

"The past is all we have to show us the way toward the future," she commented cryptically. "You are from across the ocean. Your voice is mellifluous."

He nodded a humble thanks, and Annja thought he was blushing, but his face was as dirty as hers so she couldn't be positive.

"Annja Creed is also an archaeologist," Santos said, and his mother directed her attention to Annja.

"Strong hands," Mamma pronounced. "Skilled warrior."

That assessment was strangely true. Annja nodded in acknowledgment and didn't challenge the assessment.

"And this," Santos winced, and said dismissively, "is Doug Morrell, a television actor."

"Oh. The media." Mamma's voice was as toneless and dismissive as her son's had been.

"Not an actor or host, like Annja. I'm a producer." Doug stepped forward, offering his hand to shake, but Mamma merely looked at it. He continued to hold it out, perhaps hoping she'd read his palm. She stepped back to gesture that they all sit around the table, where there was a bread board with half a loaf of rosemary bread and an open bottle of spirits.

Fresh-baked, Annja decided, breathing in the rosemary-sweetened air. She recalled rosemary was for remembrance. At the very least, she hoped it would help Mamma remember all the details Luke would ask after.

"It smells delicious," she offered.

"My own recipe," Mamma said. "You cook?"

Annja shrugged. "Never have the time."

The woman nodded, as if expecting nothing less.

Santos poured pale wine into small blue aperitif glasses and passed them around. When Luke took an obligatory sip, he nearly choked. Annja, too, had to keep from making a gasping choke. It wasn't wine, but rather some sort of high-proof moonshine, she guessed. Beside her, Doug groaned, but didn't choke or cough it up. It was a challenge, though, not to let his eyes tear up.

"I make this myself," Santos said, "from caramel-ized gooseberries. They're very tart but sweeten up nicely in vodka."

"Sweet?" So this was his idea of sweet?

Annja set the glass down and waited until Mamma, after finishing a few sips, turned to face them with a decidedly stern look.

"You diggers of history have stirred up the *mullo*," she said flatly. The gesture she made could be con-strued as an evil eye, her pinky finger out as she rattled her fist, but Annja sensed it was protection against the dead. "You think us ignorant and super-stitious, but I know the truth of the world. There are things we dream to only imagine that are flesh, blood and soul. If the dead are not respected, they will return for vengeance."

"With all respect, Mamma," Luke began, "the bones we've uncovered are from the mid–nineteenth century, at the earliest. It's possible it's been over one hundred fifty years since that body was buried. The bones are not going to rise, I can promise you that."

"Vengeance waits," she simply said, folding her hands together and looking to Santos. "You have told them?"

Santos shook his head.

"Why not?" Mamma sighed. "Children have gone missing."

"That can't be related to the *mullo*," Doug said quickly.

"Doug." Luke cast him a look. "Let me do the talking, okay? You just…listen, and record in your head."

Thankful for Luke's command, Annja nodded to Doug that he heed the man's suggestion.

"We've seen the wolf," Mamma said. "It was howling close to our homes last evening."

"The *mullo* that shape-shifts to wolf form?" Doug hurried out.

Luke and Annja both glared at him.

"We heard a dog on the way over here," Annja added. "Are you sure it was a wolf? They can sound familiar."

"I know my dogs from the *Canis lupus*," the woman said flatly.

"When were the children taken?" Luke asked. "Have you notified the authorities?"

Mamma made a dismissive gesture and sat back, elbow crooking over the back of the chair. She eyed the blue glass. "The local police do not take notice of the Roma. We cannot get help if we walk into town on fire."

An unfortunate truth. Annja's heart went out to the woman, and she wasn't even the one in trouble. Had grieving parents already gone to the police about the missing children, only to be turned away?

"Is there any reason to believe someone has a grudge against the Romani who live in the area, and who might have done such a thing as to steal a child?" Luke asked.

Annja clenched her teeth. This was a case for the police. And not at all related to burning bones.

"If you could tell me what you think the discovery of the bones has…conjured…" Luke prodded gently.

"The *mullo!*" Mamma crooned, ending in a keening note that raised the hairs on the back of Annja's neck.

"Dai," Santos chided.

"You have a better explanation for what took Melanie's son?" she said abruptly. "What of—?"

Beating the table with a fist, Santos marched out of the kitchen, the sword gleaming at his back.

Mamma shrugged and offered her guests another glass of gooseberry spirit. Both men refused. And

Annja wanted to go after Santos and talk to him, but she sensed she'd get the best information from Mamma.

"The *chavo,* Tomas, was taken four days ago," Mamma said as she settled forward, her elbows catching the table. Her eyes avoided Luke's and Annja's in favor of the old wooden cuckoo clock on the wall behind them. "The day after you discovered the buried undead."

Annja was about to correct her, but held her tongue. To protest the undead, and the fact that no one would have known about Luke's discovery if Daisy hadn't spread the word like a blazing forest fire, held no value right now. Mamma was allowing them a peek into her life, into her beliefs. She would respect that opportunity for what it was.

Aware that Santos hadn't left the small house, that he may be sitting in the next room, Annja nodded for the other woman to continue.

"My son cannot talk to you about this because he had harsh words with the boy's mother a day before Tomas disappeared. He feels the guilt of his words, and regrets them deeply."

As he should, Annja thought, if the man believed the dead would come back to take revenge.

Mamma continued, "Tomas was found a hundred yards from his home last evening. Stumbling, raving about monsters."

"He's alive?" Doug asked.

"Did you call the hospital?" Annja demanded.

Mamma shook her head and poured more goose-berry spirit from the decanter. Sadness weighed her down.

"He died shortly after his mother laid him in his bed. Early this morning. The *mullo* had opened him up."

"Opened him up?" Annja asked. "Did he have… bites?" It was too incredible to ask, but perhaps the boy had been attacked by an animal.

"Across his back there was a large wound, stitched up with black thread."

Annja exchanged a look with Luke. How often did a monster take the time to stitch up its victim?

"Did the authorities remove the boy's body?" Annja asked.

The other woman raised her head and looked Annja straight in the eyes as she replied, "We did not call the authorities. It was too late. There was nothing they could do for Tomas."

"Well, then…could we meet with his mother? And…see the boy?" Annja asked hesitantly. He may not have been buried yet. There would be a funeral ritual to follow.

"Yes," Luke added. "If we could inspect the wounds? I promise we would leave Doug outside."

The producer began to splutter, but Annja cut him off. "If there is someone harming your children—"

"Harming? The boy is dead. And I will not allow you near his body. The family would take that as a great insult. The lamentation has already begun and we are fasting. This bread is for after the funeral. In the morning we bury Tomas."

With a brick in his mouth? Annja wondered.

What beliefs would these people have for a murdered child? Could they imagine the boy might return from the dead to attack them?

It was now apparent Annja had stepped into something that had nothing to do with her work at the dig site.

Luke laid a hand on her wrist and he gestured with a tilt of his head that they should step outside. Mamma sat nursing her vodka, her eyes focused on the dark hallway leading into the living area where Santos had disappeared.

"If you'll excuse us," Luke offered, and got up to follow Annja out into the moonlit yard.

Along the side of the house stood a tin washbasin with an old-fashioned washboard and wringer, and beside that a wooden stool painted with flowers. Half a dozen bikes in all states of repair were lined along the side of the house where Luke wandered.

He turned to Annja. "We should head back to the site, get in the car and never return."

Doug sauntered up behind them, hands stuffed in his pockets. "That's not an option. Don't you see?" he said. "Someone is using the legend of the *mullo* to cover something darker and more vile."

About to protest and suggest they call the authorities, Annja paused to run Doug's suggestion over in her thoughts. It could indeed be a clever cover-up. But it was also something she didn't want to involve

Doug or Luke in. They'd already been kidnapped. Apparently more than one child had been kidnapped and murdered. Although Tomas had been kidnapped and released, only to die shortly after his return. That was strange.

And Garin had gone off in a helicopter with a cooler that sickened Annja to think of what could have been inside.

"I don't know." Luke toed the rusted wheel rim of a bicycle, his heel landing on a red-clay brick.

"It's what I feel in my gut," Doug said. "I'm not always right, but this is too weird any other way. But I do want to get away from here and head back to town."

"Uh, we'll probably need Santos to show us back through the forest," Luke pointed out.

"I can navigate," Annja said. "It was just a few bends and the path was obvious. And I've got a flashlight in my hip pack."

"Great." Doug turned toward the forest, which was completely black. "Wolves in the area, eh?"

Yes, wolves. But were they real or imagined, Annja couldn't help but wonder.

"Where's Santos?" Doug asked as Luke strode by him on his way into the trees.

"He said to follow the path. Gave me a flashlight." Luke wielded the small mag light near his shoulder, sweeping the beam across Doug's face.

"It's a mile, give or take," Annja said. "I've got a light, too. We'll be fine. Come on, gentlemen. And you, Doug, what's up with not wanting to trek into a dark, creepy forest in search of vampires?"

"I prefer my vamps a little less sanguine than the ones rumored to stalk these parts."

"Oh, you mean you like them to sparkle?" Luke asked.

Annja laughed at the jibe as she stepped onto the path through the brush.

Within seconds they were surrounded by utter blackness. The flashlight beams couldn't permeate the dark farther than a few feet. Annja let Luke take the lead.

A person forgets how dark it is away from the city, she thought. And the night had chilled measurably. Wishing she'd worn long sleeves instead of the T-shirt, she trekked onward, thankful the biting insects were avoiding them.

Doug stepped on Annja's heels for the third time, and she swung around to laser the flashlight right into his eyes.

"Annja!"

"Do you want to hold my hand?" she asked.

"No. But I wouldn't mind walking alongside you."

"Children," Luke admonished from the lead. "The faster you move, Doug, the quicker we get to the other side."

"I'm taking the middle." Doug stepped around Annja and they trekked onward.

"Did you hear that?" Doug's voice vibrated nervously.

"The squirrel in the tree above us?" she asked calmly.

"Probably smells the bread you stuffed in your pocket," Luke called back. "Did you have to do that? The woman was kind enough to offer us food, and then you make off like a homeless bandit."

"Just be quiet, Doug. We can navigate better if we can hear," Annja said.

After a few moments of silence, they heard a long howl somewhere out in the darkness. A chill ran up Annja's spine, and the muscles across her scalp tightened.

In front of her, both men looked at each other. Nobody spoke for a brief moment.

"Just a dog," she finally commented, though she wasn't sure about that. The difference between a wolf and a dog howl was negligible. Though wolves rarely barked, when they did, the sound was quite distinct from a dog's.

They heard the howl again, low and angry-sounding.

"Far away," Luke whispered.

"Not really," Doug said. "It sounded close. Like it could be at the opening where we went into the forest."

"If it is a wolf, then keep walking," Annja said. "The dig site isn't far. I can smell the smoke. Just keep moving."

"Don't look it in the eye," Doug said. "I think that's what I know about wolves. Or is it, look them in the eye? Show them you're the alpha?"

"Wolves rarely attack humans," Annja added.

Unless they were hungry or the humans had encroached on their territory. And they had the ability to bite fast and hard, so fast, in fact, that a human couldn't predict the hit and get out of its way in time. This close to the Romani encampment, she hardly expected a wolf to attack.

They moved more slowly since hearing the howl. Luke's flashlight blinked out. Doug swore.

"Take mine!" Annja called. She tossed her light toward Doug, who missed it, and the flashlight landed on the ground, a tiny glow in the leaves. The undergrowth and tree trunks were all the same, deep shadows upon darkness.

That's when they heard a low, panting sound. Annja twisted to look behind her.

"Annja?" Doug whispered.

"Right here, Doug." She reached out and he grabbed her arm. The smell of his fear was strong and acrid, and his fingers clutched her shoulder.

"If it's a *mullo,*" he whispered, his fingers tightening into her muscle, "it shouldn't have a grudge against us. We didn't do anything wrong."

"Except dig up its bones," Luke muttered from the darkness. "Found it!"

The light beam swung toward Annja and Doug and then traced the path border. Two gold eyes flashed in the brief swing of the light beam.

"Keep walking, slowly," Annja murmured. She'd thought that the dig site hadn't been far off, but she couldn't see a glimpse of the flame. She should see it by now.

There was a rustle of leaves and suddenly the eyes were on the path in front of them. How it had moved that fast, she had no idea.

"We need to walk in that direction," Luke said. "It's standing in our way."

The wolf growled quietly, revealing its teeth. The light should have blinded it. It was a good height, perhaps the size of a German shepherd, but leaner, the legs longer and the body more muscled.

"The flashlight is making it angry," Doug said.

"You want me to turn it off?"

"No!"

"You see a branch or something to use as a weapon?" Luke asked.

"There's a thick one." Doug's voice wobbled.

"Where?"

"By the wolf's foot."

Overhead, an owl hooted, startling Luke into jerking the light upward.

The wolf dashed toward them. Luke stumbled backward, the flashlight slipping from his grip and rolling up against the branch.

13

Teeth grazed Annja's thigh, and she swung out with the sword, but didn't catch the animal. She didn't want to slay the wolf, just wound it.

They stood in darkness. Luke's breaths came quickly to her left. She didn't want to accidentally slash the blade across a man, either.

Doug's yell chilled Annja's blood. She stepped across the path, careful of the branches she couldn't see, using Doug's voice as a guide. The wolf barked and Doug screamed again.

Overhead an owl screeched and Annja could make out the flapping of the great bird's wings as it flew away.

"Guys?" she called. "Luke?"

"I'm here," Luke answered. "I'm okay. But what about Doug?"

At the sound of an animal tearing into clothing Annja's throat tightened. The wolf yelped and a high-pitched whine was abruptly cut off. Annja felt fur against her leg, a tail twitching, as the wolf landed on the path before her. Its eyes caught the muted flashlight glow. She swept the sword in warning in front of the wolf. The creature didn't flinch. It only growled, exposing its teeth threateningly.

"Doug?"

"I'm…here," he said weakly.

The idea of killing such a beautiful animal made Annja's gut clench. They were encroaching on its territory.

With a snapping growl, the wolf lunged for her. She managed to swing the sword, but it cut through air. The wolf's forepaws landed against her chest. Instinctually, she knew she couldn't move the sword to perform a wounding cut, so she dropped it into the otherwhere and grabbed the wolf's jaws with both hands. Teeth cut into her palms as she forced the jaws wide.

The animal yelped and, shaking its head out of her grasp, stumbled away into the brush. They could hear high-pitched whining as it retreated from them.

Luke was at Annja's side in a heartbeat. He'd claimed the flashlight and swept it over her body, stopping at her bleeding palms. "You're hurt."

"It's wounded," she said, "but that doesn't mean it's down. We need to get out of here. Doug? Where is he? Direct the light over there."

Luke fumbled with the mag light and swept it over the body of the prone man. The leg of Doug's jeans was torn but they couldn't see much blood.

"He's been bitten."

Doug gave Luke the thumbs-up. "Dude." Then he passed out.

LUKE PACED THE hotel room floor in front of the bed where Doug lay sprawled. Annja had placed a wet cloth to his forehead and then brought in the first-aid kit from the Jeep. She'd cut Doug's jeans to below the knee where the teeth had penetrated into muscle. She'd cleaned the wound with alcohol and soap and bandaged it tightly.

Now she suggested he go to the hospital for a rabies shot.

"In the morning," he said. "I'm tired and just want to sleep. Can it wait?"

"I suppose," she said reluctantly. "We'll find a clinic in town tomorrow."

"I survived a wolf attack," Doug said proudly, tossing the cloth off his head.

"That you did."

"And the worst part?"

"What's that?"

"I don't have it on film."

Ever the producer, she thought with relief. "Would have been difficult filming in the dark while trying to fight off the big bad, eh?" she offered with a grin.

Doug would work this one for days, weeks, surely. Wasn't every day he was attacked by a wolf, and to walk away with just a scratch?

"You think it was the *mullo?*" Luke asked as he took Annja's hands to inspect the wounds. Turned out only one tooth had punctured her palm, and she was only beginning to feel the pain now that her adrenaline was fading. Thank God her shots were up-to-date.

"Of course it was a *mullo*," Doug retorted in a rapidly weakening voice.

"You buying into the idea of a dead man returning from the grave with the ability to shift into wolf shape now, Luke?" Annja asked. "I leave you with Doug for a day and your whole belief system goes topsy-turvy. Ouch!"

Luke tossed the alcohol wipe into the trash can, then grabbed the roll of gauze Annja had used to bandage Doug's leg. "He could have been killed. You, too. I'm responsible. This is my dig. The fire, and now this wolf attack. What next?"

"Time to get out the garlic and stakes," Doug said, his eyelids shut.

Annja allowed Luke to bandage her hand, knowing she'd peel it off in the shower, but it was his way of compensating for how badly he was feeling.

"I wonder where the thing came from?" Luke muttered.

Much as she wanted to believe Santos hadn't thought anything wrong with sending three people out in the middle of the night, she felt a twinge of suspicion, and always trusted her instincts. She hadn't seen the dog Mamma had claimed they owned. Could it have possibly been a wolf?

"I should talk to Santos first thing in the morning."

"The funeral is tomorrow," Luke said. "Wouldn't be wise to go there while they're mourning. Although I certainly would have liked a chance to look at the child's body. I'm no surgeon and forensics is far from my specialty, but I keep thinking about what Mamma said about the stitched-up wound. My mind goes to those crazy stories about people waking up after a drunken binge in a tub full of ice, with stitches and a note telling them to get to the doctor because their kidney has been removed. Could someone have taken out one of Tomas's body parts and then sent him on his way?"

"And if so, did they place the organ in a white cooler?" Annja whispered.

Luke grabbed her by the shoulders. "What did you say?" His gaze was so intense, she almost flinched from it. She felt his desperation in his grip.

"There was a cooler," she said. "Garin and I tracked the people who kidnapped Doug to a country cottage outside of Liberec, and after we took out half a dozen, there…was a cooler. One of the men was waiting for a handoff, which, I assume, meant handing over the cooler. I didn't get a chance to look inside, but they said it had been sealed and whatever was inside would be ruined if the seal was broken."

"Body parts?" Doug asked, his voice hollow and weak. "That's so wrong."

"You think that was what was in the cooler, Annja?" Luke asked.

He rubbed a palm across his temple. Anxiety lined his sun-browned skin and she sensed his unease. He'd come to Chrastava to excavate, not become involved in organ trafficking.

"Garin, the friend who is not a friend, mentioned something about seeing bags of blood at a warehouse he works—well, er, a warehouse he walked through."

"Blood? Now the vampire connection comes to light," Doug muttered from the bed. "Well, I mean it fits in there somehow. You think there was a human body part in that cooler? What the hell?"

"We were following the trail. Garin decided I wasn't an asset and took off on his own. I should have stayed on him." She touched her jaw. The bruise no longer hurt, but it was now changing from purple to green and black.

Annja wandered to the window. Putting her back to the men made it easier to think, to reason.

A child had been kidnapped and returned home days later with a strange wound, and then had died. It was possible illegal blood donations were taking place in a warehouse outside Chrastava, but blood transfusion didn't create a wound that required stitches.

If only she'd had the opportunity to look inside the cooler. If only Garin would answer her phone calls. Had this all started because of the skull Luke had uncovered?

"Guys, the more I think about this…" Doug sat up and eased a leg off the side of the bed. He touched the bandaged wound carefully. "Maybe I shouldn't say anything. Annja never puts much faith in my theories."

"Tell us, Doug," Luke said. "I want to hear your theory."

Giving the gauze bandage a pat, Doug leaned forward and explained. "Someone is using the Romani's beliefs in revenants—the myth that the dead will rise and seek revenge—to cover for what happened to the kid. Child goes missing? It's the work of the vengeful chewing dead. Yes?"

"But how could anyone have known the skull would be discovered?" she posited. "It couldn't have been planted. The flooding uncovered it. It's been in the ground for over a century."

"Possibly," Luke added. "It's looking newer than that to me every time I go over the thing. Could be as new as a few decades."

"Really?" Doug gestured to the skull. "But it looks old. What could cause a skeleton to age so rapidly as to look centuries old?"

"Malnutrition. Anemia. Many other factors that a bone specialist could answer. I need to get the bones to London."

Annja heard Luke's heavy sigh over her shoulder. "We should get some rest. It's been a long day fighting fire and battling wild animals. You guys take the bed. I'll toss a pillow on the floor."

"Thanks, Annja." Doug, never one to subscribe to chivalry, lay down again with a dramatic flop and a groan. "Don't worry, Luke. I'm not a spooner."

"You should take the bed," Luke said as she passed him, pillow clutched to her chest. "Or I can rent you a room to yourself."

"I sleep well on a hard surface," she said. "Slate riverbeds, underneath a picnic table, crashed on the open plain. It's all good. Besides, I got your pillow. We'll all have clearer heads in the morning. Deal?"

Luke nodded, and collapsed on the bed beside Doug, who had already begun to snore.

ANNJA WOKE BEFORE sunrise and slipped out of the hotel room. Commandeering a coffee from the front lobby, she downed the strong brew, then headed out to the dig site. It was a disaster. Kindling had been thrown over the pit and a huge pile of ash now covered it.

What she'd come for lay about one hundred yards into the forest on the well-worn path that this particular Gypsy camp obviously used a lot.

Now with the daylight filtering through the leaf canopy, she noted tattered strips of cloth on trees designating break-offs from the path, and assumed they used the area for hunting. Although she wagered they only hunted fox, squirrel and perhaps a wild pig on occasion.

And wolves.

Kneeling before the body of the creature she'd tussled with last night, she smoothed a hand over the brown and black fur. It had died, after all. She hadn't meant to strike to kill, and knew she hadn't. Who knew that pulling its jaws apart would be the coup de grâce.

"Sorry," she said. "I had to protect my friends."

She sighed heavily at the sight of a collar around

its neck. A heavy black leather collar with a square electronic device attached. A shock collar? Owners used them to train their pets. She and Bart McGilly used to debate the pros and cons of using this means to train a dog for hours, but ultimately it fell to the integrity of the trainer.

The animal beneath her palm was a wolf, not a dog that looked like a wolf, but she suspected this one had grown up tame, with a family. Perhaps later it had been trained to attack on command, or even trained as it had matured. Into a killing machine?

On the other hand, wild animals could never be tamed, no matter how amiable or family-oriented they appeared to be.

She tapped the wolf's canine teeth. Most animals' canines weren't pin-sharp, but these had either broken at one point and had worn smooth, or had been altered. Which meant they weren't designed to pierce, but simply maul. Doug had been very lucky to get away with the small wound, and that explained why she hadn't received more damage to her hands.

She assumed the electronic box could issue simple commands the wolf understood. Many shock collars were now outfitted with GPS. Wouldn't the owner have gone looking for the wolf if it hadn't returned last night? It was early yet.

She remembered the man at the dig who had revealed the scars on his chest. She had thought they were from a bear. Maybe they had been from a run-in with this wolf.

Who could've unleashed this animal on them? Only someone who had known they'd been in the woods. Was the Gypsy woman involved in sending a deadly wolf after innocent archaeologists and a film producer?

But more likely someone who wasn't pleased that they'd encroached on his territory.

"Santos."

Unclasping the collar from the animal's neck, she headed north into the forest.

Luke sipped the coffee Doug had procured from the hotel lobby as he copied down the words the man on the other end of the phone line recited.

The tiny slip of paper he'd found in the brick had easily unrolled after being closed up in the steamy bathroom. The words were Romani, yet even though Luke knew the language, he couldn't decipher them so he'd called a colleague in London.

Chester Rumshaven had been the one to suggest Luke do his research on the Romani schoolchildren last year. The old man had grown up in a small hamlet in southern England and had used the fight circuit and his knockout left hook to bring him to the big city. London. Eventually his fight earnings had added up to a tidy sum; enough to pay for schooling, which had been his dream.

"You know Romani isn't a written language," Chester's voice bellowed on the other end of the line.

"Yes, it's conversational. Used by families among

themselves in public places. My great-grandfather, who was a Kale Gypsy living in Wales, spoke Welsh Romani, but I can't recall anything of it."

"Exactly. Because of its secretive nature. Here goes—'may the sun always shine,'" Chester said. "That's what your words translate to. The words are Indic, with a Baltic influence, one of the oldest Romani dialects. Last time the original Romani language was spoken anywhere in the world was late nineteenth century, possibly a generation longer in your neck of the woods, Wales. Which could date your skull to early twentieth century."

"But what does 'may the sun always shine' mean?"

"It's an old Gypsy blessing. At first I thought it strange to find those words inside a buried skull that was suspected of becoming revenant. You'd think they'd curse it, or at the very least put some kind of binding spell on it. But no, a blessing."

"Perhaps they thought gentle words would keep the corpse down?" Luke tried.

"Very possible. Though strange. Pagan curses are believed much more effective than a few kind words, that's for sure."

"What is it?" Doug asked when he entered the bedroom and saw Luke engaged. Luke shoved the notebook in which he'd written down the translation toward him. The producer sat on the bed and studied it.

"Anything else I can do for you, Spencer?"

"At the moment, no. But I'd appreciate being able to call you if I've got further questions."

"Not a problem. I enjoyed the puzzle, though it wasn't that much of a challenge. Next time give me hell, old buddy." He clicked off, and Luke leaned over the tiny paper he'd found inside the brick.

"This is rich," Doug offered. "'May the sun always shine.' It's so Dracula, it's not even funny."

"Why Dracula?"

"Well, Dracula was weak during the day, when the sun was out. So to leave this message with the corpse was like saying, 'Dude, don't let the coffin door slam you in the face. Go out and enjoy the sunshine on your pasty white skin. And burn to a bloody crisp while you're out there.' Clever."

"I knew unearthing the skull would immerse me in the subculture that's fascinated with vampires, but who would have thought it could be so real for some?"

"There are people out there who actually believe they are vampires. Drink blood, too. Supposedly the blood is given with permission. That kills me."

"This coming from a man who has his own set of fangs?"

"I only use them for parties and the occasional date."

"A date. Seriously?" Luke held his hand up. "No. I really don't want to know. I need to do some online research."

"About vampires? Ask me anything. I bet I have the answer."

"I bet you do." And that troubled Luke more than the fact that the man was sitting on the bed picking at the blood-crusted gauze on his leg. "Tell me all you know about *mullos*."

"*Mullo* means one who is dead. Generally *dhampirs* must kill them. That is, if the stakes or bricks or iron needles driven into their bones at burial didn't keep them down in the first place."

"We know all that already."

"Sorry, but the various renditions of vampire, as they pertain to each country, I'm not too keen on. The Dracula myth is my specialty."

"Anything in *Dracula* about consuming organ blood? Or taking organs from a human body to feed the vampire?"

"Not particularly, but the whole wolf thing was in there."

"Right. I don't think you were attacked by a shape-shifting *mullo,* Doug."

He inspected the abrasion, which strapped below his knee and had already begun to scab. "I know, but still, it was a real wolf."

"That it was. We should get you to a clinic for a rabies shot."

"Check online for a clinic."

"Sure. Though we may have to drive to Liberec." Luke pulled Annja's laptop across the table and opened it up to the browser. Within minutes he had the address to the local clinic.

"Let's wait for Annja before we go anywhere,"

Doug said. "I'm going to shower quick." He strolled into the bathroom.

There was a clinic in Liberec, so Luke noted the address and searched further for some driving directions. With those notes tucked in a pocket, he then decided to surf for Dracula and revenants and the buried undead. The legend was vast and encompassed so many different breeds and forms that he felt sure it may be more of an exercise in futility, but he had the time.

He thought to type in *mullo* in the search engine, but on a sudden whim, decided to bring up the browser history. What secrets would Annja's laptop reveal to him?

The bathroom door swung inward, emitting a gust of steam. Doug danced out in a towel and grabbed his backpack. "Forgot my stuff." The door closed behind him.

The browser showed much the same searches as he'd attempted. A few were not. One site was for brand-name knockoff shoes.

"She doesn't strike me as the stiletto type," he murmured, then smiled to imagine Annja in a dress and high heels. With her toned body, she could work the little black dress. He bet she cleaned up rather nicely.

"You snooping?"

"No." At Doug's reappearance, Luke lowered the laptop cover, then realized that he looked guilty and reopened it. "A little. I might have checked her browser history."

"No porn?"

"From Annja? Doug, you really don't know your employee all that well, do you?"

"I do. Just teasing. Did you kiss her again?"

"You've been right there with us since that first kiss. Have you seen me kiss her again?"

"Is that your way of telling me to give you two some alone time?" The man actually made a fluttery eye move and smacked his lips in a kiss.

"No. It was just something that happened. It was a moment. I took it."

"You've got it, man. What you do with it now is all up to you." He grabbed the iPad. "If you decide to do some real research, why don't you look up the red lady?"

"What red lady?"

"Just popped into my head right now. She's a myth. I remember reading about her once. She has fangs and can shape-shift into a wolf, and consumes people whole. And red ladies usually go after children. I think she might be more faerie than vampire, though, but it's worth a look. Good thing we're dealing with legends and myths. I hate to think that a real person could be out there doing this to kids."

"It is a real person, Doug. Wrap your brain around that."

"Right." Doug shook his head. "Right." He sat on the bed and sighed. "This is getting heavy. Too heavy for *Chasing History's Monsters*. I can't use any of this stuff if a child really has been killed by someone who is using the vampire as cover. That would be ethically wrong to try and sensationalize it on the show."

"Depends on your moral compass."

"I do have one. And it just popped a spring."

14

Santos was strolling out of the house toward his pickup truck when Annja cleared the forest. When he noticed her he immediately set back his shoulders, straightening. Sunlight glinted in the diamonds at his ears. He made to reach behind his back, though Annja did not see the sword sheath strapped across his chest.

"Hold your steel," Annja said. "Even if it is a bluff." She tossed him the wolf collar, which he caught.

Santos turned the leather strap in his fingers, then tucked it in a back pocket. "Where did you find it?" he asked.

"Took if off the dead wolf that attacked my friends last night. You remember Luke and Doug. We were all here at your invitation?"

"My wolf is dead?"

"You were expecting to hear something else? Like maybe one of my friends was mauled? Or me? What the hell is going on, Santos? Your wolf? I thought you owned a dog?"

"My *dai* does. I owned that wolf."

And not even slightly apologetic for it. Annja clenched her fists at her sides. "Why did you send the wolf after us?"

"I don't control it like that. What?" he challenged at her lifted brow. "You think I can order the wolf to go off and murder someone?"

"So murder was your intent? I only mentioned an attack. And any animal can be trained to obey commands. That electric collar could have delivered the desired signal. The wolf has been taught to obey. It goes after human prey."

"Get off my land!"

She planted her feet, tucking her thumbs in her front pockets, and lifted her chin. She'd measured this man's courage and he tended to hide behind weapons and his mother. Now it was time to judge his mettle against hers. She wagered he'd not last long when he didn't have a blazing fire for distraction. And his sword was blatantly absent.

"We are in mourning this day," he said firmly. "You are intruding."

"I'm not going anywhere until you tell me the truth about what's going on around here."

"Weren't you listening to Mamma last night? I've nothing more to say."

"There was no mention of attack wolves when we were talking with your mother. She mentioned you had a dog. Which I haven't seen. As a matter of fact, I haven't seen any animals around the Romani encampment."

Santos spat on the ground. "You Americans think you are so brave, so tough. You don't know the meaning of strength. Now leave, before someone gets hurt."

"I don't take threats lightly."

"Neither do—"

A wailing female entered the yard from the left. A pregnant woman in a bright yellow skirt and blue top, she stumbled toward Santos. She gripped her belly, yet she wasn't large enough to be in labor. Perhaps six months along. But who was she to know?

"What is it, Melanie? Is it the baby? The funeral?"

"Not the funeral. I could not attend in my condition."

Santos shot Annja a stern look. "You should not have come here when we are burying one of our own."

"Santos, Marcus is gone!" the woman cried. "The *mullo* has taken him!"

"You see!" Santos stabbed Annja with a vicious glare. His jaws hardened. "Look what you have started!"

She had started nothing that couldn't be explained rationally. Or criminally. "Who is Marcus?"

"Her son." Santos braced the woman and led her in the direction she had come from. Not far off more houses edged the forest. One was draped with a white ribbon across the door. The dead boy's home, Annja assumed. "You've cursed us all, Annja Creed."

The woman Annja had spoken with last night, Mamma, dashed out of her home and, giving Annja only a cursory glance, she went after Santos and the pregnant woman.

"It's Marcus!" Santos called to his mother.

"Oh, blessed mercy," Mamma cried.

Compelled to follow, Annja vacillated. With a funeral going on, she wouldn't be greeted with open arms by anyone in this tight-knit community. And now this. Another missing child?

There had to be a means to infiltrate the Romani ranks and suss out details. If a child was missing, someone should contact the authorities. Annja knew they wouldn't.

And in that case, someone had to begin tracking the child immediately. Before the trail wore thin.

SANTOS, HIS MOTHER and the grieving pregnant woman entered a house ahead of Annja, who hung back near a parked pickup truck. It was early, before noon. Luke had mentioned the funeral was in the morning, but he hadn't said where it was going to be held. If it hadn't taken place yet, the family and friends would be fasting and preparing for the ceremony, which involved a possible funeral march to the cemetery. She had no idea where they planned to bury the child. There must be a cemetery in town, because she couldn't imagine them burying the child out here after the panic regarding the *mullo*. A dinner would follow the funeral, she knew, along with singing and dancing.

Had Santos cast a glance over his shoulder, spying Annja, before smoothly closing the screened door behind him? He had to have seen her. She wasn't hiding. Just hanging back, measuring how wise it would be to barge in on the family.

There was something in Annja that could not ignore an endangered child. Most people with a conscience wouldn't. Yet having been an orphan herself… She had to learn what was going on. If the best she could achieve was to convince someone to call the police, she felt she would be doing what she could.

Marching up to the house, she slid her fingers down the rusted wire screening on the rickety wood door. The inner door was open and she could hear the woman, Melanie, wailing between sniffles and explaining what had happened. She had sent her son Marcus to the store in town to buy sugar and bread, and he hadn't returned. The father was out cruising the streets of Chrastava right now, searching for the boy.

"It was the *mullo!*" someone cried. "Taking vengeance on us through our children. What have we done?"

"Santos?" she heard Mamma ask.

Did the elder woman suspect her son had a reason to fear a vengeful undead? Santos didn't respond. He was involved in this mess beyond merely protecting his people. She felt it to her bones.

But could she connect him to Bracks? Bracks would need a man on the inside if he was using the

Roma's superstitions as he'd alluded to. What a more perfect ally than someone who lived in the community?

Yet why would Santos have reason to scare his clan mates this way? And to endanger children? He was obviously a leader. The woman had come to him after her husband had gone out in search of their child. They trusted him. Was that trust mislaid?

Enough with the speculation. Annja pushed open the screen door and walked inside through the empty kitchen into the living area. There, among the decades-old furniture tufted with loose stuffing and a matted shag carpet, half a dozen people stood, all focused on the wailing mother. They didn't immediately notice Annja.

She met Santos's gaze and felt his disdain.

"Do you have a picture of the boy?" she asked, bringing everyone around to gape at the *gorja* in the room. "You should get a picture to the police quickly, so the search can begin. Along with information about height, clothing, hair and eye color—"

"It's her!" a man she didn't recognize cried. "The one who dug up the cause of our grief."

The evil eye was flung at her from more than a few fists.

"That skull is not the reason behind your missing son," Annja protested. "Someone kidnapped him." She wanted to add *allegedly,* since who could know right now if he had been taken or had merely wandered off and gotten lost? "Real people. Not *mullos* or vampires, or any kind of vengeful dead thing."

"Ah!" The pregnant woman sank to her knees, another woman's arms about her shoulders.

"Santos, get rid of her!" Mamma ordered, then turned to face Annja. "You are no longer welcome here. Can you not see we are in mourning?"

Santos moved toward her, and Annja put up her hands in placation. She stood her own in the doorway. "I apologize that I had to come here today. I think you all need to be smart about this. Why aren't you being the smart one in the room?" she asked Santos. "They need a leader to guide them, not help them sink deeper into this nonsense about vengeful dead."

"Get out," he said, and shoved her shoulder roughly.

Annja stepped through the kitchen, the ranks of Gypsies closing up behind her and Santos to protect the wailing mother. When her back hit the screen door, she paused before pushing it open.

"You saw me follow you here," she challenged. "You could have stopped me, protected your people from the woman who dug up the *mullo*. That makes me think you wanted them to see me. For what reason? To further rile them? Are you involved with Bracks, Santos?"

"Who are you?" He swung the door open and shoved her outside. Following her, he gripped her arm to swing her around to face him. "You will leave now, or I will inform the police."

"You want to call the police on little ole me, but not for an innocent and helpless child, who could very well be in worse danger than I could ever present."

"You do not understand our ways. We will handle this—"

"Don't give me that persecuted Gypsy excuse again. I think you're helping Bracks use those outdated beliefs to hide something from your friends and family. Do you know Weston Bracks?"

"The man is—" Giving a frustrated grunt, Santos swung a fist at Annja.

She dodged and, tilting to the side, swung up a leg and kicked him squarely in the gut, sending him stumbling backward against a rusted pickup truck. The vehicle swayed on its sagging tires with his weight.

"I don't want this fight," she said, keeping her fists up defensively before her face as she waited for him to right himself. "Those people inside need someone to take charge and reassure them. And I certainly don't want to create a stir with a funeral today. But you seem to want me to be here—to need the anger my presence fuels in your people. You know what happened to the boy, don't you?"

Santos charged, bending low and grabbing her about the hips, plowing her to the ground. She skidded across grass and dirt. A fist missed her jaw and smashed her shoulder. Dirt sifted into her eyes. She managed to knee his solar plexus, and scratch his neck. The man yelped at the pain as she drew blood. Pulling away from the hit, he plunged onto her gut with his entire body weight, bruising a rib.

The man fought dirty. But Annja could give as

good as she got. Elbowing him in the jaw loosened his grip on her wrist. She tossed a handful of dirt over her shoulder and he spat and stumbled off her.

Ruling out using the sword because he hadn't drawn his blade, Annja jumped up to a squat and, as she came to a stand, swung up a roundhouse kick, clocking Santos soundly in the head.

The screen door flapped open. Those inside crowded in the doorway. One woman shouted for Santos to do something, which Annja didn't consider very ladylike.

Annja backed in the direction from which she had come, the forest behind her rustling in the breeze. "Santos, there are things we have to discuss. Things that can wait until after the funeral."

She turned and marched off along the forest edge toward the first home, which belonged to Santos and Mamma.

Twenty seconds later, Santos grabbed her by the arm and shoved her into a faster pace. "I want to see you leave Chrastava and never turn back."

"I'm only returning to the hotel. I'm not about to leave town until you tell me what I want to know."

"Then I will have to change your mind about staying."

"Is that so?"

They landed in the yard of Santos's home and he shoved her toward the forest path she'd taken last night. Not caring to be pushed around, Annja jerked her arm away from his grasp.

The man detoured to his vehicle, grabbed something from inside and came at her with the katana sword, making sure she understood his threat.

"I give you an hour to return to your hotel, pack your things and get to the train station. After that, I'm coming."

He was bleeding above the eye thanks to a well-placed kick, and at the neck from her fingernails. His jeans were dirty and torn. The sword was similar to a katana, yet he wielded it as if it was a broadsword.

Santos didn't believe in the *mullo*. Perhaps he believed whatever crime he'd gotten involved in was for the good of his people? He knew Bracks. He'd almost confessed to that during their scuffle. Which meant Santos could very well be behind stirring up the fear in the Romas.

Annja nodded, turned and walked into the forest. He had given her a deadline. She had no doubt he would come after her, especially since everyone watching had heard his threat. Now to determine if the fight was worth the trouble. Every bone in her body screamed for her to return and beat the truth out of Santos.

Swiping at a fog of gnats above her head, Annja picked up into a jog, passing by the site on the path where the wolf still lay. If the animal had been owned and trained by Santos, why wouldn't he go looking for it? To leave it lying in the forest seemed cruel, yet natural deaths would allow for much the same, she decided, and quickly passed it.

An hour didn't give her much time. And she had to be prepared for the worst.

Reaching the burned-out dig site and her rental car, she inspected the ashes, but found no sign of bone shards. It had been worth a look. Not even the skeletons in the wall of dirt had survived.

Before driving away she called Luke. "Pack your things, and be ready to vacate in half an hour," she said to him.

"What's wrong, Annja?"

"Santos may be involved, and he's developed an urgent need to make sure I leave the city, dead or alive. And I suspect his hatred for me will extend to you and Doug."

"Gotcha."

"I'm putting Doug on a plane back to the States."

"And you and me?"

"Haven't figured that one out yet. But be waiting outside the hotel for me, will you?"

"Absolutely."

She hung up, then took a moment to lament the damaged dig site and the destroyed bones. Thankfully they had the skull, which could tell them a lot about the person it had once been part of. The entire skeleton would have told a much richer story. It was a significant loss to the archaeology community.

If indeed the skeletons had been older than a couple decades, which was now in question.

For some reason, superstition was driving a dark force in this area and perhaps even feeding its power.

A business opportunist would have a field day with a situation like this.

What was it Bracks wanted from the Roma people?

15

"I got a translation for the words I found on the paper in the brick," Luke said as he loaded his supplies into the back of Annja's rental Jeep. Doug had been granted the honor of holding the carefully packed and wrapped skull, and he had already seated himself in the back. "It's a blessing!"

Annja wedged her backpack among the men's things, and swung around to climb behind the wheel. "Hop in. We've got to move. It's been over an hour, and I'm not so sure Santos can tell time."

"So we're running with our tails between our legs?" Doug asked from the back.

"Last time I checked I didn't have a tail," Annja said. "I don't know about your physical problems, Doug, but maybe you should keep them to yourself."

He laughed.

"Sometimes it's better to retreat," she added. "There's already been a fire. And the funeral is taking place as we speak. I won't be going far. Just to Liberec." She glanced at Luke. "A blessing, eh? You sure about that?" She pulled out of the hotel parking lot, navigating the quiet streets out of town and through a barren stretch of land sandwiched between hills and flood-eroded silt mounds. The rearview mirror showed a clear road behind them.

"Chester Rumshaven is the foremost expert of Romani dialects, so yes, I'm sure. And it was probably placed in the brick by whoever buried the guy," Luke said. "I'm calling him a him until we learn more. He—the skull, not the person who buried it—had big mandibles, so it's a guess. Anyway, the one who buried the body must have thought a few kind words might keep him down. As opposed to a curse."

"Apparently it worked, until a natural disaster unearthed the bones," Annja said.

"Yes, either that, or as Doug posited, the blessing was meant to lure the deceased into the daylight where presumably it would be burned because of the undead's fear of the sun. However that works."

"Too bad we can't convince the Romas of the efficacy of the blessing," Annja said. "They might start looking for other reasons why their children are being kidnapped. Another boy was taken early this morning."

"No, really? That's definitely not the work of a mythical creature. What did you learn?"

"A woman who lives in the house behind Santos's home reported her son Marcus was gone. She's pregnant, too. Very sad. I suspect Santos is in on this. He's acting suspicious."

"Is that the same suspicion that left a cut on your neck?" Doug asked from the backseat.

"Yes. And reason enough to want to leave town to give me a chance to think this through."

Annja hadn't noticed she'd been injured. She glanced in the rearview mirror and touched her neck where she'd sustained a nasty scrape during her scuffle with Santos—and spied the billowing cloud of dust fast approaching behind them on the road.

"Hang on, boys, company has arrived."

She pressed her foot down on the accelerator. Their pursuers probably couldn't win a race out here on this rutted, gravel road in an old Jeep. The vehicle behind them looked like one of the wrecks from Santos's yard.

Somehow, though, the Jeep was gaining on them fast. When the first bullet hit their rear taillight, Annja took evasive action, swerving back and forth.

"Get down, Doug!"

"I'm down!"

"Luke!"

"You think it's Santos?"

"I know it is." Annja couldn't handle this situation from behind the wheel. "You're going to have to drive, Luke. I have a gun in the glove compartment. Slide over here."

They made the switch, him sliding across to the driver's seat while Annja held herself up by the steering wheel and used the windshield frame to keep a grasp on the moving vehicle. Another bullet tore out the right side mirror. She couldn't determine if

they were a bad aim, or if the shots were intended
to warn them.

The wolf had hurt Doug; she'd bet the pursuer
was a bad aim.

She choked on dust as she dove to the passenger
seat and went for the pistol. "Keep this speed," she
directed Luke, "but swerve. Don't make us an easy
target. Looks like only two in the Jeep behind," she
said, facing backward and gripping the roll bar with
her left hand.

Right arm straight out, she aimed for the rusted
front grille and pulled the trigger. The truck behind
them swerved sharply, brewing up dust clouds. But
they were still in pursuit.

"Incoming!" Luke yelled. "A truck ahead."

"Just don't crash into them," Annja warned.

Aiming, she fired again, and the Jeep's windshield
cracked down the center. While she didn't want to
kill anyone, and knew her bouncing aim could never
land exactly where she wanted it to, she had to take
the chance in order to protect Luke and Doug.

The oncoming vehicle was a tractor pulling a
wagon loaded with stacked tractor tires. As Luke
navigated around them, and swerved off the road,
the tires struggled to grip the loose gravel and the
back of the Jeep pulled to the side. Annja could feel
the vehicle's left side tires want to take off from the
ground, and only sheer willpower kept all four tires
on the road.

Another bullet hit the dashboard above the radio.
Luke shouted a curse. He sounded impressive, having

abandoned his usual gentle Welsh tone. The wheels spun as he fought to maintain control and get back on track but he gunned the engine and that dug in the back tires in the soft earth that edged the gravel road. This time the right tires did momentarily leave the ground before dropping the vehicle in a dead stop and a billow of dust.

Annja leaped out of the Jeep and waited until Santos's vehicle had cleared the slow-moving tractor. "Stay in the car, both of you!"

She stood in the center of the road, gun aimed for the tires of the oncoming vehicle. The first shot missed. The second hit the rusted chrome bumper. The car didn't slow as it ate up the distance between them.

Drawing in a breath, Annja straightened her stance. She wasn't about to lose this game of chicken.

Firing again, she saw the windshield shatter. Springing up, her foot touched the hood of the moving vehicle and she pushed up and levered herself skyward. In midair, she somersaulted high above the same spot from which she had jumped, momentarily feeling the air hold her there as if flying. Then she landed on the ground in the car's wake, wobbling into a crouch.

Drawing her sword from the otherwhere, she swung upright and turned to stalk toward the vehicle, which had ground to a stop in a plume of hazy dirt and throat-clogging dust fifty yards beyond where her rental had come to a stop.

Santos curled around and hopped out from the

passenger's side, sword thrust before him. He wore a scarf tied around his head, and it fluttered in the breeze behind him. Determination tightened his jaw and his dark eyes focused on her.

Annja dipped low, sweeping her sword arm across her body, and when she stood upright, she cut the blade across Santos's weapon. As her body spun through the delivery, she punched Santos in the kidney with a hard left hook. The surprise jab knocked him off balance. He stumbled, grunting out an oath, his sword arm wavering.

Recovering from the momentum of that swing, Annja twisted at the waist and elbowed Santos's jaw as she swung back around to face him. He managed to swipe the blade before her, low, aiming for her shins. Annja leaped high, pistoning her knees to her chest. The blade cut the air where she had once stood.

She landed on one knee, her left hand touching the gravel for balance. Rising in the next breath, she lunged, shoulder first, and plunged into the man's chest. Her body twisted against Santos's. Grabbing his shirt, she lifted him and shoved him away to clear her personal space and prepare for another strike.

"Are you seriously going to do this?" she snarled angrily.

"I said I'd give you an hour," he said, spitting out dust. "Time's up, bone hunter."

He dashed forward, but she met his charge with a defensive thrust of her sword. Blades clashed in a clatter of steel. They fought for purchase on the dug-in tire ruts that wedged the loose gravel into mounds.

Yet Annja had never felt stronger. She stood with Joan's sword gleaming in the sun.

This was the reason the sword had chosen her.

She'd come to Chrastava for a simple archaeological mission and a salacious legend. What she'd uncovered sickened her, and she would get her answers and take them to the authorities.

"You work for Bracks, don't you?"

Santos dodged her feint, and returned a thrust that she easily avoided with her quick footwork. His height, about six inches taller than her, put his swings level with her throat, so she was keen to move quickly and keep an eye on the twitch in his elbow that signaled his thrusts.

"I've done work for him off and on over the years," he said on gasping breaths.

"A freelancer, eh?"

"You've made it difficult to enact what should have been a simple task. I notified Canov the moment I heard about the skull. Thought he'd be interested. And he turned me on to Bracks."

Canov. She'd heard that name before…from Garin. "Bracks uses innocent people's fear and superstition to cover his dirty work?"

"Yes, but we didn't need someone like you to preach to the Roma how foolish their beliefs were. To make them doubt."

"I don't see that I accomplished anything close to that. They're burying a child today and all the Roma believe Tomas will come back from the dead to avenge himself."

"Leave them alone. Let them have their beliefs."

"Wait! Are you afraid of the child's revenge, Santos?"

He slashed at her, losing all skill in that moment of anger. She'd struck a chord. He did fear revenge for his crimes. Otherwise, why pursue her so relentlessly?

"Is Bracks the one who ordered you to sic your wolf after us?"

The man shoved the scarf off his head, wiping away the sweat in one rough sweep, and tucked it in a pants pocket. He stepped to the side, double-stepping to not lose balance. Annja sensed he was tiring under the hot sun. "You killed my wolf," he muttered.

"What is Bracks's game?" she pressed. "Does he take the children, then sell their blood? Their organs? And why a child? If the man is dealing in human flesh and blood why not an adult?"

Though a child would prove easier to abduct and subdue.

"I have no idea—I only find the kids for him."

"You're lying." Annja's steel cut Santos's arm and he winced, yet maintained his defense.

"I don't know what he does with them!"

"You saw the boy who returned with a wound that had been stitched up. They take more than blood," she surmised. "They're harvesting organs." Had to be. "It's a sick crime, Santos. How can you allow it to happen to your own people?"

"You've become a nuisance, Annja Creed. Besides

that, you're deadly. I think my driver took a bullet. He could be dead!"

"You're next." Annja thrust low, driving the edge of her blade along the inside of Santos's leg, cutting the jean material and opening what she hoped was the femoral artery. She wasn't going to hold good on that threat; it would be wiser to keep him alive so the authorities could question him. "I need some real answers, or I'll leave you here to bleed out."

The blood spurting from his leg, Santos fell to his knees, his sword arm falling slack. Slowly, he collapsed onto his side, gripping his thigh and cursing her. He wasn't going to give her any more information. Good thing she didn't subscribe to the power of a Gypsy curse, either.

Releasing the sword back to the otherwhere, she could still feel the lingering warmth of the hilt.

Santos was quickly growing weaker. If the man lived, he could talk to the police.

She raced to the Jeep where Doug, still in the backseat and strangely shirtless, leaned over the front seat tending Luke. Frantic, he looked to her, then to Luke, and shook his head.

"What is it? Is he hurt?" she asked as she arrived at the driver's side. Blood covered Doug's hands, and he fumbled with the T-shirt he'd removed to press against the side of Luke's neck.

"He took a bullet to the neck right before we swerved to a stop. He's bleeding a lot. I don't think he's dead. Hell, Annja, this is not happening!"

"He's not going to die."

She didn't know that. She had no idea how bad the wound was. If it had skimmed the carotid, or merely opened flesh and abraded the skin like Doug's wolf bite.

"Help me get him onto the passenger seat. I remember seeing a hospital in Liberec not far from the train station. I'm going to get Luke some medical care, then see you off to the States."

"Is that guy back on the road dead?"

Annja climbed behind the wheel and shifted into gear. "Not yet."

THE HOT AFTERNOON SUN boiled in the bubbling wound on Santos's leg. He was growing dizzy and his mouth was dry, yet sticky. He knew he had to get to a hospital, and fast. The sword cut was deep and the blood flow had slowed. Or maybe it hadn't.

He blinked. The bright sun flashed in his eyes and made it difficult to see anything.

The driver, a friend for over a decade, must be dead. He hadn't moved or come to help Santos.

Annja Creed was some kind of crazy. The operation should have gone smoothly, the Gypsies in his encampment seeing the American woman had lifted a horrible curse from the ground, and causing them to believe it had come to fruition when their children started to disappear.

They did believe that.

Mamma didn't, though. She'd spoken to Annja Creed and it was as though the two had known, had seen beyond the lies to the truth. Mamma had cursed at him for whatever he was involved in and told him he had to make amends to the families for their missing children. She hadn't known he was behind Tomas's disappearance, but she felt he'd been a part of it somehow.

But shame no longer affected Santos. The only emotion he still felt was anger. After losing Mica two years ago, he had nothing left to care about. His child hadn't been stolen by a fictional creature or an evil man. Mica had died two days after Santos's wife had given birth to him. Laura had died the moment Mica had taken his first breath.

Santos had lost so much. There was nothing left to give.

Somewhere close a tinny buzz vibrated against his hip. Santos spat blood and moaned. He had his phone! He could call for help. And luck upon luck, someone was making it easier by calling him.

He flipped open the phone and, gasping for breath, muttered, "Help me."

"Santos? What is your status?"

"Dying," he said, realizing the voice on the other end belonged to his boss. And that meant he'd get no mercy and no help from him.

"Hell," Bracks said. "What went wrong?"

"The woman...she is smart."

"Annja Creed? The same woman who challenged me in the hotel room, and who then followed my men to the cottage out of Liberec? You said she was an archaeologist."

"She fights like a man and carries a big sword."

"Is that so? Interesting."

"And she knows things. Has it figured out…"

Though Santos himself wasn't clear on the real reasons behind Bracks wanting the children. That Tomas had returned home with stitches had shocked him. He'd thought the kid would never be seen again.

He gasped and choked on the blood that fountained up his throat. If his driver were only still alive, he could get to a hospital.

"I'm ten miles out of…Chrastava…south…"

The phone clicked off, and Santos tasted metal on his tongue. The wicked sun blurred bright orange spots in his vision. Sweat dripped into his ears and down his neck.

He laid his head on the rough gravel and reached for the sword his father had given him. His father had stolen it from a man who had once threatened to kill him with it. One should never threaten a Gypsy without following through because that threat will come back to haunt you. They protected their own.

Santos had not protected his own. Didn't matter. Mica was all that had mattered to him.

Whether or not death took him today, he would return to haunt the American woman.

Dragging himself across the gravel, he cried out at the pain in his leg. In the distance, he heard a man's shout.

"CLOSE UP THE operation in the Czech Republic. Damn it!" Bracks stubbed out his cigar and waited for his assistant to leave the room. Wayne Pearce was on the phone, currently driving through France. The man was sightseeing when he should be back in London. "And send someone out to clean up the debris. What a wasted effort that was."

He settled into the easy chair behind a massive mahogany desk and put up his feet on the open drawer. He'd jumped at the opportunity to use the discovery of the skull as cover for his operations.

In Egypt he'd used a mummy's curse to obtain gold relics and scarab jewelry from a relatively insignificant tomb. He still carried one of the gold beetles with him because the weight of it in his pocket reminded him of his clever foray.

In Italy he'd manipulated the rumor of a serial killer, and had gotten out with half a dozen children without raising suspicion.

Only three children from Chrastava.

Yet the demand didn't cease. It was a profitable venture but the supply could never meet the demand, and coming up with covers was making it not worth the effort. Almost. He wasn't one to abandon business ventures until they'd been proven profitless. Up to fifty thousand per child, sometimes more, was nothing to sneeze at.

But he had a problem. Annja Creed.

Who the hell was she? That he had connected her to Garin Braden added a new and interesting twist to the game. He did love to toy with Braden. The diamond caper a few years ago in Abu Dhabi had been a marvelous snatch. And Braden had followed up with an elegant yet subtle twist of the blade into Bracks's Japanese uranium securities.

Garin Braden was a fine opponent, a match to Bracks's ingenuity and criminal daring. And the man was strong, another thing Bracks appreciated. He kept fit by boxing and practicing mixed martial arts every other day. Proper nutrition and meditation kept his mind and body at peak performance. The only one he'd found with the mettle to stand against him was Garin Braden.

Was the female archaeologist involved with Braden? He'd already stolen a girl from Garin once.

Annja Creed was a looker. And if she had taken out Santos, then he wanted to meet her, alone, and get to know what made her tick. Garin wouldn't appreciate it if Bracks tortured that knowledge out of her.

He smirked.

He did admire bruises on female flesh.

16

The small clinic in Liberec was open when Annja drove up. Together, she and Doug helped Luke inside. He drowsily muttered, "You're so beautiful," as she helped him from the car and had given her a smile.

Leaving him in the exam room with a nervous nurse and an elderly doctor who yawned after every sentence, Annja paced in the waiting room painted a sterile 1970s shade of lime green while Doug ransacked a vending machine across the street in front of a combination pool hall/Laundromat/massage parlor.

She checked with the receptionist. "Do you have the number for the police?" she asked, and when given it, she punched it into her cell phone. "Thanks."

Stepping outside the front doors of the hospital, she dialed the Chrastava police and left an anonymous tip that two children had gone missing from the Roma camp outside the city and that an adult male was bleeding out from a gunshot wound on the other side of the forest from the camp.

She could hear the dispatcher placing a call for

an ambulance and a police escort for the wounded, then asked her name, which Annja skirted by going into a description of the man.

"The Romani are frightened," she said. "They need help."

"Our officers will speak with them, Miss…?"

Annja hung up. She'd have to get rid of this mobile phone. But first…

Garin Braden answered after five rings. "What do you want, Annja?"

"Now you're answering my calls?"

"I'm in no mood."

"Again with the mood. Fine. There's only one thing that could possibly give me reason to call you. What did you learn tracking the cooler? Anything?"

"Nothing."

"Is that an 'I'm still tracking Bracks and haven't been able to get close to him' nothing, or a 'she doesn't need to know all of my business' nothing?"

"Figure it out for yourself."

She stared at the cell phone for a moment. He was particularly abrasive and she suspected the man had done a one-eighty regarding helping her. On the other hand, she didn't recall him ever agreeing to help her.

Garin Braden never did stand on the side of anyone but himself. She knew that, and expected as much. But the few times they had worked together he had genuinely helped her and she had accidentally expected as much this time.

"What was in the cooler?" she asked.

"What makes you think I looked?"

"Was it blood or a body part?"

"Annja."

"You're involved in this," she stated, angry that he was keeping a tight lid on this when anything they learned could help innocent children. "That's why you don't want me breathing over your shoulder. And when I learn the connection between you and Bracks, I'm bringing you down, too."

"When making a threat, Annja, I suggest you've the moxie to back it up."

"You know I do."

"Not today you don't." The phone clicked off.

With a curse, Annja shoved the phone in a pocket on the thigh of her cargo pants. Garin and Bracks? She didn't even want to start doing that math.

She stormed back inside the hospital to continue pacing.

As soon as Luke was finished here, she should head back to the States and leave whatever it was going on with the Romani children to the police. She would put Doug on a train. Luke could finish up at the dig site. And the Roma could handle their own troubles, superstitions be damned.

Only, it didn't work that way in Annja Creed's world. She'd been embroiled in this situation for a reason. The sword always led her to trouble, and she always followed it.

Children had gone missing. No one was protecting them. And her heart squeezed inside her chest for what they were going through. She knew she could make it all stop if she found Garin Braden. Because wherever he was, she felt sure Bracks would be close.

Doug entered the waiting room with a handful of potato chip bags and chocolate bars. He tossed her a protein bar.

"Figured you'd like that one."

"Thanks, Doug." She dropped onto the hard plastic waiting room chair that wobbled thanks to two missing rubber pads that should have tipped the steel legs. "You get a train out?"

"Tomorrow morning," he said, crunching loudly on the chips. "You sure you're going to be safe here? Alone?"

"I've got Luke."

"Dude's getting a bullet wound patched up, Annja."

"And still standing, so that puts him in the capable category. Don't worry, Doug. I never unnecessarily put myself in harm's way."

Her producer paused midbite, eyebrows lifted.

"I can handle it," she insisted. "But what I'm about to handle isn't fodder for the television show."

"I agree. Whatever is going on out at that dig site and in the Gypsy encampment has gone beyond mythical monsters." He crunched a few more chips, then fell silent and became very still. "Do you think the monsters are human, Annja?"

"I do think that. And I've called the police about Santos. Hopefully they'll get out there and pick him up before he bleeds out. I want to make sure the plight of the Roma children gets some attention."

"If Santos was behind it," Doug spoke slowly,

working things out as he went, "that means he betrayed his own people."

"He didn't seem like a very upstanding man to begin with."

"No, but his mother was nice. In an eerie, Gypsy, read-your-mind kind of way."

"I think she knew her son was up to no good, but didn't have a clue how horrible it could be. I still don't know the facts."

At that moment Luke wandered into the waiting room. His eyelids were drooping heavily and his smile wavered. "Painkillers," he mumbled. "They've signed me out—payment's all taken care of. And you are still one gorgeous woman."

"Let's get you back to the hotel," Doug said, catching the man's arm over his shoulder and leading him outside to the rental. "Unless you want the gorgeous woman to help you?"

"Just get him in the car," Annja said.

THE NEXT MORNING Luke took a phone call from a colleague in England while Annja excused herself to have a shower. She and Doug had slept on the floor last night after Luke had literally sprawled across the entire bed.

Doug had left for the train station an hour ago. He'd emailed himself the footage he'd filmed on Luke's iPad, but didn't erase it, so Annja intended to scan it as soon as she dried off. Shrugging the towel over her body, she rubbed her hair, then combed it out, tugged on her underclothes and a T-shirt, then wrapped the towel around her waist and returned to the main room.

"The university upset about the fire at the site?" she asked while shuffling through her backpack.

A reasonably clean pair of black cargos were made less dusty with a smart snap. She pulled them up under the towel while Luke watched from his position as he leaned over the table. The Welshman didn't take his eyes from her.

Sliding onto the bed and leaning on one elbow she gestured to Luke's work on the table in front of him. The skull was still wrapped in the plastic beside the microscope.

"Luke?"

"Uh, sorry." He exhaled and riffled a hand through his hair. "Really sorry."

He exhaled again, and this time made a show of sorting the few items on the table before him: iPad, tweezers, lab slides. But before launching into what she hoped was an answer to her question about the fire, the man tilted his head and winced. "They weren't pleased, but also understand that these sort of things are hazards of the profession. I'm to report back to work next Monday."

That cut their time much shorter than she'd thought. "You mentioned the blessing in the car. What was that about?"

"Yes, the, uh, scribblings on the paper are actually Romani. Chester Rumshaven, a colleague of mine, interpreted it as 'may the sun always shine.' A blessing, he believes."

"Appropriate for one who would fear a vampire coming after them. But the vampire legend hasn't always embraced the not being able to walk in daylight trope, has it?"

"Exactly, so it's baffling. Makes it difficult to date the skull preceding the twentieth century, that's for sure. This adds fuel to the idea that it's rather new." He tapped the paper with the tip of a fine set of tweezers. "Perhaps five or six decades? Or who knows? It could have been planted a year ago before the floods. I've no means to test the paper for aging methods, and we have no proof the brick was originally placed in the skull's mouth. The flooding moved the soil around the bones and completely destroyed the original placement."

"A plant? Someone might have engineered the whole thing? What better way to deflect suspicion from the real monsters than by tossing some false monsters into the mix," she decided. "The Roma's beliefs are so strong they would first believe in the *mullo,* especially if encouraged by someone they trust, like Santos. But we dug that out of the dirt. It was embedded. I've dug up pots that have been put in the ground to look like artifacts. A person can usually determine a plant from the real thing."

"I agree. Though with the flooding and all the movement in the earth, well—"

"Santos knows. He has to. I shouldn't have left him out there on the road. I need to question him further. I wonder if the police reached him in time to save his life. If Garin would have only been more forthcoming…"

Luke turned on the chair and propped an elbow on the back of it, leaning toward her.

"What's our next move?"

"I'm going to find Garin. I think he'll lead me to the man behind the kidnappings. The skull was a diversion. The real danger is in Bracks."

"So…this is where my job ends," Luke said, then hesitated. "I'm not sure how I can help you with your friend Garin. I'm an archaeologist. You, on the other hand, are something I'm not sure how to define."

"I'm an archaeologist who occasionally hosts a TV show about monsters."

"Yes, but you're so much more, Annja. So much more."

She shrugged, not so much uncomfortable with his admiration as unsure. "The trail's growing cold."

"Then you should get to it." Luke reluctantly turned back to his work. "Or—" he looked over his shoulder at her "—I could call the university and get a reprieve. Come with you…?"

Annja slid off the bed and walked over to Luke.

After all, the morning was still young.

17

"In the 1950s the government forced sterilization on the Romani camps. It was a horrible thing. Women would go to their local clinics for a free checkup and come home unable to conceive. Very sad," Luke said as they traveled west in Annja's rental car toward Liberec.

They had been planning to take the train to Berlin, meet up with Garin there, then hop a flight to London until Annja had called Garin's estate in Berlin. His butler had told her the master of the house was currently in London. Luke was pleased to be heading straight home, skull in hand.

The train didn't leave for another four hours, so they took their time as they drove to the station in Liberec.

"The Romanis have always been persecuted," he continued. "They're an easy mark. It's obvious why they've been singled out now, in this incident."

"Singled out by vampires," Annja commented. She steered sharply right to avoid a goose crossing the road.

"Don't tell me you've fallen victim to the legend?" Luke's eyes were concealed behind sunglasses. "Annja?"

"I mean real vampires. Which I interpret as cruel people who kidnap children. And I have reason to guess they steal their blood and organs. That's the worst kind of vampire, don't you think?"

"Yes, true. If we can prove to the Romanis that, indeed, it is men behind the missing children, then we could empower them. We need to do that for them, Annja."

"I have a feeling Mamma could change the thinking of the clan. If Santos were out of the picture, Mamma might be able to step up."

"Yes, and I want to help her do that."

"I need to track Bracks and ensure he's put away for what he's doing. I don't have time to steer a Gypsy camp from their ingrained beliefs."

"I should have stayed behind. I've got four days still until I'm due back in London. I've got reasonable doubt the brick wasn't originally in the skull's mouth when the person was buried. I need to talk to Mamma."

She admired the man's conviction. This adventure had been the start of a long-lasting friendship.

Navigating a hard right, she spun the car around the back tires. With laughter at Luke's surprise, Annja sped back toward Chrastava to deliver the Romas a determined savior.

IF HE COULD get a bead on Bracks and take him out, then the matter would be done with. Or would it?

Garin knew that Bracks was smart, but he hadn't gotten where he was on his own. The man controlled a vast, worldwide network. And where a man worked with many, one or more couldn't be trusted. Garin had learned that over the course of centuries.

That he'd been in the same room with Bracks in Chrastava did not soothe his ego now. He bet Bracks was having a good laugh at having eluded him. And he guessed this operation had never intended to be an affront to him, like one of Bracks's usual plays against him. It had been coincidental that he'd stumbled onto this mess. And he could use that to keep Bracks on his toes and guessing.

But it was time he dealt with Bracks. Permanently. Shouldn't be so difficult to erase the problem child and get on with business. And because it was proving such a pain in the ass, Garin knew he was dealing with something that ran much deeper than he'd first guessed. Something that nudged at his sense of justice and compassion.

He did have compassion; it was somewhere, tangled with the hardness and distrust ingrained over the centuries.

"Creed, why do you always get me in these messes?"

But really, Annja wasn't to blame for his headache this time. This was his mess. She was merely inextricably involved.

I will take you down. She'd said that to him over

the phone after putting two and two together and deciding that he was somehow allied with Bracks.

He had no doubt that she would. Yet on the other hand, the woman knew he was a man without a traceable past. Would she leave him to fend off the authorities' questions and investigations? Not that he couldn't handle a little heat. But yes, he suspected she would hold good on her word.

And that meant Garin had to stay one, or two, steps ahead of Annja Creed from here on out.

A diversion seemed necessary. Did he know of any major archaeological digs looking for a superstar to heighten the appeal of their mission? Could he send her an anonymous juicy tidbit about a lost Mayan ruin that promised adventure and which would be right up her alley?

"No," he muttered, then smiled. "I'd hate to take her out of the game at this point. She could lead me to Bracks."

He just had to play nice and make her understand he was on her side.

For now.

ANNJA DECIDED IT was best to leave Luke on his own to talk to Santos's mother because she had left the woman with a less-than-stellar opinion of her. Surely, fighting her son hadn't endeared her to the woman. And the entire Gypsy camp seemed to lift their hackles and send Annja the evil eye when she walked through.

Where was Santos? Was he in jail, in the hospital or at the morgue? She had no idea.

Back in town, she checked outgoing flights from Berlin to London. After mailing the skull from Liberec to her address, she booked coach for an evening flight, then drove to the train station. The train to Berlin didn't leave for another two hours.

With time on her hands, she vacillated on calling Roux. If anyone would have more of a clue than she did on Garin Braden's whereabouts, the saucy old Frenchman would. Yet she snapped her cell phone shut after pushing the speed-dial number for Roux.

Intuition told her this time around he wouldn't know any more than she did. Garin was involved in dirty dealings, and though the two men had been known to partner in crime on occasions, this one felt too deep for Roux's interests, which tended toward art and, always, women.

But what the crime was, Annja still hadn't a clue.

Tugging out her laptop, she jacked into the train station's Wi-Fi using an app to go online from where she sat in the parking lot. Her initial search for *mullo* only verified the information Luke had given her. When she added "kidnapped children" to the search, it brought up an article completely unrelated to mythical vampires.

"Voodoo?"

One article detailed a particularly grisly murder a few years ago in London. An eight-year-old boy's body had been found in the Thames, his arms and legs cut off and organs removed. Missing for over three months, he had eventually been traced to a Romani family from Bulgaria.

"Do I have a connection?" she muttered, scanning the article, and finding it lacking in detail and links to further information. It merely stated those few facts, and that the authorities were looking into it. No perpetrators had been charged as of the date on the article, which was two and a half years ago. No follow-up articles were found.

"Disappointing," she muttered of the lack of information.

One link took her to a man who claimed to be the son of a voodoo witch doctor, and confirmed the use of children in rituals because the young were thought to have pure souls. That helped to answer her question as to why children would be taken as opposed to adults.

She closed her eyes against the image of a child, alone, tied up and beaten. To not know what would happen to him, all alone and away from the safety of his family. It was too horrible, and she shook her head to clear it.

Yet another article, dating back a few years, tracked missing Nigerian children to a trafficking ring in London that had been loosely linked to voodoo rituals.

Missing organs and copious amounts of blood, Annja read. The suspects were never arrested. The bodies had been found in the Thames, and one had been disposed of in a trash bag in a dumpsite near Kew Gardens. The identity of only three children had been verified and matched to dental records, though other body parts could not be matched. They suspect dozens of children could have been murdered.

She sat back in the seat, closing her eyes. The soft strains of Czechoslovakian folk music over the radio didn't quell her disturbing thoughts. That a human being could have the capacity to harm a child sickened her. But she knew it happened all over the world, from pornography, to trafficking and prostitution, and now this. Organs may have been harvested from innocent children for bizarre voodoo rituals, and blood drained from them, as well.

"Real-life vampires indeed," she said.

And for once she wished Doug's image of the fanged and caped monster had been more real and they'd been mistaken about the missing children. Just a vampire risen from the grave to scare everyone, folks. Your children are safe.

But that particular mythical monster didn't exist, and human ones did.

This information and the white cooler that had led Garin to London on Bracks's trail had to be related to the missing Romani children. As Santos had claimed, the traffickers had used the legend of a *mullo* to distract from the real crime. Made a macabre kind of sense. It would easily explain away the missing children if the Romani believed the lie. They would never go to the authorities, because to claim such superstitious nonsense would see them laughed at.

Bracks walked away clean from the kidnappings and any connected macabre crimes.

"Clever. Too clever."

Someone must have alerted Bracks about the skull. Daisy's bragging, possibly. Someone, Santos or Bracks, had known it would work as a diversion. Santos and Garin had both mentioned a man named Canov. She scribbled the name down on her field notebook.

Such a cover story had only net them a child or two from the Roma camp. Bracks could hardly operate a trafficking operation with such a poor source. It didn't add up. But then, Annja decided the authorities would have a better handle of the criminal aspects of this case. She had no evidence to call London and report the possibility that Bracks was involved in child trafficking.

Garin could help her with that.

Annja pulled out the cell phone again and dialed Roux's number.

"Hello, Annja," Roux said, answering on the first ring. "What are we going to do about Garin?"

MAMMA GREETED LUKE with reserve. The woman wore a flour-dusted apron and gestured for him to sit at the kitchen table where she had six plump balls of dough sitting on strewn flour. His mother had always been a bread baker, and he inhaled the aroma of yeast and flour as if an addict sinking into a field of opium poppies.

Beside the door sat a box of toys and children's

clothing. It drew Luke's eye because he hadn't seen a child in the home or been aware that Mamma had a grandchild.

"If I'm disturbing you, I can return at another time," he offered. Annja had dropped him off here. He wasn't sure how to get back to town, except to walk the few miles, which shouldn't be a problem. So he expected to accomplish what he could while he was here. "Rosemary bread?"

"Leftover from the funeral," she said coldly. "Not many had the stomach to eat following the service, and I can't let all this dough go to waste."

"Are you expecting a guest?" he said, glancing at the box near the door.

"No," she answered abruptly, and continued kneading the dough.

"Must be selling some old things, then."

The family of the deceased sold all the dead's property because to keep an item would prove bad luck—and possibly lure the *mullo*.

"What have you come here for, Mr. Spencer? And where is that archaeologist who thinks she can go after my son with a sword?"

"Er, Annja has other business that's taken her out of town. Your son went after her with his sword. She was only acting in self-defense."

He caught the woman's frown and winced. Had to be cautious of the evil eye in these parts.

"She is not natural," the woman said. "And now…" She lifted her chin and stared through the archway that led to a darkened room. Luke thought he caught the scent of incense burning. "Speak what you've come to say, then leave as quickly as you arrived. I've work to do, as you can see."

She fisted a ball of dough, sending a plume of flour into the air, and began to roll and knead.

"I wanted to give you this." Luke pulled out the small plastic bag in which he'd placed the slip of paper with the blessing. "I think it only right I return it to you. And perhaps, with this blessing, you can take back your power."

"Return it? What makes you believe it was once mine?"

"Oh, I didn't mean it that way. I don't know the origin of this blessing, but like I said, you seem wise and will probably know what to do about it."

The woman stopped punching the dough—Luke noticed her taut biceps and decided she was not a woman to mess with—and held out her hand for the item.

He left it in the bag, since her hands were covered with flour, and handed it to her.

"What is it?" She looked over it carefully, pressing the plastic to read the paper inside.

"It was tucked in the brick that was in the skull we unearthed."

The woman hissed and almost dropped the bag. She narrowed her eyebrows and studied it closely before glancing toward the darkened living room.

Judging from the chill at the back of his neck, Luke suspected Santos was inside the room. So he was alive, then.

"Whoever put that in the brick wanted to lure the deceased into the sun. Or so that is what I and my colleagues guess. Sort of a sneaky blessing, if you will. As if to say, 'I wish you brightness and light—and I also know that will be your death.'"

"And you're going to take the skull back to London? What do you think it will tell you about us?"

"I, er…I'm not sure. Have you got something to hide?"

She kneaded faster, making no reply.

"I'm not investigating the mystery of the missing children. I am an archaeologist and I simply want to learn about the origin of the bones. Such information can tell me about who it was, and perhaps give some clue as to why someone believed it would rise again. The decedent may have had purperia or some sort of mental condition that indicated madness. It's my job to answer questions like that. Otherwise, I'd have no reason to do what I do."

"It's time for you to leave," the woman said, and gestured to the door.

"I, uh…" Luke stood from the chair, unable to come up with a good reason to stay and argue when the woman was obviously in pain and—hell, she was making food leftover following a funeral.

He nodded, and walked to the door. "I thought if you told your neighbors about the blessing, they may be reassured. Can you use it to convince the others in your camp that it's all right? Nothing is going to harm them. Nothing mythical, anyway."

"I said, go!"

Luke pushed open the screen door and stepped out into the sweltering noonday sun. Barging through a cloud of gnats, he spat them out of his mouth.

Now that had been odd. The woman's entire body had tensed, and she'd gotten that look of recognition Luke sometimes saw when he taught students out in the field. A knowing look before they were sure what it was they had uncovered.

Had she recognized the blessing?

Landing at the edge of the property, he eyed the long dirt road that led toward town. Should have packed a hat and sunglasses. But he did have a cell phone. Annja was on her way to Liberec to catch the train, so he wouldn't think to bother her. He didn't have the number for a cab company in town, but he did have Siri.

MAMMA STALKED INTO the darkened room and flicked on the light near the green plaid sofa where her son lay. His eyes were open and he nursed a clove cigarette.

"What did he give you, *Dai?*" Santos asked in that drowsy tone she associated with him checking out on life. And drugs.

Ever since Mica's and Laura's deaths, he hadn't been the same. And she didn't know how to reach through his grief to pull him back to the surface. And earlier he'd come home limping, and bleeding through a bandage on his leg. She hated herself for allowing him to fall so far.

She bent and gripped him by the shirt. He protested with a shout that he was injured. She didn't care anymore if she did hurt him. She'd had her suspicions when he hadn't attended the funeral, and had set out the box of toys and clothing this morning. Toys that had belonged to Tomas, the boy who'd been buried. She had babysat for Tomas on occasion, and he'd slept in Santos's room when he'd had to stay overnight because his mother worked a night shift in town at the steel factory and the father was often out boozing it up with other women.

"What curse have you brought on our family, my son?"

AFTER TWENTY MINUTES of walking in the sweltering noon sun, Luke decided it had been a while since he'd made a trip to the local gym, or even lifted a weight that wasn't a hunk of dirt with an artifact stuck in it. Curls of smoke from the factory at the edge of town that made pressed components for cars disappeared into the white sky. He estimated that he had another half hour to forty-five minutes of walking, unless he got lucky and someone drove by.

Wiping the sweat from his forehead with the stretched hem of his shirt, he paused, hand to his hip, and bowed his head from the hot sun. Had his thoughts been anywhere but drifting back to the night he'd spent with Annja, he might have heard the slow approach of the vehicle behind him in the distance.

He never even noticed when the truck pulled over, and a man got out and jumped on Luke's back with an animal yell and fit his hands about his neck.

18

Stumbling forward, Luke fell to his knees at the weedy roadside. Body swaying, he rolled to the side and back, managed to loosen the attacker's hands from his neck. Instincts taking over, he rolled up into a crouch and lunged upward to stand face-to-face with Santos, who didn't look much better than Luke felt. The man's face dripped with sweat, and the dark shirt he wore was wet with perspiration.

Luke's eyes fell to the dark stain on the man's thigh. Santos had been wounded when fighting with Annja yesterday, and was still bleeding. If he had been bleeding since the fight, how in the hell had he been able to follow and jump him? Despite his own injury, Luke guessed he had the advantage in this duel.

Until Santos stretched an arm behind his back and drew out the katana.

At that moment, another vehicle drove up and skidded to a stop, stirring up a plume of dust around the men. Luke turned quickly, but his ankle twisted and he lost his balance. Before he could answer gravity's call, his body was wrenched backward, and the cool edge of a steel blade cut up under his chin.

Annja Creed jumped out of the new rental Jeep, wielding the remarkable and mysterious battle sword. Where she'd gotten it, Luke didn't care. He just hoped she had the sense to talk this crazy man out of killing him.

"Hold steady, Santos," Annja said calmly. She remained near the hood of the Jeep. Santos's blade didn't move from where it was against Luke's neck. "He's done nothing to warrant such treatment."

"He upset my mother in her home!" Santos hissed, his spittle wetting Luke's neck. "Telling her lies!"

"The lie that you're involved in trafficking children for voodoo rituals?"

Voodoo? Much as he should be worried about the blade, Luke couldn't help but feel a twist in his gut to imagine the horrors the missing children must have experienced. What monsters would do such things? And how had he become involved in this? By merely unearthing a skull? It was too incredible.

No matter what fate offered him in the next minutes, Luke knew Annja would find the men responsible and stop them.

"I know nothing!" The blade tugged sharply at his skin and Luke felt his own warm blood seep down his neck.

"Let him go, Santos! And if you tell me where to find Bracks, Mr. Spencer and I will walk away and leave you and your family alone."

"You are lying!"

The tall man stumbled, wobbling forward. The abrupt move almost causing Luke to go down, which would have led to his decapitation—but Santos caught himself, jerking Luke back with the blade, which cut deeper.

"Bracks is in London, right?" Annja pleaded. She'd taken two steps forward, and held out her sword to the side, nonthreatening. Her eyes tracked to Luke and held his gaze briefly, yet betrayed neither worry nor confidence. "Where in London can I find him? We need to protect the children."

"I don't care about the children."

"Because you lost your own?" Luke guessed. The toys in the kitchen could have belonged to the dead boy, or perhaps to a man who had once played with his own child.

The blade cut even deeper, and Luke swallowed.

"Is that true?" Annja asked cautiously. "Did you lose a child, Santos?"

"None of your damn business."

"I'm sorry for your loss, but that doesn't mean you have the right—"

"Annja!" Luke managed to say. Now was no time to lure the man with the sword into recalling devastating memories.

"I don't know where Bracks is," Santos insisted. "Do you think he would tell me? He's smarter than that. Everything I did was approved by Canov."

If Luke swallowed, he guessed the blade would cut so deep blood would run down his esophagus.

"But he must call you, this Canov," Annja insisted. Luke could feel the urgency in her voice waver through his system and he felt light-headed. Ready to face fate. "Your cell phone," Annja urged. "It might have his phone number and we can track him that way. Santos, please!"

Annja's shout was the last thing Luke processed as his knees bent and he fell. He didn't gauge the impact of his body hitting gravel as his oxygen had been depleted and he blacked out. The release was quick and sweet.

SANTOS EXECUTED Luke Spencer right before Annja's eyes. Her breaths choked. Heartbeats stopped—then stuttered back to a thunderous race.

As Luke's body fell slack onto the grassy roadside, she charged the Gypsy. A warrior cry erupted from her lungs. She leaped over Luke's fallen body, swung her sword through the air and brought it down across Santos's chest as he stumbled away from his violent deed. Her blade cut across his leather jacket and she smelled blood, but couldn't know if it was his or Luke's.

Drawing back the sword, she readied for another punishing blow as she couldn't drown out the awful choking gasps she'd heard Luke make before going down.

A split second of wisdom stopped her from slashing her blade across Santos's neck.

He killed an innocent man!

Her fingers tightened around the sword hilt.

While he may have murdered Luke, Annja did not relish answering to the authorities her reasons for killing Santos. Vengeance was justified only in the eyes of the weak and criminal.

"May your most feared curse accompany you to hell," she spat out. "If I guess correctly, that will involve the vengeful undead."

Shoving Santos to the ground, she landed on his chest with a knee and stabbed the sword into the loose gravel beside his head. Grabbing him by the scruff she lifted his head.

"Where is Bracks?"

"London," the man blubbered. "Canov mentioned it. That's all I know. He doesn't give his location to field scouts."

Field scouts who located children for the man's evil endeavors.

"Give me your phone!"

"It's in my back pocket!"

Annja fisted the man in the jaw, knocking him out cold. Turning him over, she took the phone from his back pocket and shoved it into one of the cargo pockets on her thigh. Standing, she found she couldn't walk away without first kicking his jaw. Swinging the sword out angrily to cut the air, she almost slashed it down and across the bastard's neck. But some force greater stopped her.

Joan of Arc's spirit?

Annja opened her fingers and released the hilt, sending the battle sword off into the otherwhere. No spirit, just her own conscience.

She could have killed with it. She should have. But she would not have this bastard's death on her hands.

Rushing to Luke, she knew he was dead before lifting his hand from the ground. The cut had gone deep, exposing the spinal column and surrounding muscles. He had likely choked on his blood.

Swearing, and with a glance to Santos, she gave one last thought to committing murder. *It won't change things, except to lower you to his level of unscrupulous morals.*

With a shake of her head, she stood and dialed the police number she'd entered in her phone at the hospital and reported the site she'd found on the road out of Chrastava. A colleague of hers had been walking, and she'd found him dead. She suspected his assailant was the one lying nearby.

Slapping her cell phone shut, she knelt over Luke and pressed her arms over his warm torso and bowed her head. She should have never left him here by himself. She'd thought he'd be safe talking to Mamma, and hadn't considered Santos could have survived their earlier battle and would be lying in wait for Luke.

Only, she had been compelled to return while waiting outside the train station. Call it intuition.

Call it the sword beckoning her.

"I'm so sorry," she whispered.

Had Luke not called her about the archaeological find, he may have still encountered the angry Romani, urged on by Santos and whoever this Canov was, and yet would have never learned the truth behind the mistaken beliefs.

Was it good that she'd traveled here and had learned what she had about the evils taking place, when wherever she went people died? People she grew to care about?

She had to find Bracks and make him pay for the dead children, and for Luke.

She waited for the ambulance and police to arrive and spent half an hour answering questions and explaining repeatedly that she had found the men exactly as they were, sprawled on the road. Santos was still unconscious and couldn't deny her story. Yes, it appeared as if both had been wounded by swords, and no, she hadn't noticed another weapon in the vicinity. Luke was a colleague and they had been working on the dig near the Roma camp. She had reported Santos chasing them out of town last night. Mention of her duel with Santos was unnecessary. The emergency techs reported the cut on his chest was superficial, but he would probably not survive the blood loss from a previous injury on his leg.

"Justice served," Annja muttered as she walked toward the Jeep after being told she was free to go.

She left her new cell phone number with the authorities and gave them Luke's home number to contact family in London. She vacillated between remaining in town or leaving while the coroner's office processed Luke's body, so she could then accompany the body back to England.

Death had taken people she cared about before. It never got easier.

And was she to blame, or was it that fate colluded to ensure she remained alone, a woman unattached and always available to answer a quest? If so, she'd give back the sword in a heartbeat to have her loved ones all back. Yet she knew that was impossible. She had taken ownership of the sword and all that came with it, good, bad or horrible.

The best thing she could do right now was to find Bracks and stop his reign of terror.

"WE MEET AGAIN," Garin said to his freelance help, Slater.

The man nodded, hands folded before him as he awaited instructions. He stood beside a man tied to a chair. Wayne Pearce, who Garin had once seen at Bracks's side. An assistant of sorts. He'd been found in a nightclub popular with celebrities, hanging on a leggy young thing, dosing on Ecstasy like it was going out of style. He was high now, and though his hands were bound behind the chair he sat on, and his ankles were secure, as well, he grinned a stupid smile.

"Break time?" Garin asked.

"Less than three minutes," Slater reported with a slam of his fist into his opposite palm.

"I'll give you two."

Slater worked his head upon his neck, side to side, stretching and bouncing on his feet like a boxer. "I do like a challenge."

The echo of fist meeting jawbone was followed with a pitiful whining yelp. Pearce's front teeth dropped onto his lap and he begged for mercy after the second punch.

WAITING AN HOUR for her flight to take off in the Berlin Brandenburg Airport gave Annja time to call the London coroner's office. It wasn't to notify them of Luke's incoming body; the authorities would take care of that. Annja had a contact there. Not a friend so much as a spy. Years ago, Daniel Newton had contacted her online to tell her how much of a fan he was of *Chasing History's Monsters,* and to let her know if she ever needed his help for a future show he was ready and willing. He was also an amateur archaeologist—a hunter of coins in his neighbors' backyards.

Never overlook the value of having an inside man in a coroner's office. It was where she had hoped the organ in the cooler had been taken, and if not, then she was at a dead end.

She'd never spoken to him personally, beyond the online contact, so when Daniel answered, and realized it was her, he gasped and stuttered enthusiastically before Annja was finally able to ask him for a favor.

"Anything!"

She winced and turned down the volume on her cell phone. Wandering to a corner in the airport terminal, she squatted against the concrete wall, feeling the strain in her calves and thighs.

"A few days ago you may have received a white cooler with bags of blood or possibly human organs. I suspect it was a police confiscation. I assume it made it to your office, or hope it did."

"Sounds intriguing. Wait! Yes, it did. It was retrieved from a fire, though the firefighters were able to put it out fast enough and the cooler was intact. Benedict, the head guy here in the shop, has been working on it exclusively. Very hush-hush stuff. What's this about, Annja? Have you got information on the case?"

"No." She didn't need to get embroiled in the criminal investigation of something she truly had no solid evidence on. "But I do find that certain events in my life parallel the need to know more about what was in the cooler. I would never step on police authority, but I know a family who lost their child."

"Oh, Annja, that's a terrible thing. The organ did belong to a child. Oh, hell, that was classified information. But you won't tell anyone, will you?"

"Never."

"Do you think it's related?"

"Probably not, but who knows. I've been reading articles about missing children who were dismembered for voodoo rituals. Terrible stuff. I'm wondering if there was anything odd or unusual about the evidence."

"Hmm, well, I haven't had a hand in the project. It might take some doing to suss out information since, like I said, Benedict has been protecting this one. But I'd do anything for you, Annja. Is it for one of your shows?"

"Not exactly. You run into any vampires lately, Daniel?"

"No. But really? Is that what you're working on for the show now?"

Hell, she'd had to give him that one. He deserved it. And if she was going to get anything from the guy she had to make him believe he was helping not only her, but possibly the show. It was a huge lie, but she had no clue how else to proceed with this mystery, and felt sure the information might lead her to Garin.

He wasn't answering her calls, and she'd tried him twice now. She wasn't one to beg, or act like a rebuffed mistress, so she'd take this route and meet him in the middle, whether or not he approved. Of which, she guessed, he would not.

"Give me two secs, will you, Annja? Benedict takes a lunch break soon. I'll slip into his office and see what I can learn."

"Don't do anything that would jeopardize your job," she said, but hoped he wouldn't take the warning to heart. "Just let me know if you find out anything unusual. Thanks, Daniel. You can reach me at this number for another hour before my flight leaves."

"Oh, thank you, Annja! This is so awesome. I'm helping you with your research."

"Yes, well, you're helping me quietly, right?"

"Oh, yes. Quiet. Shh. I can skulk around with the

best of them. I'll call you soon, Annja. I have your number now. Yes!"

She hung up before another excited shriek made her question her sanity in calling the man. Daniel would prove useful. And sometimes useful demanded sacrifices. But she'd look into changing her phone number once she returned to the States. Wasn't like she hadn't had to do that many times before.

GARIN LOOKED OVER the pummeled man wilted in the chair before him. Very little damage to his face because the teeth had done the trick.

"The men's club on Rossmore Road, not far from Hyde Park," he said. "Good job, Slater. I do believe that was less than a minute."

"He was a wanker," Slater said. "Pretty boys always go fast. They don't know what pain is, and when they experience it, they start crying for their mommies. Isn't that right?" He lifted the man's head by a hank of his hair, but he was out cold. A mercy, knocking him out. One Slater generally didn't grant his subjects. "You need me for anything else?"

"No, that's good. We'll talk soon, I'm sure."

"Always a pleasure."

Slater strolled down the hallway to the washroom to clean up, and Garin checked his watch. It was ten in the evening. The nightclubs wouldn't get rolling for another few hours. But a pool hall would be quiet this time of night. Which made for easier pickings when he wanted to catch someone unawares.

He pulled out his cell phone. Three messages—

all from Annja Creed. She was trying to find him, and if he answered, she may be able to track him to London. He wasn't stupid. But she wasn't, either, and he'd probably be seeing her sooner rather than later.

That was fine. Because he expected her research on Bracks to parallel his, and maybe, just maybe, her pieces would fit into his and together they'd form a solid lead on the man. Because he knew the men's club was only a front, a resting place for the man when he needed to do local business or chill with the boys.

On the other hand, he could get lucky and come face-to-face with his nemesis tonight.

"CALABAR BEAN EXTRACT," Daniel whispered over the phone line. "Or, more properly, *physostigma venenosum*. It's a perennial indigenous to an area in Africa called the Calabar region."

The flight had started to board, but Annja needed to take this phone call from Daniel. "What is that?"

"The seeds are a natural poison. Black magic potion."

"Black magic," she said, thinking it sounded out of place, but then, why should that be so? Her research had alluded to voodoo. It was easy enough to associate the two.

"It's used to paralyze a subject. And in that state of paralysis, they remain conscious. Annja, the extract was laced through the blood and organ of this child. Whoever gave it to the child may have removed the organ while the kid was conscious yet unable to move."

Annja gasped.

"The child may have felt everything," Daniel said solemnly. "It's perfectly horrible. What are you working on, Annja? This doesn't sound like anything for a television show."

"I'm not sure anymore, Daniel." She felt sick. At least she hoped the people who had intended to drink the blood would also be affected by the extract laced through it. "Was that it?"

"Yes, that's the notation that Benedict circled and entered on the lab report for the police report. I'm sure Scotland Yard will investigate as soon as the report is turned over. Funny, this feels familiar. I feel as though there was something in the papers about this years ago. I should look into that."

"Do that, please, but be careful. This is a police matter. Whoever did this to that child must pay. Uh, my flight is at final boarding, I'll have to go. Thanks, Daniel. I owe you one."

"If you're ever in London, I'll take you up on that."

Since she was heading to London, she figured she might have to make good on that offer.

WHILE FLYING ACROSS Europe, Annja surfed for information on voodoo clubs in London and found very little beyond some pseudoclubs that played on the idea and exotic allure of voodoo, but it was apparent they weren't involved with real practitioners.

Of course, any genuine hits were likely secret societies, and one generally had to know who to ask for to learn more. She considered putting a call out on the archaeology forums she frequented, but then decided she didn't want anyone to ask questions this time. Normally, she invited questions and suggestions regarding her research and expeditions.

She paged through a few new-age shops that sold gris-gris, voodoo spells and fancy incense burners and crystals. Aboveboard stuff, not genuine, nasty voodoo shops that she'd been in a time or two before. They gave her the chills. It was a dark and mysterious religion that Annja was forced to respect. She'd landed on the wrong end of a voodoo curse more than a few times.

Using a child's organs to gain riches, beauty or extended life? It sounded horrible, but Annja knew there were desperate people who would pay for that kind of macabre fix. Again, her heart went out for those children. She couldn't get it out of her mind that they may have been conscious when their organs or blood had been removed. Children had paid an unconscionable price.

The cursor blinked next to an entry for *discreet vodou.* Clicking on it brought up a black page with a single line of text in a red font that was difficult to read. It indicated, *All your dreams answered if you can pay the price.* A symbol, or *veve,* swirled two white serpents parallel to each other, fading on and off the page with a clever animated gif. No contact email, but there was an address. She tapped the key-

board. Probably a false lead, or another curio shop.
But she typed the address into her cell phone. Just
in case. She'd drive by when she reached London,
and check the place out.

Meanwhile, she scrolled down to Garin's phone
number, and then tapped into the tracking program
on her laptop. She'd set it up to track after her conversation with Roux. If Garin made a phone call,
it should snap up the location and enter it into the
GPS field.

And there it was, an address, which, checking the
London map, placed him in Hyde Park right now.
The man certainly wasn't strolling around the gardens admiring the landscaping. Her best guess? A
nightclub. If he was partying with women and the
narcotics that tended to accompany his adventures
she wouldn't have a problem confronting him.

But if he were tracking Bracks, she would welcome the challenge of insinuating herself onto his
trail.

The pilot announced their impending landing. She
could make it to the address within an hour.

19

Garin left the loud, grinding techno music in the London nightclub behind as he angled down a dark, narrow hallway. He passed by a few red doors, but didn't want to know what was going on behind them. Really, he didn't. It was either drugs, gambling, illicit sex or all of the above.

No one would ever catch him indulging in vices in a dive like this.

A stairway led him down a red shag-carpeted walkway with walls paneled in dark wood. Flashing back to the seventies—an era he had found innocuous and dull—he winced as the decor declined rapidly. Behind the next red door, he heard the clatter of pool balls on felt and knew he had found what he was looking for.

Bracks had a few hiding places. Some of which Garin was aware of. But this new one Slater had unearthed.

Garin grunted to himself and cracked his knuckles. Adjusting his cuffs, and unbuttoning the top button of his starched Armani shirt, he opened the door with the upside-down number seven on it, and strode inside the pool hall. The two-story room was open to the balcony and again was furnished in early seventies wood paneling. There was even a cheesy stained-glass beer lamp hanging over each of the pool tables.

He wasn't immediately noticed, and wouldn't be remarkable, except for his impeccable clothing among the jeans and T-shirts. Eight or nine men were gathered around the half dozen pool tables in game, or tilting back glass mugs of beer and whiskey. A pair of bruisers stood by an old-fashioned jukebox that flashed bright neon lights, and chuckled over some ribald gossip. To top it off, a Bee Gees tune proclaimed he should be dancing.

Garin did not see the man he was looking for, but the stairway along the north wall, carpeted in more of the hideously matted red shag, led up to a door, behind which, he suspected, would be a good place for a business opportunist's office. A man sat on the fourth step from the bottom, long legs stretched the length of the stair riser, crossed at the ankles. Steel-toed cowboy boots featured a white *Día de los Muertos* skull etched on the bottom of each sole. His eyes were fixed to Garin as he strolled the edges of the room.

Always wise to pinpoint the lookout, and vice versa.

Garin hadn't entered carrying a gun because of the security check at the nightclub entrance. He didn't need one. These men were lackeys. Well-built, a few of them, including the lookout, but he didn't worry about the scrawny set bent over the table near the stairs, so that took three out of the equation. The odds were against him, but he'd never been an odds man.

Walking to the center of the room, he stood there a moment, taking in the energy, the foul cigarette smoke imbued in the ancient rug and the molding ceiling tiles. With a crack of his neck to one side, he then gave his arms a shake and clapped his hands together.

"Gentlemen!" Garin called. "I'm looking for Weston Bracks." The room fell silent, except for the annoying falsetto still pleading him to dance. "Anyone have an address book or speed dial? Facebook friend?"

He smirked, gauging how long it would take before he'd be in hand-to-hand combat. Five seconds?

"Who wants to know?"

The idiotic, but necessary, question. He flicked a glance to the man on the stairs, who now stood, fists coiled and arms arching at his sides as if preparing to quick draw.

"None of your damn business." Garin twisted at the waist and thrust up his right arm to block the punch from behind. His attacker strained against his arm to push him off balance, but with a shove, Garin sent him tumbling to the floor at the base of a pool table.

Ten seconds. He was losing his ability to rouse a good fight. On the other hand, these men did not plan to disappoint. Turning, he gut-punched another bold attacker, sending him sprawling across an empty pool table.

He heard the swing of a pool cue through the air behind him. It missed his head by three inches. Garin growled, and grabbed a cue from a table, which happened to be decorated with skulls. He broke the white-maple stick in half, and outfitted himself with a worthy yantok, or short stick used for eskrima-style fighting. Spinning it and ending in a redondo, he challenged anyone to come forward with a lift of his chin. Two men charged. He swung the stick out in a forward strike, connecting with a shoulder, but it only slowed the one man. The other slammed him against a table.

Garin used the momentum, his body falling backward, and lifted his attacker with his legs, sending him over his head and sprawling across the table. Jumping high and landing on his feet, his palms on the table, he defied the man who spidered up to a crouch on the green felt. He swung at Garin's face, missing. Garin grabbed his wrist and crushed it against the table, slamming the butt of the stick down on the back of his hand. Something snapped, either wrist bones or tendons. A painful yelp signaled surrender.

Garin pushed away, stick spinning in his fingers, and turned to face the next challenge.

Thankfully, no shots had been fired, which gave him hope he was fighting unarmed men. Didn't make things easier, but taking bullets out of the equation did make for an equal fight and an easier grip, since blood tended to make the skin slippery.

Slapping a hand against one man's face, he used the force of the blow to slam his head into the swinging fist of another one's attack. The puncher cursed the fact he'd hit his friend, and twisted back on the defense, fists up, bouncing on his toes before Garin. The one he'd punched landed with his arms across the table, his jaw slamming the edge as he went down hard.

Donna Summer now crooned about love, and the music grew louder as fists met flesh, and bones took the impact and tendons crunched.

Garin ran up the stairs, turned and clocked his pursuer—one of the scrawny ones—up the side of the head with a fan flick of the stick. Blood spattered from the man's mouth, and possibly a tooth, but tenaciously he clung to the stair rail, and grinning a crimson sneer, he gripped Garin's ankle and brought him down hard on his ass. Some landings were more vicious than others, and that one crushed his tailbone up into his spine and made him groan. And in the process, he'd dropped the stick.

But he wasn't out. The attacker dragged him down the stairs, and Garin padded each bumpy step with his forearms, cursing his judgment when his aggressor packed powerful strength in those lean muscles. When he reached the bottom, Garin grabbed the railing and kicked high, landing the man under the jaw. Bones cracked, and his assailant went down, his unconscious body tumbling into the next who would try to take Garin out.

Righting himself, and assessing that five were still standing—three groaning and one out cold—Garin wished he had a magical weapon like Annja possessed. Would be great if he could call a Glock out of the otherwhere and send a few rounds through bodies right now.

But the old-fashioned way with fists it would be. Besides, he was just getting started. The adrenaline was racing and his breaths were even and strong.

"Bring it," he muttered.

Catching the swing of a pool cue across the back of his neck, Garin cursed himself for not being more aware as he stumbled forward, avoiding tripping over the fallen man. He collided into another who charged him, grabbed him by the face and slammed his cheek into the wall. Blood spattered Garin's face. He let the man drop.

Turning, he swung, but a forceful block stopped his punch with an echoing *smack*.

The man who caught his punch cracked a tobacco-stained grin. And from behind, Garin's left arm was wrangled. The two men worked in tandem, twisting his arms around behind him painfully. And when the bruiser from the stairs approached with a length of thick chain in hand Garin began to rethink the game plan.

PALM PRESSED FLAT to the red door with the upside-down number seven on it, Annja listened to the noise on the other side. She'd thought it was supposed to be an underground pool hall—one of those places you had to know someone to be invited into the fold, or better, work for a criminal underlord. What she heard now sounded more like a gym or boxing ring.

She smiled. If Garin was inside, that offered perfect explanation for the fisticuffs. And he would probably be alone, fending off more than a few.

For long seconds she vacillated about turning the doorknob. Garin would likely curse her out and wouldn't thank her in any way. He'd insist he had the situation under control. And he'd find some way to make it look like it had been her fault if he received so much as a bruise.

How could a girl possibly walk away from all that praise and appreciation?

With an inhale, Annja opened the door and strolled inside, quickly assessing the situation. The ridiculous song "Disco Duck" quacked out over the speakers. A stained-glass beer lamp swung dangerously back and forth over the table, half of the glass dangling by the lead inserts. Lights from a jukebox flashed over a pair of men brawling, their faces blinking from pink to violet and revealing bloodied scowls.

She didn't have time to count how many were, indeed, against the burly German. Instead, she walked right up to Garin's bleeding and bent-forward face. Two men held his arms, and another stood ready to kick him from the side.

"Now that's going to hurt," Annja said.

"It's your damn fault," Garin spat.

"Naturally."

Adjusting her weight to her back leg, Annja tilted her torso, swinging a high kick to land on the hip of the one who delivered the kick to Garin. The man's boot didn't connect with Garin's jaw. And Annja's blow sent him stumbling backward to land against the ugly paneled wall in a surprised sprawl.

"You're welcome," she said, and left Garin to get out of the hold with a couple well-placed shoulder shifts.

She bent over the man she had laid flat and punched him squarely in the nose. Cartilage crunched under her knuckles, and she winced. But damn that had felt good. She wanted to kick some ass. Adrenaline rushing through her veins, she swung up and met the next man who wanted a piece of her.

"Your trollop come to save your ass?" he shouted, and laughed, revealing a bloody grin. He swung for Annja's shoulder, but she delivered a high kick that caught him across the throat, her hiking boot leaving a waffle impression on his skin as he stumbled, clutching and gagging for breath.

"She's not my trollop," Garin called, more as a denial than in defense of her virtue. He held a man's head in the vise of his bent arm. Gripping the guy's hair, he swung him out and released him, sending him straight toward Annja.

She caught him across the throat with her arm, clotheslining him efficiently. Garin winked at her. About the only thanks she expected to get.

"Good thing I decided to stop in," she called.

"I had it under control!" Garin shouted. He elbowed another man in the temple, and the guy went down without a sound. Garin was no slacker. "Who invited you?"

Annja leaped to avoid the grabbing hand of a man on the floor. She landed on the edge of a pool table on one thigh, rolled backward and across the table, and scissored her legs high to connect with the man who waited on the other side. Pushing off the table and leaping over that fallen goon, she landed solidly on the floor and straightened.

"It upsets me you didn't put my name on the guest list," she called to Garin. "You here in London, making new friends and having all this fun. I'm affronted."

Two opponents remained standing—plus Annja and Garin. Annja charged the one aimed for her, caught his upper arm and swung him around. Garin performed the same move with his attacker, and they swung them about to meet with grunts and an exhausted and painful hug. Garin kicked the one in the jaw, laying him out, and the other, a man with white leather skulls on his boots, simply wilted, either from fear or exhaustion.

Garin stepped over to Annja and wiped what she noticed was a smear of blood from her forearm. "You think I needed your help?"

"No."

"Of course I didn't—no?" He thrust back his shoulders. Adjusted his shirtsleeves, which were spattered with blood. He'd lost a cuff link, and poked a finger through the buttonhole. "Right, then. I want to take a look upstairs in the office before leaving."

"I'll hold down the fort."

Annja let her eyes wander across the fallen. A few were conscious, but she didn't expect they'd give her much trouble. But to be safe, she picked up a broken pool cue stamped with skulls. The blood on it added the perfect touch.

"Take your time!" she called after Garin as he climbed the red-carpeted stairs to the balcony. "Might get in a game while you're snooping."

She heard his grunting scoff and smiled. Any day she got to tweak Garin Braden was a good day. But who was she kidding? He could have handled this on his own. Maybe. It had felt damn good to let out her aggressions on this tattered bunch, though.

But it would never make up for her churning anger over Luke's death.

Don't think about it. Not until you've put this case behind you. Find Bracks. You can mourn Luke later.

Aiming the cue toward the black eight ball, a silver glint beside it caught her eye. A cuff link. Who knows? It might be Garin's. Not many of the men scattered around the floor were wearing good shirts. Sliding the broken stick over her finger, she hit the cue ball. It rolled toward the eight, which knocked the cuff link into the side pocket, before rolling into the corner pocket.

GARIN HADN'T FOUND the man he was looking for in any of the balcony rooms set around the upper perimeter of the pool hall.

Annja had returned his silver cuff link, which didn't seem to do much to lift his mood.

Now they stood a few blocks down from the nightclub in the opening of an alleyway strewn with the daily newspaper, watching as young kids in sexy clothing—focused on their cell phones more than their dates—headed toward the action.

At least the music wasn't disco, Annja thought, glad she'd missed that era. Eighties music was some of her favorite, but she'd been too young to go to the clubs then. She'd never been a club girl. Couldn't see the point, really. It was much more fulfilling to have a conversation over a centuries-old stack of bones or ancient pottery.

"How'd you find me?" Garin asked. He leaned against the brick wall of the building, while Annja stood with her hands in her pockets, facing the sidewalk and observing the passersby.

"Nowadays they have an app for everything, don't you know? I tracked your phone through a GPS app."

"Remind me to beef up my personal security."

"Yes, well, Roux was worried about you, as well."

"That old bastard."

"Coming from another old bastard, that slur hardly holds water."

"Annja, I'm in no mood."

"Fine. Let's cut through the small talk and get to the point. We both want Bracks, so let's overlook the fact you laid me flat in the field out of Liberec, and share our knowledge of the man."

"Why do you want him? I thought you were digging up bones in the Czech Republic. How does a vampire skull relate to an international smuggler of weapons, art and data?"

"Is that Bracks's official title? Bigger mouthful than 'business opportunist.' But I like it. Tells a person exactly what to expect."

"Annja."

"Garin."

She sighed and turned to face him. Though the night shadowed his face, the streetlight cast a sharp angle to his already square jaw. "Sometimes the things I dig up lead me to real, contemporary problems that need solving. You know how it is with the sword. And I have reason to believe Bracks is kidnapping children."

Garin didn't say anything for a moment. "You have proof of that? He's never been into the flesh trade, that I know of."

"You seem to know a lot about the man."

"I have many enemies. Kind of expected, don't you think, for all the centuries I've lived?"

"I suppose. And Bracks has never dealt in trafficking?"

"Not that I'm aware of. Though I'm not privy to his every move. That still gives me no explanation for why you are here in London, seeking the man. Leave this to me, Annja. I'll take care of the matter. You go back to your artifacts."

"Are you telling me to sit tight and be a good girl?"

He sighed heavily and nodded slightly. "I would

never say that, because I know it would only fuel your determination."

"You got that right."

"So I'm stuck with you?"

"You're the guy with the clue about Bracks. So yes, I'd call it stuck."

"I've reached a dead end. The pool hall was the last place I have information on him."

"What about a voodoo club?"

Garin quirked a brow, which she only saw half of in the shadows, but she felt his surprise and curiosity. He hadn't cottoned on to that clue yet?

"My research leads me to guess that the kidnapped children may have been used in voodoo rituals, or else they had organs removed for the same."

"That's a hell of a guess. You're grasping."

"The toxicology report on the blood found in the cooler after the fire, said it was full of Calabar bean extract."

"What the hell is that?"

"It's derived from an extremely poisonous plant. The extract paralyzes a person while leaving them conscious. Think about it, Garin. A child fully conscious while some monster removes his kidney. Now dare to tell me to step away from finding Bracks."

He looked aside, his eyes tracking the passing groups of colorful nightclub partiers. His jaw pulsed. "Fine. Voodoo clubs? I may know of one in the city. Access is through the underground. They hold group rituals that involve sex and bondage, but I suspect the closed-door rituals are the ones in which body parts may be used."

"I'm not even going to ask how you know about something like that."

"Best you didn't."

"Where is this club and how do we gain access?"

"Do we need to gain access? If Bracks is supplying voodoo practitioners with body parts—the words on my tongue sicken me—then he's not getting his hands bloody by entering the clubs. I followed the cooler to a local doctor."

"And?"

"He was selling directly to the practitioner, or, I suspect, those rich and demented enough to attempt the rituals on their own. There are those who would do anything to get what they want most, Annja."

"Surely Bracks has to rub elbows with a few?"

"I don't know. The voodoo club feels like the wrong angle. We've found the source, and you have a good idea of the output. To find the man behind the curtain we need to throw a wrench into his operation."

"I have a feeling the Chrastava operation has already been brought to a halt, what with Santos failing. He's one of Bracks's men. He killed Luke, the archaeologist I was working on the dig with."

"I'm sorry about that. Although all's fair—"

"Don't even say it, Garin. There may even be another child still missing. One woman—Melanie—her son disappeared. The local police need to find him."

His false compassion was the last thing she needed right now.

"Santos mentioned another named. Canov."

Garin hissed out a breath.

"I take it from that reaction you know the man."

"Yes. But he's an underling. And I'll wager he's gone way underground by now if you've been sniffing around and taking out Bracks's men."

"If you've dealt with Bracks in the past…"

"Never made a deal with him, only engaged in some turnabout play."

"Then let's lure him into a new play."

Garin's brow lifted.

"What if we gave him a new supply?"

"That's insanity."

"It is, but I don't have any better ideas at the moment."

"I have a better idea."

"Shoot."

"I think he'd like to know we're allies."

Annja fisted her hips. "We're not allies."

"Bracks doesn't know that."

"So you think he'll want to…what? Kill me? Take me away from you?"

"He's already stolen one woman from me. I think we'll need to sweeten the bait."

"You are not putting me in a dress again, Garin."

"You are so not like any normal woman, Annja. Have I mentioned how much that appeals to me?" He snorted.

Annja sighed. "Name one of Bracks's weaknesses. You must know."

"Weapons. And art."

"I'm not keen on either." Though she knew they were on Garin's radar. "What about artifacts?"

"If it were rare and valuable enough. You have access to anything like that?"

Annja shoved her hands in her pockets. "Give me the night to think about it. I'm sure I can come up with something. But the problem is, even if we can lure him into a trap, we need to prove he's had his hand in the kidnappings and organ theft. I still think the voodoo club is something we should check out."

"Fine. You go back to your hotel room and take a shower and snuggle into a nice sleep and let your mind wander. I'll look into gaining access to the club I know about."

"I'd prefer staying close to you, because I don't trust that you're not going to cut me out of the action again."

"I make no promises." He smacked a fist into his palm. "I'm sorry about the jaw."

"It still hurts, but I'm a big girl. Where are you staying?"

"I've a suite at the Ritz. You want to share my bed?"

"How about you set me up with a room nearby."

"So this is my treat?"

"Yes. It'll make up for the bruise on my jaw."

"Fair enough," he conceded, laughing.

"I'll hail a cab."

"Let's walk."

The Ritz was across town and a good hour away. No matter how late, Annja was always up for a jaunt, but she was surprised Garin was. "You up for it, old man?"

He shrugged and joined her on the sidewalk. "I thought if we walked it would make it easier for whoever is following us to continue to do so. If Bracks comes to us, that'll make things easier."

"I see your point."

"Two men. Dark suits. Two blocks west."

"A walk, it is. Let's stop in at a fast-food restaurant on the way. I could eat something big, greasy and served in Styrofoam."

"Such class, Annja. Such class."

20

Annja lingered in Garin's room before going to hers, which was adjoining. He offered her wine, champagne and caviar. She refused them all.

Exhaustion was her excuse.

But really, she didn't want to imbibe in the vicinity of Garin Braden. She had to stay on her toes around the man. Not that she expected him to try to seduce her. It was her own inhibitions she worried about.

No, it wasn't that, either. She couldn't get Luke, and the intimacy they'd shared, out of her brain.

"So tell me about you and Bracks. What is it between you two?"

"None of your business." He relaxed into a Louis XVI chair, propping an ankle across his knee and dangling a goblet of champagne at his side. "Next question?"

"It has to be something deep," she announced, and leaned against the door on the opposite side of the room from him. "You've been going at each other for years?"

"I said next question."

"It's a woman," she guessed.

"Annja."

"It's always a woman when two men clash."

"Doesn't have to be."

"But it is?"

He shook his head and tilted back the champagne in one swallow. So the guy didn't want to talk about the sensitive stuff. Annja never had been one to skirt delicate issues.

"Someone you loved?" she asked. "Have you ever been in love? You must have loved many times."

"Annja."

"Just indulge my overtired brain right now. Please?"

The man dipped a finger in a saucer of caviar that sat on crushed ice and popped the roe into his mouth. "I have been in love, many times, over the centuries."

"I knew it."

"But not lately. Love is…tough."

"I imagine so for someone like you. I mean, I've seen the *Highlander* movies." Stupid, Annja. "I know that's fiction, but the idea of a man living for centuries, falling in love and watching those he loves die…"

"You romanticize things. I'm surprised at that. Didn't think you had a romantic bone."

She sighed and spread a hand down before her body. "It's in here. Somewhere."

"Have you been in love?"

"No."

"Said with such immediate certainty I have to question the truth of that statement."

"Nope. I've been in extreme like a few times, but never love."

He nodded, accepting that. Resting the goblet against the chair arm, he asked, "Would you know love?"

"I'm sure I will." Luke hadn't been love, just extreme like. Hell, it was going to be rough forgetting him. "And you are skirting my question. This isn't about me, it's about you."

"It's not a woman between me and Bracks. Although he did steal a woman from me, and killed her, actually."

"Oh." Annja tilted her head, suddenly seeing the man in a new light. That he had watched lovers come and go seemed sad, yet to have one murdered must have been the cruelest blow. *Because now you know what that feels like.* She shivered. "I'm sorry."

"Thank you. I extend my sympathies toward you for losing Mr. Spencer. I won't make assumptions about the two of you. Anyway, I've learned that life never warns you before it's going to smack you hard. A man learns to deal with it."

"You still haven't told me what's up between you and Bracks."

With a growling sigh that indicated good old grouchy Garin was back in charge, he finally said, "It's a simple matter of pride. Male ego. There's not room enough on this planet for the both of us."

"So…a little like your love-hate relationship with Roux, then. And, what, you're going to take him out? Has to be a better reason to justify murder."

"You're annoying me."

"Someone has to." She gripped the door pull. "I need to get some sleep."

"I'll have breakfast sent up for you. No champagne and caviar?"

"I'll stick with bacon and eggs, and orange juice."

"Whatever makes you happy."

"You don't really care about my happiness, Garin. You're only nice to me because you want to get your hands on my sword."

"I would never deny that."

Always truthful with her, though sometimes his omissions felt like lies, she knew better than that. "Good night, Garin."

"Sweet dreams of extreme like and fire, Annja Creed."

She startled at his mention of fire, but didn't allow him to see he'd touched a nerve. Annja smoothly opened the door and closed it behind her.

"Fire?" She shook her head and closed her eyes. "The man's cruelties are razor sharp."

ANNJA was sitting on a wooden chair, hands tied behind her and ankles secured together with a leather band—perhaps a belt—but not tied to the chair.

So Garin had been right. The cat had followed the mice.

Weston Bracks was seated at a desk across the room from her, his feet up on a desk drawer and his fingers rapping the mahogany desk. Hair slicked back from his face, he was neatly shaven, and she could smell his aftershave from the ten-foot distance between them.

As it was, she wore a white T-shirt and her cargo pants. Good thing she'd slipped out for the newspaper during her usual four o'clock lying awake in bed and staring at the ceiling anticipating the day and had fallen asleep reading it or she'd be in a state of undress right now.

"Do you know how amazing you are?" Bracks asked as he dropped his feet to the floor and leaned forward on his elbows. "Tracking me all the way to London? Or is it that you simply wanted to meet up with Braden?"

"Santos told me I'd find you here."

"Here? In this office? Or the city? I don't believe the Gypsy had my exact location."

"The city. And it must have been Canov who provided those details to his underlings. Santos is bad off, by the way. If he's not dead."

"At your hand, I suspect."

"What makes you think I'm capable?"

"I've heard reports from my men. You've left a path of injured in your wake, pretty lady. You're much more than meets the eye, I must say. Extremely interesting to me. I've read your profile online. You've quite the arsenal of talents—and to learn that you've got martial arts skills *and* beauty…?"

"You forgot the part about where I can part large bodies of water with a single wave of my hand."

"And funny, too! Oh, Annja, you and I are going to get along famously. That is, if your lover doesn't mind."

"My lov—" Apparently his research had led him to guess at the sensational. "Garin Braden and I are not lovers."

"Huh. That explains why he's not here right now. The man is slacking. I expected him an hour ago, not long after you were brought here. Guess you're not as important to him as I had hoped."

"Guess not."

"Well. We'll wait, all the same. He did put you in the same hotel—and right next door—so he wanted to keep you close. And he's after me, so he'll come after one or the other of us soon enough. In the interim, what shall we talk about?"

"How about this is the part where the evil villain details the reason behind his horrible crime?"

"No, that's boring. Besides, there are too many crimes. I wouldn't know where to start. You, on the other hand, fascinate me. You host a television show about monsters, and you venture across the world in search of treasure and mystery."

"It sounds more exciting than it is. Adventure is ninety percent toil, ten percent reward."

"Still, I could use a woman like you on my payroll. I find many an opportunity falls onto my lap that requires someone who possesses your skill set and thirst for adventure combined with archaeological knowledge."

"I think this is the part where I tell you to go do something nasty with your mother."

"Sadly, she's passed. As are your parents, eh?"

He knew too much about her. That was never good. But she didn't suspect he was going to use it against her because what means did he have? He was an enigma, and she wanted to hear him confess. Yet what good was confession if the authorities were not here to record it? It would be her word against his, and it wasn't like she had the superstitious Romani backing her up, either.

Worrying at the rope about her wrist, Annja could easily call the sword and cut through the thick hemp. Screw the questions Bracks would have about the sudden appearance of a battle sword into her hands. She owed him nothing.

He stood, and walked around the side of the desk. The man reminded her of Garin. Finely tailored suit, well groomed, handsome in a bad-boy criminal sort of manner. Entitled. Probably too smart for his own good. That's usually the way it went with the ones who used their brains to commit evil. And those psychopathic brains could always justify their atrocities.

"You've murdered children," she said, peering into his pale gray eyes and not finding the compassion or glint of humanity she hoped to see. "How can you sleep at night?"

"On a king-size air mattress. You know the kind

that adjusts with a remote? Amazing and so comfortable."

"You're the real monster," she hissed. "Those Gypsies believed in something that rises from the grave to exact revenge upon them, and you used those beliefs to serve them a much worse punishment."

"As I've said—" He crossed his legs at the ankle, and proudly announced, "Business opportunist. Don't look so angry, Annja, it puts a crease in your brow. And I have murdered no one. I tend to keep my hands two to three degrees away from the dirty work. The fact this one came back to me has made me rethink some of my safeguards. I've sacked the Chrastava operation, you'll be glad to know."

"The only thing I can be glad for is that I'm here now, and I will make you pay."

He leaned forward, hands behind his back, bringing his face a foot away from hers. "I do admire a boastful woman. Puts a delightful shiver up and down my spine. What are you going to do to me?"

Annja could feel the sword hilt in her hand, the warmth of it. A knock on the door stopped her from calling it.

It wasn't exactly a knock. More like a heel kicking in the wood door. Garin Braden.

"I've been expecting you," Bracks said, pulling a pistol from his suit pocket and positioning himself beside Annja. He jammed the barrel against her temple. "Took your own sweet time. She not worth it to you?"

Garin heaved out a heavy breath, and produced the Heckler & Koch, but instead of aiming it at Bracks, he held it to his chest, arms crossed, and barrel flat against his shoulder.

If he wasn't going to do anything, Annja wasn't about to sit here any longer and remain a helpless victim. The sword slid silently into her grip. She noted Garin's attention diverted above her head, where he must have seen the blade tip of the battle sword.

"No, Annja," he said, then to Bracks, "This ends right now."

Bracks, who still hadn't realized Annja was armed, maintained the barrel against her temple. "Really? You'd end it with a single bullet after all we've been through over the years? Come on. You know you enjoy the game as much as I do. So you lose a few guns or a valuable piece of art now and then. I still visit my brother's grave every winter. He killed my brother," he said to Annja.

"You killed Louisa," Garin countered.

Louisa? Must have been the lover, Annja decided. This was fast becoming a maudlin duel of one cuckolded man against another. And Garin had almost convinced her it wasn't about a woman. Well played, old man, well played.

"I'm finished with the game," Garin said. "For good. Put it away, Annja!"

Before Bracks turned to look at her, Annja sent the sword back into the otherwhere. She smirked up at the man, shrugging as if she hadn't a clue what Garin was talking about.

"Let her go," Garin said firmly. "This is between the two of us."

"Up for a bit of a tussle, then?" Bracks asked, lowering the gun and tucking it at the back of his pants.

"If that's the way you want to end it…" Garin tucked away his gun and removed his suit coat, tossing it over the desk, and following by unbuttoning his sleeve cuffs. "Then let's do this."

Annja heard the sound of a switchblade opening behind her. Her wrists dropped free, and she wiggled her fingers.

"Back by the wall, Annja," Garin directed.

And, inclined to let this play out between the two men, she did as she was told.

Bracks tugged his tie free and zipped it out from his shirt collar, tossing it aside. "This will be a treat for you, Miss Creed," he said, unbuttoning his shirt and tugging it off. "Braden and I are matched equally. I'll count on you to call the draw when you've become uncomfortable with the bloodshed."

Annja quirked a brow at Garin.

"It's not going to end in a draw," he announced, then swung a fist toward Bracks.

Annja pressed up against the wall, content to let the testosterone patrol go at it. Each man managed to land a punch square to the other's jaw, ribs, kidney, and then it got interesting. The kicks were high and delivered with deadly precision. It was difficult not to wince when either man took a hard rubber heel to the chin or the solar plexus.

Dragging the chair out of the way, Annja moved

along the wall until she reached the doorway and closed the door, leaving the men alone in the room. She had no idea if others were in the building, but the fight had not brought out any armed guards. They could be alone.

She still had no evidence on Bracks's involvement beyond the confession to go to the police with. And to do so would get Garin arrested, as well.

The door rattled against her shoulders. Felt like two hard, brute bodies had collided with it. She heard very little grunting and only the occasional oath. They were two extremely fit and trained men going after the thing that had pushed them to an edge.

They'd been going at each other for years? Sounded like something Garin would engage in. And now he'd grown tired of the game. Again, sounded like him. He enjoyed the challenge, but when that challenge started to bite, he'd as soon shoot it than endure another wound.

And that's when Annja heard the pistol shot.

Summoning the sword into her grip, she turned and grabbed the doorknob. She listened for movement, anything that would clue her where the two parties in the room stood so she wouldn't be charging in with a target marked on her forehead.

"It's over," Garin called.

She opened the door and saw Bracks standing in the center of the room, a gun very slowly falling from his hand. A bullet had pierced his skull at the temple, boring through a small crimson hole. It exited in a spray out the other temple, and hit the wall next to a previous bullet hole, with a splash of blood to the papered wall.

Annja swung the sword toward Garin, and tipped it up under his chin. "Why? We should have called the police."

"It wasn't going to end any other way. And I'm getting too old for rock-'em-sock-'em." He held up his gun hand, fingers slipping from the trigger, in surrender. "One of us was going to die in this room, Annja."

"You've murdered the one man who could answer to the Romani for their lost children."

Garin lifted his head and looked down his nose at her. He then bowed his head and the tiniest shrug lifted his shoulders. An unspoken apology for what he had just done. Perhaps, for many other things he had done.

"I ended a long and tiresome feud, and I don't regret it. Now put away your pretty little sword before I get angry enough to take it away from you."

"Try me," she challenged, aware now that Bracks's body had finally dropped over the chair she'd been tied in. His lifeless hand landed on top of her boot. "Take it if you dare, Garin. But I warn you, I won't make it easy."

He slashed his pistol across the blade, sliding the barrel along the steel. Twisting, he reached with his other hand, and clocked her aside the jaw, in the same place he'd hit her previously.

Annja released the sword to the otherwhere, rather than risk him actually getting his hands on it. When she straightened from the blow and showed him her empty hands, the man grunted. She would call it a growl.

"Get the hell out of here," he said, tugging down his shirtsleeves. "I'll clean up the mess. If I see you again, Annja, it'll be too soon."

"You know we'll see each other again, and again. The sword ties us together, like it or not."

"Today I don't like it."

"I can get behind that sentiment."

The two held stares for long seconds. Annja was certain she saw regret in Garin's dark gaze, but pride would never allow him to voice it. He was old and set in his ways. She should be thankful a dangerous man was now dead, unable to harm another child.

"If you're going to clean up," she said, "then make sure Bracks's underlings are dealt with, as well. Canov is a name I have."

"Canov has already been dealt with," he said.

That's right. He'd admitted that Canov had been on his payroll. "What about the other men who work for Bracks?"

"Don't ask for the world. All I can give you is this small piece, right here, right now."

She paused in the doorway and tilted her head down, fighting the urge to look at the man she would indeed see again, and knowing it would be too soon, as he'd said.

He and Bracks could not have ended this encounter any other way, she instinctually knew that. And while she had no clue as to what strange alliance had forged the criminal games between the two, she also didn't want to know.

She wasn't sure whether or not to mark this one as a win or lose, but it felt less than triumphant.

Walking away, without looking back, she made plans to stop into the university and talk to Chester Rumshaven, Luke's colleague.

THE STUDIO WORK for *Chasing History's Monsters* was always tedious for Annja. But the fact it gave her a moment to sit down and blow out a breath after filming could not be denied as a good thing. She read over Doug's script for the segment they planned on the chewing dead. It was very good and included the history of so-called vampires across the Slavic nations. It also detailed the burial rites that had seen stakes, iron rods and even bricks put into bodies to keep them down and dead.

As she scanned through the edited segments, she was impressed as well by Doug's renditions of corpses rising from the grave after having chewed through their funeral shrouds. Cheap actors with even cheaper makeup, but it worked.

It was sad to see the interview segments featuring Luke. Doug had asked her if he should cut them out, and she said she'd let him know after viewing them. Luke had been genuinely concerned for the Romani and had hoped to help them move forward from a history of beliefs that even he knew could never happen.

She couldn't decide whether or not to leave the

segments in. A few days to let it sink in and perhaps she'd have a clearer head to make the right choice.

She finished narrating the segment with a few cautious words of her own, advising viewers to stick to horror-movie monsters, and to leave the legends buried.

Before leaving the studio she called the Chrastava police and mentioned Luke's name in order to speak to the deputy he had befriended a year earlier. He had been the first one to report to the scene after she'd called in Luke's death and Santos's wounds. Annja expressed an interest in the Romani encampment, and how they were holding up in the wake of the children's disappearances. All the deputy could offer was that the Romani camp had moved on. The homes were empty and vehicles gone. Surprising, considering those who owned property generally remained where they were.

It turned out Santos had died in the end. After his funeral, which the deputy had attended out of respect for the family after investigating the whole child-abduction case, he'd been offered the chance to buy a nice weapon. A katana sword, which he had purchased, and then, when he'd gotten home with it, the niggling worry that it was probably evidence tore at him, and he'd sent it to forensics.

Forensics had detected blood, and they were typing it out right now, and hoping to do a DNA match to the database.

"Interesting," Annja had said, then had thanked the deputy and hung up.

"Blood on Santos's sword?"

Annja knew it was Luke's, and yet, it could also be hers. The deputy had taken surprising initiative in having the sword tested. She hoped the DNA didn't lead them back to her. This particular case was closed in her mind. She didn't want to see another skull with a brick, or even a stake run through a corpse's heart, for a very long time.

LATER THAT WEEK, in her Brooklyn apartment, Annja reread the last few paragraphs of the article she was completing about the Romani burial rituals and beliefs. She wasn't going as in depth as Luke had intended, incorporating their superstitions and beliefs, but she was doing the best she could with the firsthand information she had witnessed. She'd downloaded Luke's notes from the cloud server, and thanks to his details and meticulous notes, she had mostly filled in the blanks. Luke would have wanted her to finish this for him. She would publish it under her name, with a postmortem attribution to Luke Spencer.

The idea to do an article on the chewing dead was fleeting. She'd leave the sensational vampire stuff to Doug Morrell.

She leaned back in her office chair and eyed the cardboard box that sat open, packing material still tight about the contents. The skull she'd had mailed from Liberec had arrived a few days ago. She intended to turn it over to Chester Rumshaven, who had offices in New York and London. He'd know what to do with it. All of Luke's projects would be cataloged and his personal belongings forwarded on to family.

She hadn't known his family, but had been honored to be his friend, colleague and someone he had trusted.

Pouring a finger of whiskey into the shot glass beside her laptop, she saluted. "To Luke!"

The liquor burned in the sweetest way. This adventure had been bittersweet, but in the end, Luke's tenacity and determination had prompted her to remain involved and they had saved children, she knew that to her very marrow.

She would have liked to have brought Bracks to justice, but suspected he was serving it already.

As for Garin Braden, they had clashed this time around.

There was always a next time.

"It's done. I played the final move against Bracks."

"You always did like to win."

Prepared to protest Roux's acerbic comment, Garin stopped himself from sounding like a prideful old bastard.

"Indeed, I like to win," he agreed. "Annja sends her love."

"Does she now? The two of you come to terms and play nice?"

"She did spend the night in my hotel room, so take that how you will. Good night, Roux." He hung up, smirking. Roux would eventually decide that Garin had been baiting him, but to know he'd initially be shocked and upset thinking that Annja Creed may have spent the night with him was a win too sweet to ignore.

* * * * *

JAMES AXLER

DEATH LANDS®

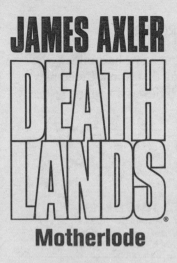

JAMES AXLER

DEATH LANDS

Motherlode

A struggle for survival at the end of the line

Motherlode

Seeds of Sustainability

Desperately short of supplies, Ryan Cawdor and his crew approach the prosperous-looking ville of Amity Springs. Hired to retrieve a stolen relic, the band is quickly caught in a power struggle between two strong-willed lady barons. Each covets the predark goods buried in Amity's backyard. But they are not alone in their zealous desire. All that stands between a mother lode of buried bounty and the destructive power of unchecked greed are grim warriors determined to survive another day in the Deathlands....

Available November wherever books and ebooks are sold.

GOLD EAGLE®

GDL113

TAKE 'EM FREE
2 action-packed novels plus a mystery bonus

NO RISK

NO OBLIGATION TO BUY

EXPLOSIVE DEMAND

Banking on destruction

The Executioner is gunning down a high-level conspiracy to destabilize the U.S. and Chinese economies by flooding the global markets with counterfeit money. The enemy is powerful, intelligent and well armed. And dangerous criminal kingpins—an ex-Spetsnaz Russian mafia boss and a Thai pirate—are the key to getting to the conspiracy's brilliant mastermind: a Russian power broker gunning for the rebirth of the Soviet Union as a superpower. Bolan has just one battle strategy for this merchant of doom: scorched earth.

Available October wherever books and ebooks are sold.

The Executioner®
Don Pendleton's
SLEEPING DRAGONS

Lethal nerve gas falls into the grasp of a Libyan terrorist.

When a British CIA operative in Hong Kong dies moments after sending a cryptic text message, the government needs a special kind of help to deal with the foul play—under-the-radar Mack Bolan expertise. Ambushed at every turn, Bolan soon discovers that there's a new weapon of mass destruction on the market, a Sleeping Dragon, and a fanatical Arab plans to use it to take back Libya, killing millions in the process. His enemies believe they know their devils, but they haven't met the Executioner.

Available October wherever books and ebooks are sold.

GOLD EAGLE®

GEX419